THE CONFESSION

Blythe Bonniwell, rich and untouchable! At last Charlie Montgomery, facing certain death on a dangerous war mission, could reveal the love he had been too shy to show. Now Charlie dared to touch the slim girl, to crush her in his arms and press his lips to hers.

It was a love she had dreamed about. This shy football hero who had never spoken to her before this passionate farewell.

But while Charlie fought for his country, his hometown rival, Dan Seavers, wove a web of intrigue to trap Blythe into an alliance she despised . . .

Bantam Books by Grace Livingston Hill
Ask your bookseller for the books you have missed

GRACE LIVINGSTON HILL

MORE THAN CONQUEROR

*This low-priced Bantam Book
has been completely reset in a type face
designed for easy reading, and was printed
from new plates. It contains the complete
text of the original hard-cover edition.*
NOT ONE WORD HAS BEEN OMITTED.

MORE THAN CONQUEROR
*A Bantam Book | published by arrangement with
J. B. Lippincott Company*

PRINTING HISTORY
Lippincott edition published 1944

Grossett & Dunlop edition published March 1951
2nd printing ...... October 1954   4th printing .... January 1964
3rd printing .. November 1956   5th prinitng .... July 1965
6th printing .... May 1967

Bantam edition | February 1969
2nd printing .... June 1969   4th printing .... February 1971
3rd printing ...... October 1969   5th printing .... February 1972
6th printing .... March 1980

ISBN 0–553–13772–7

Published simultaneously in the United States and Canada

PRINTED IN THE UNITED STATES OF AMERICA

0 9 8 7 6

MORE THAN
CONQUEROR

Chapter 1

A TALL YOUNG soldier swung off the bus at its terminal and walked briskly up Wolverton Drive.

He was a handsome soldier, though he did not seem conscious of it. He had strong, well chiseled features, heavy dark hair and fine eyes. He walked with a kind of grave assurance as if this was something he had fully made up his mind to do, though not as if this broad avenue were an old haunt of his; more as if he were driving himself to a sacred duty.

Oh, it wasn't the first time he had walked that way of course. In his school days he had passed up that road, had carefully studied its substantial houses, admired them each, and later come to search out and be interested in one particular house. He had never stepped within one of them, for his life had not been blessed with wealth and luxury, but he had admired a girl in school who lived here and he had taken pains to find out where she lived. Not that he had a personal acquaintance with that little girl in the grade school. Oh no! They had been only children then, with but the passing acquaintance of classmates as the years progressed. But he had been interested enough to find out where she lived, and when he had found her home he had been glad, as his eyes took in the lines of the fine old stone mansion. There had been no envy in his glance. He was glad she had a background like that. It was satisfying to know it. It seemed to finish out the picture for him. But he had known then, and equally he knew now, that *he* did not belong in this setting. He even knew that the circumstance which had brought him here now might not be recognized by anyone belonging to her

1

as justifying his coming. Nevertheless, he had come, and having started he was not to be turned back now at the last minute by any qualms of reason or conscience that might have made him hesitate in the past.

At the third corner the soldier turned sharply into a broad driveway, sweeping up in a pleasant curve to the old gray stone house that gave evidence of having been built a goodly number of years before.

As if he were accustomed to treading this way he walked quickly without hesitation, mounted the stone steps and passed within a stone arch.

As he stood awaiting an answer to his ring he cast a quick comprehensive glance up and down the broad piazza, with a look in his eyes as if the quiet elegance of the place was pleasant to him. There was satisfaction in his expression.

As he stood there he looked as if he might fit into that setting very easily. There was courtesy, strength, grace in his whole bearing, and the elderly servant who opened the door did not seem to see anything incongruous in his being there. These were days when men of the army and navy were honored guests everywhere. Moreover his attitude and manner showed the culture of one to the manner born.

"I would like to see Miss Blythe Bonniwell," he said, stepping into the hall as the servant swung the door wide and indicated a small reception room where he might sit down.

"She's still in," admitted the woman. "She's gone up to get ready to go to her Red Cross meeting."

"I'll not keep her long," promised the soldier understandingly.

"Who shall I say is here?" asked the woman.

The young man turned on her a winning grin.

"Why, you can tell her it is Charlie Montgomery. I'm not sure she'll remember the name. It's been some time. Just tell her I'm an old schoolmate and I'd like to see her about something rather important. That is, if she can spare just a minute or two."

"*Mr.* Montgomery, did you say?" asked the woman with dignity.

"Yes, I suppose you might call it Mr. but I doubt if she

would identify me that way," said the soldier with a grin. "It wasn't the way I was known, but it's all right with me if she remembers."

"Just sit down," said the woman with a disapproving air. "I'll call her. She'll likely be down in a short time."

The young man entered the room indicated, and sat down in the first chair that presented itself, dropping his face in his hands for an instant and drawing a quick breath almost like a petition. Then he straightened up, but he did not look about him. This was her home, her natural environment, that for long years he had often wished he might see, but he did not wish his mind to be distracted now. He must be alert and at attention when she came. This was probably a crazy thing he was doing, and yet he felt somehow he had to do it.

He heard a light step, and glancing up he saw her coming down the wide staircase that he could just glimpse through the open doorway. She seemed so like the little girl she had been long ago. The same light movement, as if her feet had wings, the same curly brown hair with golden lights in it, the same ease and poise and grace of movement.

She was wearing a slim brown dress that matched the lovely brown of her eyes, and there was a bright knot of ribbons in her brown hair, green and scarlet, that looked like berries and a leaf. It was like a jewel in a picture. His heart quickened as she came, and he felt abashed again at the errand which had brought him here.

She entered the room eagerly and an interested smile dawned on her sweet face.

The soldier arose and stood awaiting her. A salute—*that* was her due, yet he didn't want to flaunt his position as a soldier. But she was putting out her hand, both hands, as if she had a warm welcome for him. It occurred to him that perhaps she did not remember him—had possibly taken him for someone else. Or was it her habit to welcome all soldiers in this warm-hearted gracious way? But no, she just wasn't that free kind of a girl. She was welcoming him as someone she knew intimately and was glad to see.

The look in her eyes, the warm touch of her hand seemed so genuine that his own plans for distant courtesy seemed somehow out of place. And so for a moment he could only stand there with her hands in his and look down at her as she spoke.

"I'm so glad to see you!" she said. "It's a long time since we met."

"You remember me?" he asked in wonder. "You know who I am?"

"Why, of course!" said the girl with a happy little lilt in the turn of her voice. "You're the boy who sat in the very last seat in the first row in our senior high school year. You're the one who always knew all the answers all the way through our school years. Because you really studied, and you cared to know."

He looked at her in astonishment.

"Did I seem like that to you?"

"Oh, yes," she said, drawing a happy little breath. "You seemed to be the one student in our room who really cared to learn, and knew what it was all about. And I have often wondered whatever became of you. Did you go away to college, or go to work, or what?"

"Oh, I went to college," he said modestly, not even showing by so much as a glint in his eyes, what a march of hard work and triumph that college course had been. This young man was one who took the next thing in his stride and did his best in it as he went.

"And now you're in the army," she said, her glance taking in the insignia on his uniform. "You're—?" she paused and gave him a troubled look. "You're going overseas pretty soon?"

"Yes," he said coming back to his purpose. "Yes, if it hadn't been for that I would scarcely have ventured to come to see you."

"And why not, I'd like to know?" asked the girl lifting her lovely eyes, bringing into her face all the old interest she had had in this fellow-student who had been so much of a stranger to her, bringing a light of genuine understanding and admiration.

"Why not?" He laughed. "Why, I had no acquaintance with you. You belonged in a different class."

"Oh no," said the girl with a twinkle in her eyes, nestling her hands in the big strong ones that still held hers. "Have you forgotten? You were in my class all through school. And what's more, you were the very *head* of the class. It was my main ambition to try and keep up with you in my studies. I knew I never could get ahead, but I wanted to be at least second in the class! So don't say again that you weren't in my class."

He laughed, with an appreciation of the way she had turned the meaning of his words, and the fine color rolled up into his face gorgeously.

"You know I didn't mean that," he protested. "I knew you were the lovely lady of the class, and that you gave me a wholesome race as far as studies were concerned. But even so, that didn't put me into your class. You, with your lovely home, and your noble father and mother, and your aristocratic birth, and your millions, and your fashionable friends."

"Oh," said the girl with almost contempt in her voice, "and what are they to separate people? Why should just *things* like that have made us almost strangers, when we could have been such good friends?"

He looked at her with a deep reverence.

"If I had known you felt that way, perhaps it wouldn't have taken me so long to decide whether I ought to come to you today."

"Oh, I am so glad you came!" she said impulsively. "But come, let's sit down!" Blythe, suddenly aware that her hands were still being held closely, flashed a rosy light into her cheeks as she drew the young man over toward the couch, and made him sit down beside her.

"Now," she said, "tell me all about it. You came for some special reason, something you had to tell me, Susan said when she announced you."

"Yes," said the soldier, suddenly reverting to his first shyness, and to the realization of his appalling impertinence in what he had to say. "Yes, I have something special to tell you. I know I'm presuming in speaking of it, and perhaps you will think me crazy for daring to tell you. I'm sure I never would have dared to come if it hadn't been that I'm in the army, and that I have volunteered to undertake a very special, and dangerous commission about which I am not allowed to speak. It is enough to say that it means almost certain death for me. And that's all right with me. I went into it with this knowledge, and it's little enough to do for my country. But when I came to look the fact in the face, and get ready for my departure, which is probably to be tonight, I found there was something I wanted to do before I go. There was just one person to whom I wanted to say good-by. And that was you. I have nobody else. My mother has been gone two years. She was all I had. My other relatives, the few that are left, live far away, and do not care anyway. But there was just one person whom I wanted to see before I left, and that was you. I hope you don't mind."

"Mind?" said Blythe, lifting dewy eyes to his. "I think that was wonderful! Why should I mind?"

"But we are practically strangers, you know," he said with hesitation. "And in the ordinary run of life, if there were no war, and things were going normally, we would probably never have been anything but strangers. I am not likely ever to become one whom your family would welcome as one of your friends—"

"Oh, but you don't understand my family," said the girl, putting out an impulsive hand to touch his arm. "My family are not like that. They are not a lot of snobs!" She was speaking with intense fervor, and her eyes implored him to believe.

"Oh no," he said, "I would not call anything that belonged to you by such a name. I don't want you to think that, please! It was never even in my thoughts. I have only thought of them as being fine upstanding conservative people, with a high regard for the formalities of life. It would not be natural for them to pick out a 'poor boy' as a friend for their cherished daughter. But I thought, since this is probably the last time that I may be seeing you on this earth, it would do no harm for me to tell you what you have always been to me. You have been an inspiration to me from even my little boyhood when I first saw you in school, and I have loved to watch you. And in my thoughts I have always honored you. I felt as if I would like to tell you that, before I go. I hope it will not annoy you to be told, and that you will remember me as a friend who deeply admired—and—yes, *loved* you from afar, and who for a long time has prayed for you every night. Will you forgive me for saying these things?"

Impulsively he put out his hands, laid them upon hers again and looked at her with pleading eyes. But her own eyes were so filled with sudden tears that she could not see the look in his.

"Forgive!" she said in a small choking voice. "Why, there is nothing to forgive. It seems very wonderful to me that you should say these things, that you should have felt this way. And of all the beautiful thoughts, that you should *pray* for me! Why, I never knew you even noticed me. And I'm glad, *glad*, now, that you have told me! It seems the loveliest thing that ever came into my life. But oh, *why* do you have to go away? *When* do you have to go?"

He gave a quick glance down at his wrist watch, and said with distress in his voice:

"I ought to be on my way now. I have things to do before I take the noon train. I waited on purpose until the last minute, that I might not be tempted to stay too long and annoy you."

He sprang to his feet, but her hands clung to his and she rose with him.

"Oh, but I can't let you go like this," she pleaded, her eyes looking deep into his, her face lifted with the bright tears on her cheeks. "I *can't* let you go. You have just told me that you love me, and we must have a little time to get acquainted before you go. I—oh—I think I must have been loving you, too, all this time." Her own glance drooped shyly. "There was no one else ever who seemed to me as wonderful as you were, even when I was a little girl. Please don't go yet. We *must* have more time to get our hearts acquainted."

He looked down at her, his very soul in his eyes, his face deeply stirred, and then suddenly his arms were about her and he drew her close, his face against her tear-wet cheek, his lips upon hers.

"Darling!" he breathed softly.

She was clinging to him now, trembling in his arms.

"Darling, if I had dreamed it could be like this!"

Again he held her close.

"God forgive me! I've got to leave you. I'm a soldier under orders, you know."

"Yes, I know," she said softly. "I must not keep you.

But oh, I wish you had come sooner, so that we might have had a little time together."

"I'm afraid my coming has only made you unhappy!"

"No, don't say that! It is a beautiful happiness just to know what you have told me. And you know—*I* shall be praying—too. May God take care of you, and keep you and bring you back!"

He took her in his arms again, and their farewell kiss was a precious one to remember. And then suddenly a clock above stairs with a silvery chime told the hour and he sprang away.

"I must go at once!" he said.

"Yes, of course," gasped the girl sorrowfully.

It was incredible how hard it was to separate when they had only just come together. It was breath-taking.

Hand in hand they went out to the hall, to the front door, trying to say many last things for which there wasn't time, things that had just begun to crowd to their attention.

"But you will write to me?" said Blythe, lifting pleading eyes. "You will write at once?"

He looked at her with a sudden light in his eyes.

"Oh, may I do that?" he asked, as if it was more than he had dared to hope. "I hadn't planned to hang on to your life. I don't want to hinder you in any way. I want you to have a happy time, and—to—well, *forget* me. Think of me just as somebody who has gone out of your life. I mean it. I don't want the thought of me and of what I have said to hinder you from having friends, and going places. I want you to be your dear happy self, just as you have been all through the years before you knew I cared. That will be the best way to keep me happy and give me courage to go through with what I have undertaken. I mean it."

Her hands quivered in his and clung more closely.

"How could you think I could forget you and go on being happy? You have told me that you love me, and it has—well, just *crowned* my life!" She looked up at him with a kind of radiance in her face, that beamed on his heart like a ray of sun and warmed him through and through. He had been so humble about telling her, that he hadn't dreamed it would bring this response. It thrilled him ineffably.

"Darling!" he breathed softly and caught her to him again, holding her close.

Then upstairs another clock with a silvery voice chimed a belated warning, and they sprang apart.

"You must go!" It was the girl who said the word. "You mustn't let me make you late. And—how can I write to you? We have so much to say to one another."

"Oh, yes, I forgot!"

He plunged his hand into his pocket and brought out a card.

"A letter sent to this address will be forwarded to me whenever I am where it could reach me. Good-by, my precious one! You have given me great joy by the way you have received me, and you haven't any idea how hard it is for me to leave you now."

He touched his lips reverently to her brow and then dashed out the door.

She watched him flashing down the street, her heart on fire with joy and sorrow. Joy that he loved her, sorrow that he must go away into terrible danger. He wouldn't tell her how much danger, or what he was supposed to be going to do, but he had spoken as if it were plenty. "Probably death!" he had said, and yet even that terrible prospect had not been able to still the joy that was in her heart. Whatever came he was hers to love, she was his! Whatever came there was *this,* and for the present she could only be glad. By and by she knew that anxiety would come, and fear, and anguish perhaps, but still he would be hers.

How strange that she should feel this way about that boy with whom she had scarcely had a speaking acquaintance, a word, a look, a hovering smile, all the most formal, had been their intercourse thus far. And yet he had loved her so that he could not go away into possible death without telling her how he felt. And she had loved him well enough to recognize it at once, though she had never used that word even in her thoughts with regard to him. It seemed as if it were something that God had handed to her as a surprise. Something He had been planning for her all through her life, and she hugged the thought to her heart that she had always admired him, even when he was a little boy. He had beautiful intelligent eyes that always seemed to understand; a tumble of dark curly hair and a way of disappearing into thin air as soon as the business of school was over for the day. He never seemed to take part in social affairs of the school,—he just vanished. But his location in the room had always seemed to Blythe like a light for the whole class. Something clear and dependable to give their grade tone. It had been that way right along through the grades.

Just once in those years they had stood side by side at the blackboard working out a problem, their chalk clicking, tapping along almost in unison driven by sharp brains, quick fingers—and they had whirled around with lifted hands almost at the same instant, the only two in the class that had finished. They had given one another a quick look, a flashing smile, and that smile and look had lingered in Blythe's memory like a pleasant thing, and helped to complete the picture she had of that wise young scholar with a well controlled twinkle of merriment in his eyes.

The memory flashed at her now as she stood on the steps of her father's house and watched him stride down the driveway. She followed down to the end of the drive and watched him away down the sidewalk. Then she saw the bus coming. Was he going to make it? She held her breath to watch. Oh, had she made him late to something most important? That would be an unhappy thing to remember, if she had.

Then she saw him swing on inside the door just as it was about to close. Was he looking back? He was too far away for her to see.

But there were footsteps. Was someone coming? There were also tears on the verge of arrival. She turned like a flash, hurried up to the house and vanished inside just as one of her friends reached the gateway and called out to her. But she was gone. She couldn't, *couldn't* talk to anyone now. Not after what had happened. Idle chatter of friends and neighbors would put a blur over the precious thoughts that were in her heart, if she allowed them to come now before they were firmly fixed in memory. The morning was too rare and precious to be mingled with the commonplaces of life. She must get away by herself and savor this wonderful thing that had come to her.

So Blythe sped to her room and locked her door on the world that might have interfered.

For a moment she paused with her hands spread behind her on the closed door and looked about her. It was the same room it had been a few minutes before. There lay her coat and hat across the chair, just where she had dropped them when Susan told her she had a caller. There on the bureau lay her handbag. She had been all ready to go down to that Red Cross class, and of course she ought to be going at once. But she couldn't just walk out and go down to sew, until she had a chance to catch her breath and realize what had happened. Anyway, there were women enough there to run the class without her. It would be all right for her to wait just a few minutes and get her poise again. If she went down at once there would be a kind of glory-shine in her face that everyone would see. She was sure some of those catty women who had so much to say about other girls, would ask her about it. They never let any little thing go by. It seemed sometimes as if they were putting a magnifying glass over her to study her every time she came into the room. The questions they asked were impertinent questions about her home life, her family and friends, just so they would be able to tell about it afterwards: "My friend Miss Bonniwell went to the orchestra concert last night. Yes, she went with young Seavers. You know. They run around together a lot." She could fairly hear them saying things like that. In fact she had overheard some of their talk that ran a good deal after that fashion and she couldn't bear the thought that they should look into her face today, and by some occult power they seemed to possess, search out that grand and glorious thing that had happened to her this morning.

She sank into her easy chair and put her head back happily. This was her own haven. No one had a right to call her out from here now.

Then she closed her eyes and drifted back to the moment when she had gone downstairs, scarcely able to believe the message Susan had brought, that Charlie

Montgomery, her childhood's admiration, was really down there and had come to see her.

Oh, she had thought, it probably wasn't anything that mattered, some technicality, perhaps, about the business of their alumni. Though she couldn't remember that he had been interested in their plans about the alumni, but perhaps they had drawn him into it in some way. Those had been her thoughts as she hurried downstairs with her hands out. Had she been too eager, shown her pleasure too plainly at first?

But no. He loved her! He had come to tell her that he loved her. Amazing truth! That anything so unforeseen should have come to her. The joy in her heart seemed almost to stifle her.

And then she went over the whole experience bit by bit. Her delight when she recognized him. Her instant knowledge of her own heart, that he was beloved! Her hands held out to greet him, the touch of his hands, the thrill! Was she dreaming, or had this all been true? Oh, if he could but have stayed a few minutes longer. Just so that they might have talked together and gotten their bearings. And he was going away, into what he seemed to think was pretty sure death! Could it be that they would have to wait for Heaven to talk together? Oh, the joy and the sorrow of it! The memory of his arms about her, his lips on hers! It was wonderful! It was beautiful!

And it wasn't anything she could tell anyone about! Not yet anyway. Not even her mother. Her mother wouldn't understand a boy she never had known telling her he loved her. And she couldn't bear to bring the beauty of that newfound love into the light of criticism. And that would be inevitable if she tried to make it plain. They would only think he was one of those "fresh" soldiers, as her mother frequently disapproved of some of the very young, quite gay, boys at the canteen. And her mother would never understand how she could have so far forgotten her upbringing as to let a stranger kiss her, hold her in his arms, even if he *had* gone to school with her years ago. No, this was something she would keep to herself for the present. Herself—and God—perhaps. She didn't feel that she knew God very well. She would want to pray to Him to guard her lover as he went forth into unknown perils. She would have to learn to pray. She would want to do this thing right, and she did not feel that she knew much about prayer, that is, effectual prayer! Oh, of course she had said her prayers quite formally ever since she was a tiny child, quite properly and discreetly. But seldom had she prayed for things she really needed. She had seldom really needed anything. Needs had always been supplied for her before she was even aware that they were needs. But now, here was a need. She wanted with all her heart to have Charlie safe, and to have him come back to her. She wanted to feel his arms about her again, to see him look into her eyes the way he had done when he told her so reverently that he loved her—that he had prayed for her.

Where could she learn to pray aright? Since she could not tell anyone else of her need, would God teach her?

And just then Susan tapped at her door.

"You're wanted on the telephone, Miss Blythe," she said, and Blythe's heart leaped with sudden hope. Could it be possible that Charlie had found a way to telephone her?

"Coming, Susan," she sang out, springing from her chair and hurrying to the door.

Chapter 2

CHARLIE MONTGOMERY, striding down Wolverton Drive, was quickening his pace with every stride until he was fairly hurling himself along, straining his eyes toward the highway. Was that the bus coming? Yes, it was. And he must catch it! He couldn't possibly do all that was to be done before he left unless he did.

But the glad wonder was in his heart even though he hadn't time to cast a thought in its direction. Was he going to make it? He scarcely had breath for the shrill whistle that rent the air and arrested the driver as he was about to start on his route, but it reached his ear, and looking around he saw the soldier coming. One had to wait for a soldier these days, of course.

Just in time Charlie swung onto the bus and was started on his way; and not till then, as he dropped into the seat that a smiling old gentleman made beside him, did his mind revert to the great joy that he was carrying within him.

He had come this way full of fear and trembling lest he was doing the wrong thing. Lest he would be laughed at, scorned, for daring to call on the young woman upon whom his heart had dared to set itself, and she had not only received him graciously, warmly, gladly, but she had listened to his words, had owned that she loved him, had let him hold her in his arms and kiss her. That much was the theme of his joy-symphony. It was enough for the first minute or two till he got his breath.

"Well," said the kindly old gentleman next him, "you going back to your company?"

Charlie suddenly became aware that someone was addressing him. He turned politely and gave attention.

"Why, yes," he answered hesitantly, recalling his thoughts from the house up Wolverton Drive, and the girl he had gone to see.

"Where are you located?" asked the old man with kindly interest.

"I've been in Washington taking some special training," he said evasively.

"Yes? That's interesting. What special service are you doing?"

Charlie twinkled his eyes.

"I'm not supposed to discuss that at present," he said. "Sorry. It's kind of you to be interested."

"Well now, I beg your pardon, of course," said the old man, and he looked at the young soldier with added respect. "But I—I really didn't know that a question like that couldn't be always answered."

"It's all right, sir," said Charlie with his charming smile. "It's not my fault, you know. And, I beg your pardon, this is where I change buses. You'll excuse me please." Charlie swung off the bus as its door opened, and tore across to another that was standing on the opposite corner. Fortunate that he could catch this one. He had been expecting to have to wait ten minutes more for the next one, and that would have given him little time to pick up his luggage and catch his train.

And now when he found himself almost alone in a bus, with time to get back to his happy thoughts, it already seemed ages since he had left the girl he loved. He began to wonder if it had surely happened? Perhaps he just dreamed that he had been to Bonniwell's and talked with Blythe. And then suddenly the sound of her voice whispered in his heart, her eyes seemed to look into his, the feeling of her lips on his! No, it was not a dream! It was real. Joy, joy, joy!

Just at present, in the midst of his tumult of realization that memory brought, the possibility of his own probable death in the offing, the fact that had loomed so large before he had dared to come to her, seemed not to count at all. He was simply rejoicing in the unhoped-for love that had been given him, and could not think of the days

ahead when death would probably come down and wreak
its vengeance. He was just exulting in the present, with no
thought or plan for the future as a normal lover would have
done. It was enough for the present moment that she
loved him, and was not angry that he had told her of his
love. It made her seem all the dearer than he had
dreamed, it gave a glimpse of what it might be to have her
thought, her love to carry with him on his dangerous
mission. It was enough that he could sit back in that bus
and close his eyes and remember the thrill of holding her
close in his arms, his face against hers.

With such thoughts as these for company the ride
seemed all too brief, till the bustle and noise of the city
brought him back to the present moment and its necessi-
ties. Tenth Street, yes, here was the corner where he must
get off and pick up those packages he had ordered yesterday over the telephone, to be ready this morning. And
over on Chestnut Street was the place where he had
promised to stop and pick up a book some kindly stranger
had offered him. He didn't think he would be likely to
want the book, but he did not like to hurt the man's
feelings, for he had a few days ago gone out of his way to
get an address for him that he wanted. Well, it wouldn't
take but a minute. He glanced at his watch. There was
time. He could give the book away, or conveniently lose it
if it proved a bore. He didn't at all know what the book
was. The kindly friend had not told him. Just said it was a
book he might like to have with him, and it was small,
wouldn't take up much room. So, well, he would stop in
case the first packages were ready on time.

And then to his surprise the packages were not only
ready, but waiting near the door for him, and a smiling
proprietor handed them out with a few cheery words, and
it suddenly came to him to realize how exceedingly kind
everybody was to men of the service now. The world had
really taken on an air of kindliness. Was it only for the
soldiers and sailors, or was it everybody?

He hurried over to his other stopping place and was
handed a small neat package with a letter strapped on
with a rubber band. The man himself was out but the
salesman handed it out smiling. More kindliness!

He put the little book in his pocket, thankful it was not

large, and went on his way. A glance at the clock told him he had plenty of time to telephone. Should he, dared he telephone Blythe? He hadn't dared think of that before, but now the longing to hear her voice once more was too much for him. Passing a place where there was a telephone booth he went in and looked up her number, even now hindered by a shyness that had kept him for days deciding whether to go and see her before he left. Perhaps someone else would answer the phone, that dour servant woman, or even possibly her mother. What should he say? Was this perhaps the wrong thing to do? Was there a possibility that it might spoil his happiness? But no, if such a thing could be possible it would be better to find it out now than to go on dreaming in a fool's paradise. So he frowned at the number, and dialed it quickly before he could change his mind, for now the longing to hear her speak was uncontrollable. It was going to be simply unspeakable if she was gone anywhere and he couldn't get her in time.

It was the dour Susan who answered.

No, Miss Bonniwell was not in. She had just gone out to her Red Cross class.

He felt as if the woman had slapped him in the face, but of course that was foolish. There was an instant's silence and then Susan asked.

"Who shall I tell her called?"

Charlie came to himself crisply:

"Montgomery is the name. Is there any way that I can reach her at that Red Cross class?"

"I suppose you might," said Susan disapprovingly. "She's always pretty busy though. Still—if she chooses, of course—the number is Merrivale 1616."

"I thank you," he said with relief in his voice, "It's rather important. I'm leaving in a few minutes. I wouldn't be able to call her later."

He began to dial Merrivale 1616 as if it were some sacred number.

Of course he did not know how reluctant Blythe had been to go to that class. How eagerly she had flown to the telephone a few minutes before hoping, praying that it might be himself calling, although he had not said he would—and of course he wouldn't have time, she knew.

"Who is it, Susan?" she had asked eagerly, as she passed her in the hall dusting.

"It's one of them Red Cross women," answered Susan sourly. "They act as if they owned you body and soul. They said they had to speak to you right away that minute."

"Oh," said Blythe in a crestfallen tone. "I suppose I ought to have gone to that class, but they had so many I thought they could get along without me for once."

"And so they could!" encouraged Susan indignantly.

"I suppose I could send a message by you that I have something else important to do this morning."

Blythe lingered on the stairs looking hopefully at Susan, for the woman had often helped her out of unwanted engagements, but this time Susan shook her head.

"No, Miss Blythe, you couldn't. I asked them did they want me to give you a message, but they said no, they must speak with you. They seemed in some awful hurry."

Blythe gave an impatient little sigh and hurried down to the telephone in the library.

Chapter 3

MRS. FELTON and Mrs. Bruce had arrived early at the Red Cross room, had hung their wraps in a convenient place, and settled down in the pleasantest situation they could find.

They arranged their working paraphernalia comfortably, and looked around with satisfaction.

"I wonder where Blythe Bonniwell is," said Mrs. Felton as she took out her thimble and scissors and settled her glasses over her handsome nose. "She's always so early, and she seems so interested in the work. It's unusual, don't you think, for one so young and pretty to seem so really in earnest."

"Well, of course, that's the fashion now, to be interested in anything that has to do with war work. They tell me she's always at the canteens evenings. She's very popular with the young soldiers," said Mrs. Bruce with pursed lips. "She won't last, you'll see. I'm not surprised she isn't here."

"Well, somehow, I can't help feeling that Blythe is somewhat different from the common run of young girls. I don't believe she'll lose her interest," said Mrs. Felton, giving a troubled glance out the window that opened on the street.

"Well, she isn't here, is she? You mark my words, she'll begin to drop out pretty soon. They all do unless they have really joined up with the army or navy and *have* to keep at it. This is probably the beginning already for Blythe."

"I hope not," sighed Mrs. Felton. "I'm sure I don't know what we'll do if she doesn't come today."

"Why is she so important?" demanded Anne Houghton who had just come in and was taking off her hat and powdering her nose. "I'm sure she doesn't do so much more work than the rest of us." There was haughtiness and almost a shade of contempt in Anne's tone.

Mrs. Felton gave her a quick inspecting glance.

"Why, she put away the materials last night, and I don't see what she has done with the new needles. I can't find them anywhere and we can't sew without needles. The one I have has a blunt point."

"Oh, I see!" said Anne. "Well, I should think she was rather officious, taking charge of all the needles," said Anne Houghton sitting down in the third best chair in the room. "Who does she think she is, anyway? Just because she's Judge Bonniwell's daughter, and has plenty of money, and has Dan Seavers dancing attendance on her at all hours. I can't think what he sees in her, anyway, little colorless thing, so stuck on her looks that she won't even use the decent cosmetics that everybody else uses. She'd be a great deal more attractive if she would at least use a little lipstick."

Mrs. Felton gave Anne another withering glance and went to the sewing machine to oil it and put it in running order for the day, not even attempting an answer.

"Well, what do you suppose she can have done with those needles?" asked Mrs. Bruce rousing to the occasion. "My needle has a blunt point too. I don't see how so many of them got that way. They can't be very good needles."

"Well, if you ask me," said Mrs. Noyes who had just come in, "I think it was that child Mrs. Harper brought with her yesterday. He picked up every needle and pin he could find in the place and began to drive them into the cake of soap they gave him to play with,—the idea! *Soap!* For a *baby!* And scarce as soap is now in war times!"

"Well, but soap ought not to make needles blunt," said Mrs. Felton.

"Oh, he didn't stop at the soap," said Mrs. Noyes with a sniff. "He had a toy hammer with him, and when he got his cake of soap all full he started in on the table and the floor, and tried a few on the wheel of the sewing machine. I declare I got so nervous I thought I should fly. I was so glad when she decided she had to take her child home for his lunch. I don't know why he needed any lunch though. He had bread and butter, and sticky cake, and chocolate candy and a banana along, and he just ate continually, and kept coming around and leaning over my sewing and smearing it with grease and chocolate. I had to take that little nightgown I was working on home and wash it out before I could hand it in. I don't think we ought to allow women to bring their children along. They're an awful hindrance."

"But some women couldn't come without them. They have no one to leave them with at home," said another good woman.

"Let them take their children to the nursery then," said Mrs. Noyes with a pin in her mouth. "Mrs. Harper thinks her child is too good to go to a nursery with the other children!"

"What I want to know is, what are we going to do about those needles?" said Anne Houghton. "Here I am ready to sew, and *no needles!*"

"I think I'll call up Blythe Bonniwell and ask what she did with them," said Mrs. Felton. "I've looked simply everywhere and I can't find them. She must have taken them home with her." And without further ado Mrs. Felton went to the telephone, while all the room full of ladies sat silent, listening to see what would happen.

"What did you do with the new needles, last night, Blythe?" asked Mrs. Felton severely, getting so close to the phone that her voice was sharp and rasping. "I've looked simply everywhere for them. And you know we can't work without needles. You must have taken them home with you."

"The needles? Why, no, Mrs. Felton, I didn't take them home. They are right there on the shelf where you had them before," said Blythe pleasantly.

"The shelf?" said Mrs. Felton more sharply. "What shelf?"

"Why, the shelf right over where you were sitting yesterday, Mrs. Felton."

"Well, you're mistaken, Miss Bonniwell. There isn't a needle in sight, and I'm looking right at the shelf."

"Oh, Mrs. Felton. But I'm sure I put them right there in plain sight. Someone must have moved them."

"No," said Mrs. Felton coldly. "No one could have moved them, for there hasn't been anyone here to move them, and we have looked just everywhere. I wish you would come right over and find them. You know we have simply *got* to have those needles, for there is not another one to be had in this town, and we haven't any of us time to go into the city after them. You know needles are scarce these days. I wish you'd look in your handbag and see if you didn't take them home with you."

"No, I didn't bring them home," said Blythe decidedly. "I know I didn't."

"Very well then, come over here at once and find those needles! I shall hold you personally responsible for them."

"All right," said Blythe indignantly. "I'll be right over!"

So Blythe caught up her hat and coat, snatched her handbag from the bureau where she had put it last night when she came in, and hurried away, calling to Susan that she was going to her Red Cross work.

When she walked into the Red Cross room the ladies were all sitting there in various stages of obvious impatience. They had purposely so arranged themselves for a rebuke as soon as Anne Houghton announced, "There she comes at last! My word! It is high time!"

But Blythe was anything but rebuked as she entered with that delightful radiance on her happy face, for she had been thinking about her new joy all the way down, and her thoughts had lent wings to her feet.

So, as she entered, the ladies sat in a row and blinked, for perhaps the brightness of her face dazzled them for an instant.

"Well, so you've come at last!" said Mrs. Bruce disagreeably. "Now, get to work and find those needles if you can. We've looked everywhere."

Blythe's glance went swiftly to the shelf over Mrs. Bruce's head.

"But—why there they are! Just where I told you they were!" she said triumphantly.

"What do you mean?" snapped Mrs. Felton. "I don't see any needles."

"Why, in that blue box. Don't you remember, we took the whole box because we were afraid we wouldn't be able to get more later when we needed them."

"That blue *box?*" said Mrs. Felton, jumping up and going over to seize the box from the shelf. "Why I supposed those were safety pins. I don't understand."

She took down the box and opened it, and her face took on a look of utter amazement.

"My word!" she said slowly. "I certainly don't understand. I supposed of course those were the safety pins that Mrs. Huyler brought. Well, then where are *they?*"

"She took them home again when she found this wasn't a nursery," said Mrs. Bruce grimly. "She said she would take them to a place she knew *needed* them."

"Well, upon my word!" said Mrs. Felton again. "I guess you're right and I was the one to blame. I certainly ask your pardon, Blythe."

"Oh, that's all right," laughed Blythe, swinging off her coat and hat and taking the first empty chair that presented itself. "Now, where do I begin? Do you need more buttonholes made, or shall I run a machine?"

"Make buttonholes," snapped Anne Houghton handing over the baby's nightgown she had been set to finish. "I just hate them, and anyway I always make them crooked. I don't see why *poor* babies have to have buttonholes anyway. Why can't you use safety pins? I'd rather buy a gross of them and donate them than have to make a single buttonhole."

"Oh, I don't mind buttonholes," said Blythe pleasantly. "That was one thing I learned to do when I was a little girl. We had a seamstress who made beautiful ones, and she taught me."

"Well, I'm sure you're welcome to them for all me," said Anne disagreeably.

And it was just then that the telephone rang, and Anne, being on her feet, answered it. She always liked to answer the phone. It gave her a line on other people's business, and that was usually interesting.

"Yes?" she drawled as she took down the receiver.

"Red Cross Sewing Class. *Who? Who* did you say? Miss Bonniwell? Yes, she's here. Who shall I say wants her?"

But Blythe with cheeks like lovely roses was on her feet beside the telephone.

"I'll take it," she said smiling, as she gathered the receiver into her hand.

"Well, you needn't snatch so," said Anne turning angrily away just as she was trying to identify the voice as Dan Seaver's.

"Oh, I'm sorry," said Blythe, her cheeks flaming crimson, "I didn't mean to snatch."

But Anne turned away with her head held high and went over to select a needle for her own use.

So the room held its breath to listen to the telephone conversation.

"Yes?" said Blythe quietly into the instrument, though she couldn't keep the lilt out of her voice, for she hoped she knew just who was calling her, though, of course, it might be her mother or Susan from home.

"Is that you, Blythe?" The voice on the wire was cautious, tentative.

"It certainly is," said Blythe with a light ripple of a laugh.

"Are you alone?" Again the voice was very guarded, low. Even the most attentive listener could not have understood what came from the other end of the wire, for Blythe was cupping her hand about the receiver, which was most annoying to Mrs. Bruce. She severely shook her head at Mrs. Felton who ventured to interrupt the performance by asking a question about which buttons were to go on the little nightgowns they were making.

But Blythe's voice was clear, without confusion.

"Oh, no. I'm sorry!" she answered brightly. "But—you weren't late, were you?"

"No, I got here in plenty of time. The train was late. I found I had a few minutes to spare, and I wanted to hear your voice again, even if it were only in commonplaces."

"Oh, that's nice of you!" said Blythe graciously. "Don't forget to write that down for further reference," and she rippled out her bewildering laughter again.

"No, I won't forget," came the man's voice, louder and clearer than before. "I'll write that down as soon as I get on my way, and I'll see that it gets to the proper person. And by the way, will you kindly think over what I told you, and see if you can possibly respond to my suggestion?"

"Oh—yes—I'll do that," said Blythe in a matter-of-fact tone. "I'll take pleasure in doing that, and I'll let you know later what I think."

Blythe was talking in a very off-hand tone, and she had a feeling that her eyes were twinkling over her words, across the space between them, as if he could see her and understand why she was speaking in such veiled language. But her heart was warm and happy over his voice, even though she had to strain her ears to identify every word.

"That's good of you," said the man's voice, falling into the game easily. "I'm glad to have had this little talk with you—this chance to explain."

"Yes," said Blythe smiling into the receiver. "It was so good of you to call. But how did you know where to find me?"

"Oh, I called the house first and the servant gave me the number," he explained.

"Oh, yes, of course," said Blythe letting her voice linger, glad to have the brief interlude drawn out to its utmost, knowing the listeners would not understand. "Well, it was nice of you to take all that trouble to find me and let me know."

"Oh, it was a pleasure, I assure you," spoke the young man, "and you are sure you won't forget?"

"Oh no, I won't forget," lilted Blythe gaily. "And—I hope you—are successful!" Those last words were spoken guardedly, very low, her tone full of feeling, as she gave a quick glance about the silent room full of women, sewing steadily without a word.

Suddenly the man's voice spoke sharply, almost breathlessly:

"Well, I hear it coming! I must go! Is there any chance you might be at home later in the day or evening, if I had the opportunity to call again?"

"Oh, yes," she breathed softly, "after two o'clock and all the evening. Yes, I'll be at home."

"Of course it *may not* be possible for me to call, but I'll try. Good-by—*dearest!*"

Could that last whispered word be heard by the audience? Blythe held her head high and didn't care. What did all those women know or care about her and her precious beautiful affairs?

Then she hung up the receiver, and walked steadily over to Mrs. Bruce.

"Have you one of those buttons I'm to make buttonholes for, Mrs. Bruce? I must get to work and make up for lost time."

She took the proffered button and went smilingly over to an empty chair without a sign of the lovely tumult in her heart.

Then those frustrated women sat and sewed away, and occasionally lifted baffled eyes and glared at one another, as much as to say: "Does that Blythe Bonniwell think she can get away with a thing like this as easily as all that?"

And at last Anne lifted her head with a toss and sang out clearly for them all to hear. "Well, who *was* your friend? It was Dan Seavers, wasn't it? I was sure I knew his voice. Are you and he going to the benefit concert at the arena tonight? I suppose that's what he called up about. I don't see why you had to hedge about answering him that way. I'm curious to know if he succeeded in getting tickets after waiting all this time. And I think I know where he could get a couple if he didn't. I know somebody has some who has to leave town tonight. Do you think he would like them?"

Blythe looked up with a distant little smile.

"Why, I wouldn't know, Anne," she said. "That wasn't Dan calling."

"Well, who in time was it then, with a voice so much like Dan's?"

"Oh, it was just one of my friends in the air corps," said Blythe easily. "I don't think you would know him. He was only here on a brief furlough."

Anne looked at her curiously.

"Oh, *yes?*" she said contemptuously, but Blythe was too happy to be ruffled by her contempt and went on making buttonholes with a radiance upon her lovely face that defied the scrutiny, furtive or open, of all those women. She went happily through the morning, thinking her pleasant thoughts. True, Charlie Montgomery was going from her, but he was leaving his love in her heart, and for the present that was all she needed to give her joy.

And thus thinking her happy thoughts the morning went forward with its business, and at last was over, so that she was free to go on to her home, and wait for whatever might be in store.

"Dearest?" Had he really said that? She hugged the memory to her heart.

But back in the room she had left, where the other women were purposely idling about putting on their wraps and getting ready to leave, there was a significant silence until the sound of her footsteps died away in the distance, and the ordinary routine noises of the street assured them that Blythe was well out of hearing. Then they relaxed almost audibly.

"Well," said Mrs. Bruce grimly, "she certainly has more brass! Imagine her sitting here so gaily sewing after she had been through that play-acting on the telephone. Was that really Dan who called her, Anne?"

Anne Houghton shrugged her shoulders.

"Well, I certainly thought it was. But why on earth she considered she had to tell a lie about it I'm sure I don't know. It wouldn't be of much importance, would it? We all know she runs after him day in and day out."

"I don't think she does," said Mrs. Felton. "She's too well-bred to run after anybody. Remember, Anne, her mother is a lady."

Anne shrugged again.

"That's not saying *she* is one," said Anne.

"What makes you hate her so?" asked Mrs. Felton looking gravely, steadily at Anne.

"Oh, I don't hate her," laughed Anne. "I didn't give the matter that much importance. I merely think she's so smug, and she does like to give big impressions about herself. See today how determined she was to let us think that was some soldier she was talking to, some one of those soldiers she's hostess to up at the canteen. She wants us to think that she can flirt around like the other girls."

"She doesn't flirt at the canteen," said Mrs. Stanton gravely. "I go there every night, and I've never seen her do anything out of the way."

"And I guess you'll find that Blythe is busy some nights doing evening hospital work or something of that sort. Isn't she? I'm sure I heard that," said Mrs. Felton.

"Oh, *really*? I think you must be mistaken. I saw her out with Dan Seaver last night and also the night before." That from Anne.

"Well, I suppose she must have some nights off. Most of them do, don't they?"

"I'm sure I wouldn't know," said Anne coldly. "But for heaven's sake don't let's talk about that girl any more. I'm fed up with her. She gets on my nerves every time I see her. Just say she's a paragon and let it go at that. If that's what you like in a girl then that's what you like. Good-by. I'm going out to lunch and I'm late now," and Anne slammed out of the door and her high heels clicked as she hurried away.

Mrs. Felton and Mrs. Bruce walked slowly down the street behind Anne, and watched the arrogant swing of her shoulders till she vanished around the next corner. Then after a pause Mrs. Felton said:

"Young people are awfully rude nowadays, don't you think?"

"I certainly do," said Mrs. Bruce with a heavy sigh. "It's the one thing that makes me glad my daughter died when she was a child, so she wouldn't have to live to grow up in this impudent age."

Mrs. Felton uttered a sympathetic little sound, and walked thoughtfully on until they parted.

Chapter 4

THE TELEPHONE WAS ringing as Blythe entered the home door and she hastened to answer it, wondering if it could possibly be Charlie again so soon. But it was only a tradesman calling up about something that had been ordered, which he couldn't supply yet, and she turned away with a sigh.

Upstairs her mother met her in the hall smiling.

"Oh, you're back, Blythe. I didn't think you'd be here for a half-hour yet. Well I just made a tentative engagement for you for this evening," said her mother. "It was Dan Seavers. He wanted you to go somewhere with him tonight. I forget where. But I told him I was sure you'd be glad to go."

"Oh, *mother!*" said Blythe in dismay. "Not *this* evening! I really can't go this evening."

"Why, why not, child? If it's that hospital-office work I think you give entirely too much time to that. It isn't good for your health, after you have sewed all the morning. And you really ought to take some days off and not slave *all* the time, even if it is war time. The government *doesn't* want to kill anyone, and there's no need to go to excess, even in a good thing."

Blythe was silent and thoughtful for a moment, then she looked up.

"Is Dan going to call up again?"

"No. I think not," said her mother. "He's going to be away this afternoon, but he said you could call and leave word with the butler what time you would be ready. And he'll be here as early as you say."

29

"All right," said Blythe after an instant's thought, "I'll attend to it."

Her mother turned away, smiling, satisfied. After all mother didn't know, couldn't understand why she must stay at home tonight. She would better engineer this thing herself. Later, when she could talk about this, she would tell her mother all about Charlie Montgomery. But not now, not till it was more a part of herself so that she would be able to answer questions, and make her mother fully understand.

She watched her mother get ready to go out to her war work, watched her down the street, and then she went to the telephone and left a message with the Seavers' butler.

"Please tell Mr. Dan that Miss Bonniwell cannot possibly accept his kind invitation for the evening. Something else was already planned. Thank him for the invitation."

Then Blythe went contentedly to her room and sat down to await the ring from the telephone. Would Charlie call? *Could* he call? For she was sure he would if he could.

And it was then she had her first uninterrupted time for going over, step by step, the beautiful experience of the morning. It was then she could close her eyes and visualize his face when he rose from his chair to meet her as she came downstairs. That fine lifting of his head, the sparkle in his eyes, the old humble yet assured manner he had as a boy in school. Charlie! The same Charlie she used to watch and admire as a lad in school days. Charlie, come to tell her that he loved her! It was almost beyond belief! He had never seemed to look her way before. How did he know that he loved her? He had seen her so seldom?

All the sweet hurrying eager questions that rushed upon her, each demanding to be answered at once, yet none of them shaking her faith in his love even for an instant. The breath-taking memory of his arms about her, folding her close. Why, she had never dreamed what love like this could be!

She had read many beautiful love stories of course, and delighted in them, yet none of them came up to the sweetness of those all-too-brief blissful moments while Charlie was with her. Her own lover!

There would come a time of course when she must bring all this out in the open, must tell her mother and father. Or would there? *Must* she? If anything happened to Charlie, if he did not come back, she would keep it deep in her own heart. Never would she allow even her dearest ones to speculate on what Charlie was, and what he had intended to do about all this. That was her part, and for the present it must be kept so. Precious. Just between themselves. And so, whatever came in the future, this afternoon was hers to be with Charlie in her thoughts. To knit up all the years of affection that had been so empty and barren for them both before the knowledge of their mutual love had come to make it shine like a light.

And then she turned in her mind to face that other thought, that terrible thought, that perhaps he might not come back. Not *ever!* He had spoken as if that was a sure thing. In fact it was the only reason apparently that had given him the courage to come and tell her of his love, as if it were just a kind of spiritual thing that could last through eternity, but could not be used on this earth. It seemed a beautiful awesome way to look at life, to reach such heights of sacrifice that he could smile as he said it. Would she ever reach that height too? Oh, she could not, must not, think of that now. She must only think how he was going to try to call her up sometime, today, or this evening, and she *must* be at home and be ready for it. She must have heartening words ready at the tip of her tongue, for his time to talk with her might be very short, if it came at all. Just between trains, or a stop at some station for connection, or some needed repair. She must think of all those things and be ready not to waste the time. She must have a pencil and paper ready in case he wanted her to write down some address or something. But she must have some brief sweet messages ready for him to take with him in his memory. Things he would like to hear her voice saying, ringing in his heart sometimes when he was far away, and needed comfort or strengthening.

And so she sat and dreamed it out, as if she were communing with him, knitting up those past years when they had never talked except a few scant words concerning an algebra problem.

It might have seemed to an outsider like a monotonous little round of thoughts to be so sweet and absorbing, but they were precious to the lovely girl who sat and thought them. Like some potent charm that works a change on words written long ago, brings out clearly what was invisible before, so these tender thoughts were painting over the past years, and bringing out the meaning of a young love that has grown up unknown and unacknowledged through the years. And now she could remember glances, furtive shadowed smiles, little acts of kindness and courtesy. Things like picking up her examination paper that a breeze from the window had caught and fluttered across the aisle down to his vicinity. She could read the look in his eyes, the flush on his cheek that before might have only meant embarrassment, shyness. Oh, it was wonderful, this thinking, in the light of the knowledge of that confession of his that he loved her!

Into the midst of these happy dreams, that were as yet not consciously tinged with the coming fears of possible pain and sorrow, there came the ringing of the telephone.

Blythe sprang from her chair and hurried to the instrument over across the hall in her mother's room, lovely anticipation in her face. Could this be Charlie?

But no, it was only some tiresome woman who wanted to persuade her to undertake the management of a play to be given for the benefit of a day nursery.

Feverishly, because she didn't want the telephone to be in use when Charlie called—if he called—she tried to decline, but the woman only urged the harder.

"But such things are not in my line, Mrs. Basset. I never got up a play in my life, wouldn't know how to go about it, and besides, just at present I'm doing all the war work I can possibly manage, without undertaking anything else. No, I'm sorry. I can't possibly do it. Think it over? No, I'm sorry, I can't promise to do that, even, for I wouldn't, under any circumstances, undertake to put on a play anywhere, and I'm quite sure there are more important things to do for the war than to get up a play. No, Mrs. Basset, you'll have to count me out."

She hung up at last with a sigh, and glanced at the clock. Five whole minutes wasted that way! What if he had tried to call during that time, and might have no other opportunity! But there! She must not get hysterical over this.

Quietly she went back to her room and read over the notes she had been writing down. Why, they were almost a letter! For the words came directly from her heart. She would go on writing, and when he did call she would tell him she was just writing him a letter.

With this thought in mind she went back to her writing, a light in her eyes and a sweet smile on her face.

The next interruption was from her mother, calling to say that neither she nor Blythe's father would be at home to dinner tonight, as they had met an old friend who was leaving town at midnight, and wanted them to dine with him at his hotel, so they could have an old time visit.

"Why don't you call Dan and ask him over to dinner with you tonight? That will probably just fit in with his plans," said her mother.

"No," said Blythe sharply, "I don't want to, mother. I've got letters to write and a lot of other things to do. I'll be all right, and I'll tell Susan. You needn't worry. What's one dinner, mother? And I'm tired, I really am. Have a good time, mother dear." Then Blythe went back to her pleasant thoughts, and her first happy letter.

It was five minutes of six when the telephone rang again and Blythe flew to answer, sure now it must be Charlie. But instead she heard Dan Seavers' angry voice.

"What in the name of time is the matter with you, Bly? *Can't* go? Of *course* you can go! I've been planning to take you to this picture for weeks. You know I've spoken of it several times."

"Oh," said Blythe gaily, "I'm sorry, Dan, to disappoint you, but you said nothing about going *tonight,* and I really can't do it. I had made other plans!"

"Plans! *Plans!* What are plans? Change them, then! Call off whatever you've promised to do. This comes first, and I won't take no for an answer."

Blythe drew a weary little sigh and looked with anguished eyes toward the clock. Suppose Charlie should call now? It might be likely. It would be so near the dinner hour, surely his train would stop somewhere at this time, or would it?

Her mind was turning this subject over and over while she tried to be half listening to Dan, and wondering what she could say to him that would make him understand she meant what she said, and that she was not available this evening for *any*thing but her own plans.

"Bly, you're not listening! I say I'm coming right over there and *get* you. We'll go somewhere and get dinner, and then take in the first show."

Blythe roused.

"No!" she said. *"Positively no! I simply can't.* I thought I sent you word in plenty of time for you to find someone else to go with you."

"No, Blythe, you don't mean that! You know you don't want me to take someone else."

"Why, yes, I certainly do, Dan," she said sweetly. "I'm sure you can find somebody."

The altercation lasted some minutes, and Blythe drew a breath of relief when Dan finally grew angry and hung up the receiver with a slam, furious because she wouldn't tell him where she was going, or what engagement she had that she would not break for him.

Annoyed beyond measure at the time he had kept the telephone occupied, Blythe tried to get back her happy serenity, but try as she would she was worried lest Dan had made her miss the few treasured words she hoped to hear from Charlie. And yet of course he hadn't been sure he would be able to call, and this was probably but the beginning of a long weary hopeful waiting. But she put the thought from her. She must not allow her mind to dwell on the possibility of future unhappiness. Not on this the first day of her new joy. Sorrow and anxiety might come, but she would not dwell on them ahead of time. And this was a day that must be remembered as having been all joy.

It was an anxious evening for Blythe. She was beginning to worry lest Charlie hadn't been able to telephone at all, and perhaps there wouldn't be any way she could hear his voice again, ever! She was also beginning to be afraid the call might come so late that her mother and father would arrive in the midst of it, and there would be questions perhaps, and she might have to explain at once, so that the beauty of Charlie's words might become dimmed before she could savor them fully.

But there she was, being silly and hysterical again! Why couldn't she be sensible? This whole thing was something that had come to her right out of the blue as it were, nothing she had solicited, nothing that any act of hers had brought about, and if it was something sent to her she ought to be able to trust, and not get excited about it.

It was not until a little after ten that the call did come, and she tried to go to it calmly, so that she would not be out of breath to talk.

His voice was very clear in the quiet room.

"Is that you, Blythe?"

"Oh, yes, Charlie!" she said joyously. "It is *you at last!*"

"Yes, beloved," he said. "Are you alone?"

"Yes, I'm alone, and so glad to hear your voice!"

"My precious girl! How wonderful to hear *your* voice!"

"I was afraid you couldn't make it." she breathed.

"Yes," said the young man, "our train was late and we had to make up time. New orders. And now, I've only a few minutes to talk, so we mustn't waste time. But I've written you a letter and you may get it in a day or two. It has to go through the regular routine now of course, I think, and you won't know where I am nor where I'm going. But don't mind about that. I just want to say again that I love you. I love you more than I ever dreamed I could love anyone. You opened the way into a heaven of delight when you told me you loved me. I hadn't counted on that. I hadn't thought you ever noticed me. I know I'm going to spend a lot of time rejoicing in your words, in the memory of you in my arms, your face against mine, your lips on mine. It is a greater joy than I ever had hoped could be mine. Even though it must likely be a brief joy, since I have a rendezvous with death."

"Oh, Charlie! *Don't* say that!"

"Well, it's true, beloved! You know I told you if it had not been for that I would never have presumed to tell you what I did." He spoke gravely.

"Well, I'm glad that anything made you tell me," said Blythe, happily. "But oh, I pray that it may only be a brief absence, and that you will soon come back to me."

"I shall be glad of your prayers, but don't be arbitrary about them. My mother used to say that God must have His way, and it was of no use to try to force any other. I believe God knows what He is doing, don't you? And I've committed myself to this thing, you know. I think it is right. I know it is patriotic."

"Yes, I know," sighed Blythe, "but oh, *don't* take it *for granted* that this is going to be *the end!*"

"No," said the young man's voice with a clear ring to it, "we won't take anything *for granted* now, but just our love. Shall it be that way, beloved?"

"Oh, yes!" said the girl breathlessly. "And I like the way you say 'Beloved.' I shall remember your voice saying it, *always*—till you come again."

"That's very precious of you to say. Yes, till I come again—somewhere, sometime. For I do believe there'll be a 'somewhere' of meeting, don't you? *Don't you?* No matter what happens?"

"Yes, of course," said Blythe. "But—I'll believe—you will come back. Oh, Charlie! Why didn't we know each other better before? How much time we've lost out of our childhood days!"

"Not enough to keep us from loving, my dear!" and his voice was very tender. "Please don't mourn over that or anything else. It is enough for me for the present that I can carry your love with me, your permission to receive my love. You are not angry that I told you. That gives me great joy and strength for my mission. It is more than I have ever dared to ask of life. Will you pray for me that I may be brave as I go forth to my duty? Forget that it is terrible, and think of it as something that *must* be victorious. Will you do that?"

"Oh, yes, dear. Of course."

"Then I shall go armed with courage, feeling that whether I live or die, I shall *conquer*. And now, I've only a few seconds left to talk, and how can I possibly say all that I have in my heart in that time? But I want you to understand that if you hear nothing from me, perhaps for a long time, or even perhaps *never,* still I have loved you with all my heart. They have not told me what are to be our circumstances or location, but I feel that communication with our home world may hereafter be greatly restricted, certainly limited, possibly entirely forbidden or impossible, and you will not let yourself grieve about that, will you? You will say in your heart it is all right. You will know I have not forgotten, nor changed. You will remember that?"

"I will remember!" Blythe breathed the words softly, choking back the sobs that kept rising in her throat.

"Dear girl! It was selfish of me to do this to you, and make you unhappy, even for a day. I should have kept my love to myself."

"No, no, don't say that! Please don't!" she pleaded. "Your love is the greatest thing that ever came into my life. I am glad, *glad* that you told me! I shall be glad always!"

"You *dear!*" he breathed softly. "You wonderful, beautiful dear!"

There was silence for an instant, and then suddenly, a far call, and the young man's voice alert, almost agonized:

"They are calling me. I have to go! Good-by, my precious girl. God keep you!"

And then as he hung up she could hear his voice answering to the call: "Coming!"

Chapter 5

FOR A BRIEF interval she stood still before the instrument staring hungrily into it, hoping against hope that there would yet be perhaps one more word from her lover. And then she was suddenly aware of her mother standing in the doorway, watching her, astonished.

"Why, my dear!" said the mother. "How did it happen that you came home so early? Dan told me you would probably be late!"

And suddenly the long wait of the evening with its precious thrilling climax was swept away, as if it had all been a dream, and she was back in her everyday life again, with the usual things and people surrounding her.

"Oh," she said dazedly. "Oh, why no, mother, I didn't go."

"You *didn't go*? But, my dear, I told him I was sure you would be delighted. I am afraid you must have been very rude, for he was quite insistent about it, and I understood him to say that you had known about this for some time. Didn't I make you understand that I had promised you would call him. It certainly was very rude of you if you did not."

"But I did, mother I called him right away after you went, and left word for him that I couldn't go tonight. I left the word with their butler, and then Dan called up himself later and I explained that I couldn't go tonight. I had something else to do that was important."

"Im*portant*?" said her mother eyeing her bewilderedly. "What was it, dear? I don't understand. I thought this was your free evening. I had told him that."

"Yes, mother, but this was something that came up that you didn't know about. I had promised to be at home all the evening for a phone call."

"A phone call! Why, who was calling that you felt was important enough to make you miss going out with Dan? When you had practically promised him you would go with him?"

Blythe's face flushed.

"But I hadn't promised Dan, mother. He had never made a definite date for this, and he can't expect me to dance attendance every time he speaks. I have a few other friends and interests."

"Oh," said her mother significantly. "I thought you considered Dan's wishes would be paramount. I thought you were especially fond of him."

"Oh, not *especially* fond, mother. He's just a good friend. But I wasn't rude to him, really, mother. I left word I couldn't go tonight, and when he called up I tried to explain to him that something had come up that I felt I *ought* to do."

"But who was this person who presumed to ask you to stay at home all the evening? Couldn't you have called him up and told him that you found you could not be here?"

"No, mother. I had no way to reach him till he called. He was a soldier friend who was leaving—for the front— and he had asked if he might call me to say good-by when he left. I said yes, I would be at home all the evening."

"But a soldier boy, just one of those soldiers at the canteen? Stranger boys you don't know very well? It couldn't possibly have made any difference with him. I think, Blythe, that sometimes you confuse your obligations and let trifles hinder more important things. In fact I've been a good deal worried at the number of hours you are spending in that social service down there at the canteen. Of course I want you to be patriotic and all that, but you are just sticking in the house and working hard almost every minute of your life, and it is time you had a little brightness and fun, or you will wither up and get to be old before your time."

"Oh, mother!" protested the girl, "I—you—you don't *understand*. This was a special soldier, going into danger, and his mother had died. He wanted somebody to say good-by to before he went."

"Oh, yes," said her mother a bit sadly. "They're all going into danger, of course, and of course we all feel sorry for them. But you, Blythe, can't take every one of those soldier boys on your heart and feel sorry for them. There are plenty of people over there at the center, good motherly women who would be glad to give a boy good advice before he leaves for the front. That's what they are there for. He didn't need to pick out a young girl and hold her up for an evening just to say good-by. Those boys haven't always got good sense. I have no patience with them. It is all right of course for you to play games with them, and make them have a cheerful time, but I do think you ought to hold your home time free for your own friends. Blythe, I'm really worried about you. I don't want you to go to extremes in anything, and you know these boys in their uniforms may be very attractive and all that, but when they get across the water they'll forget all about the girl that sacrificed what she wanted to do just to humor them."

"But mother, it wasn't like that! I didn't *want* to go with Dan tonight. I really didn't. I was tired and wanted to stay at home and get caught up with several things, and I had some letters to write. You see—"

Blythe hesitated and looked troubled. She was almost on the verge of telling her mother all about Charlie Montgomery, only somehow this seemed no time to bring out that precious experience and tell it in every detail. Her mother was in no mood to sympathize and understand just now. She was evidently too much annoyed about her failing Dan Seavers.

"You see," said Mrs. Bonniwell, "I had a long talk today with Mrs. Seavers. She is so pleased that you are going so intimately with Dan. She says it has made her feel so safe and happy about him, so content that he is in good company and not getting in with a wild set. She has been greatly troubled about a girl who sings at one of the night clubs, in whom he has been interested, and she was so relieved when he took to asking you to go places. I do think you ought to consider other people as well as those young boys in the soldiers' canteen. You know it would be really worth-while to help a young man like Dan Seavers. A young man in his position would have a great many temptations, and a young girl with right principles can often strengthen her young men friends by her friendship and be doing something really worth-while. You know Dan is in line for an officer's commission; and what he *is* will be an influence on all the soldiers under him. If I were you I would consider how wonderful it would be to help anchor Dan to the right kind of people."

"No, mother, that's just it. I don't like the kind of men and girls that come around Dan. More and more it is getting so that I feel uncomfortable in his company. I don't think you would like them either, mother, if you could be with us sometimes."

"Well, that's unfortunate, but don't you think a good girl can usually dominate a situation wherever she is, and show them how much better a right-minded girl is than one who is loud and coarse and common?"

Blythe looked troubled.

"No, mother, not always. I used to think so, but lately I've been places with Dan where I felt as if I were being soiled and trampled underfoot."

"Blythe!" said her mother. "You don't mean Dan would allow anybody to be rude to you while you were in his company?"

"I don't think Dan feels the difference. He doesn't understand why I don't enjoy going places with people like that."

"Oh, my dear! I'm sorry to hear that. But don't you think you might be able to win him away from that kind of people?"

"I'm afraid not, mother," said the troubled Blythe sadly, thinking in her heart that there were going to be a lot of questions to settle which she had not thought of hitherto. How was she going to make her mother understand? Oh, this was something she had to think out before she talked any more about it, even with her mother. But for the present her inmost heart told her that she had no taste nor interest in going anywhere with Dan or any other young man, now that she knew of Charlie's love, and while he was off engaged in a terrible undertaking for the cause of freedom. Oh, of course, she would have to go about as usual and be pleasant and interested in life as it had to be lived here on this side of the world, but good times were not the chief aim of her existence any more. Something had happened to her since Charlie Montgomery had told her of his love for her, and the great undertaking to which his life was pledged. To a large extent that undertaking must be hers too, hers for interest and prayers. Hers to place first in the list of daily plans. Hers to cherish as the greatest possible undertaking. Because she and Charlie were one in heart now, they must be one in purpose too. And if, in the working out of that purpose, it came about that Charlie had to die to accomplish it, well then, it was her part to die too, to a lot of interests that had hitherto been a part of her life.

But she couldn't tell all this to her mother now. Mother would protest and tell her she was crazy. Mother didn't know what it was to love someone who was going out to die. She would say she was morbid. She would turn heaven and earth to get her interested in the world, and get her out among the young people again, make her stop her delightful work among the nursery babies, and maybe make her stop the Red Cross classes. Mother would just tell around that she hadn't seemed well lately and she felt she needed a rest, maybe insist upon her going away somewhere, to the shore or the mountains or down to Florida, and there was nothing in life that Blythe wanted to do less than to go away from the home where Charlie would write if he had any opportunity to write at all. Oh, what should she do?

Of course if worst came to worst she could tell her mother the whole story, tell of Charlie's coming, and how she had always admired him, but could she make mother understand now, after all this excitement? Evidently her mother was thoroughly on Dan's mother's side, and willing to have Dan take her out anywhere, just so that his mother's worries might be appeased. But mother just did not understand, and how could she make her see it in the right way? Mother had always been so sane and reasonable. And mother wouldn't for a moment approve of the things Dan did and said when he was out among that crowd whose company he seemed to enjoy so much. Was it possible that Dan could be turned back to a more refined crowd? Was it really right that she should try to help him in this way? How the thought of it irked her, in the light of the wonderful love of a real man!

Well, she would have to think this out, try to find out what her duty was, and of course if it was duty, she must do it. But it need have nothing to do with the new joy that had come into her life. That was something secure, that was hers. So far hers in secret, but *hers,* and it was something that nothing, *nobody,* could ever take away from her. Not even death, because it was founded on that rendezvous with death that had set his heart free to come to her and tell her of his love. Oh, death could be cruel, *cruel,* and the fear of death could bring agony—the death of a beloved one! But death with all its stings could not take her beloved's love away from her. Somehow that thought bore her along over the immediate present with its problems, and bravely into the dim future that gloomed ahead with so many terrible possibilities. She must sit down and think this thing all through, and see what was the right thing to do. Oh, if she only had somebody to talk it over with.

Of course her mother, normally, would be the one, the only confidante she had ever had. But how could her mother judge aright in this thing? She would be too horrified by the unknown. Charlie would mean nothing to her now but a menace. She would not at first realize what a difference death made in the conventions of the world. Even if it were only a *rendezvous* and didn't reach a final end, it did make a difference, and by and by when this matter of pleasing Mrs. Seavers was past, she was sure it would all be perfectly understood by her mother. Anyway, it wasn't really hers to tell—yet. It was their precious secret, hers and Charlie's.

All these things flashed through her mind like a message she was reading to herself, while her mother talked on.

And when her mother, watching her daughter's changing expressions, finally dropped wearily into a chair, and said:

"Oh, Blythe. What *is* the matter with you? It is not like you to be so regardless of others' needs. Why will you not give the help you can so easily give? If you could have seen his poor mother!"

Suddenly Blythe put on a resolute look.

"Why, of course, mother, I'll do all I can to influence Dan for the right things, but you don't just seem to understand that he practically wants to *own* me, to order me around, and insist I shall go whenever he commands."

"Oh, my dear! I don't think he means it that way. He just likes you very much, and really wants your company."

Blythe's face grew serious.

"Well, perhaps," she said hesitantly. "But tonight I didn't want to go, and I felt I had a right to say no. Besides, mother, people are beginning to talk as if Dan and I were engaged, and we're *not*. I don't *want* people to get that idea! I don't like to be watched and talked about!"

"Nonsense!" said her mother. "Nobody is talking about you. That's just a sign you're getting self-centered. I don't believe anybody has ever thought of such a thing."

"Yes, they have," said Blythe firmly. "I heard them myself today as I was going into the Red Cross room."

"You heard someone talking about you? Who in the world would dare to do that?"

"Oh, it was only Anne Houghton, and she's always been disagreeable and jealous, but she was talking to Mrs. Bruce, and *she* assented to everything Anne said, and I just felt as if I wanted to get out and get away from them all. Of course I won't desert the work I've promised to do for the war. But I do think I'd rather not go out quite so much with Dan. Oh, I'll go sometimes, of course, but please don't urge me when you see I'd rather not."

"Why, of course not, dear," said her mother anxiously, "but I wish you would tell me what they said that has made you feel so uncomfortable."

"Oh, Anne was just saying that I thought I was so great because I had Dan Seavers tagging around with me everywhere, that I wouldn't let him out of my sight, and things like that. Mother, I don't like to be talked about that way. It takes all the joy out of life."

"Well, of course, it isn't pleasant," said her mother

thoughtfully. "But after all that wasn't such a dreadful thing for her to say. She's probably jealous. Maybe she admires him herself very much. However, of course, I don't want to urge you to do anything that does not seem pleasant to you."

"Thank you, mother dear," said Blythe, coming over to her mother and kissing her tenderly, and as she stood with her mother's arms about her she felt a quick impulse to tell her all about Charlie Montgomery. And perhaps she would have done so, except that her father came in just then with some news about the war that he had just heard, and the time seemed again not to be just right for the story. Perhaps she should wait and think it over a little more, plan out in her mind just how she would make them understand what kind of a boy Charlie had always been, introduce him to them as it were, bit by bit, so that they would see the beauty and tenderness of his nature. So that they would not be shocked by the abruptness of what he had done in telling her, an almost stranger, that he loved her.

Then her father turned on the radio and there came a session of reports of what had been going on in some of the war zones, men sent on secret missions behind the enemy lines, to get certain information, to spy out the enemies' plans; others flying straight into death to accomplish some great necessary destruction of the enemy's works. They were almost like a suicide squad.

Blythe caught her breath, and one small hand flew to her throat involuntarily.

"Oh!" she breathed softly under her breath, and looked aghast at her father and her mother. But they were not noticing her then. They were only looking pitiful and sad over the terrible state of the world in these war times, never dreaming that one of those young men whom they were distantly pitying, *might* be the lad their cherished daughter loved, who was even now hastening on to such a death somewhere. "A secret mission" he had called it. Oh, was this what he was going to do? Blythe did not know, could not know, perhaps would never know till the war was all over and the missing ones were counted up.

So, the moment passed, with Blythe's heart suddenly overwhelmed with understanding, and a terrible sadness settling down upon her which kept her silent. Then suddenly they were all roused to realize that it was getting late and the morrow had duties early in the morning. So they said good night and hurried away to their rest.

Back in her own room Blythe settled down in her chair, her knees still weak from that sudden startled realization of Charlie's peril. She looked about her. Was it only this morning that she had gone downstairs to hear him tell her that he loved her? It seemed that she had lived years since the morning dawned and she went happily down to pleasant duties, without a thought that this war was coming into her life. Really coming. Not just by forcing her to go without a few luxuries, doing a few unusual things, economizing; less candy and sugar and coffee, fewer beefsteaks, walking miles instead of using her car. The war had struck to the center of her being, now, through the boy she had watched through the years and greatly admired, and who had suddenly become beloved beyond anything that had ever touched her life before.

For some time she sat there quietly and relaxed in her chair, trying to think it all out.

And would the morrow bring her a letter? No, for that would scarcely be possible. Her soldier had said all mail would have to go to headquarters before it could be forwarded to her, that is, after they had really started on their mission. And now that she was beginning to understand a little what terrible possibilities loomed before such missions, her heart trembled at the thought.

But oh how she longed to get a word from him, his handwriting written *to her!* How wonderful that was going to be! A letter from Charlie Montgomery, all her own! She must get to sleep to hurry on another day, to bring that letter nearer to her.

Quietly, with her light turned out because she didn't want her mother to come in and ask her what was keeping her up, she began to get ready for sleep, and creeping into her bed lay thinking over all that had happened since morning. But, though she had been good friends with Dan Seavers for years, not one thought of him came to spoil her bright vision.

Chapter 6

CHARLIE MONTGOMERY, back in his train again, his heart warm with the sound of his dear girl's voice, tried to settle down and compose himself for rest, for he knew the journey ahead was likely to be strenuous the next day. But the joy surging over him was like a bright sunshine shining in his face, and how could he sleep when he could bask in its warmth and brightness. To think that wonderful girl was really his beloved, at least for the little time he had ahead to live. And after all, that was all that anybody had of joys, for death *might* be waiting just around the corner anywhere for anybody.

But somehow since he had talked with Blythe, and begun to sense all the joy that life might have held for him if he had not committed himself to this war enterprise, the whole thing took on a gloomier aspect. The exaltation of willingly giving himself to a great duty seemed suddenly to have faded, and his heart was beginning to cry out to have it all done with, to go back, and live like a normal human being.

With a sudden closing of his firm young lips he straightened up and took himself to task. This would not do. The preciousness of what had come to pass for him must not be allowed to spoil the greatness of the undertaking to which he was committed. He must not allow himself to sink into gloom over this. He must go smiling to the doom he firmly expected, and he must not falter.

All his life Charlie Montgomery had had to be doing something like this. Even as a child his father and his mother had wisely trained him to know that his first concern should be to conquer himself. His father once told

47

him that half the battle was won if he once was sure he could conquer himself. His mother taught him that this must also be done at no expense to the gentleness and beauty that was meant to shine in his life, but that he must learn to put his own wishes and plans aside, lay them away carefully in his heart, if there was something else that ought to come first. So, now, as he thought things over, he could almost hear his mother's voice saying: "First things first, son, and don't let personal wishes cloud over the brightness of your judgment, or make your will waver in what you ought to do. The precious things of life can wait. They will not perish. There will come a time, either here or hereafter, when their beauty will be yours in all fullness."

Yes, those words of hers were graven on his heart, and he wished with great longing that she might be here now, that he could tell her about Blythe, and see the look of love in her eyes as she understood. For she would have understood, he knew. She had been like that.

But mother had God. He was very real to her, and she drew great stores of wisdom and strength from Him. And he did not have God. At least he had never consciously drawn much strength from any slight contact he had had with his Creator. Oh, he used to go regularly to church in the days when his father and mother always went. And he went through the form of joining the church when he was quite young. He had been brought up to read his Bible and pray every day when he was a child, and he had eagerly taken in the Bible stories then. But somehow they had never taken hold of him, and he had never drawn any help from his connection with the Almighty. He supposed now, with death in the offing so definitely, that perhaps he ought to do something about this. But he wasn't quite sure how to go about it. He hadn't for a long time read his Bible, and it had never meant much to him. Prayer had been a sort of routine, a formality. Not a definite coming of his soul into the conscious presence of the Most High. Well, he ought to do something about that before he reached the end. Perhaps if they stopped at some camp for a day or so he could look up some chaplain and ask a few questions, sort of get him to intercede with God for him, for his soul that was so soon to go out to the end of this life. Since his mother wasn't here to do it, surely he could find someone to pray for him. Though to tell the truth his idea of chaplains was that most of them were more or less what the fellows called "stuffed shirts." However, perhaps there would be an exception, and he must make that a definite engagement with himself, to look up some contact with God before he finally left.

So, having settled that with himself, he composed himself to rest. He told himself that at least until he reached the next stopping place he might allow himself the dear privilege of thinking exclusively about Blythe, just as if he might be coming back some day to her. No, that wouldn't do, for the let-down would be too great when he remembered the present duties of life. He must not get a gloomy slant on what he had to do. He could never do good work in any way if he was filled with personal gloom. But at least he could rejoice in her attitude toward him, in her precious words, the look in her dear eyes, her smile, and her voice over the telephone.

Sinking into sleep with these thoughts in his heart the night was amazingly brief, and waking in the morning it came to him sharply that he was a new day nearer to his doom.

Soon after breakfast the train halted at a station and took on a lot of soldiers, also quite a number of officers. Some of the officers were most distinguished looking men. About mid-morning Charlie was summoned to an audience with the officer he had been advised would give him more definite instruction in what was before him.

Charlie had written a letter to Blythe which he had mailed at the time he had last telephoned her. And now as he returned to his seat after his interview with the officer he reflected that he was glad he had done so; for he had learned among other things, that hereafter, while he was in this special service, all communications with the outside world would have to pass through the censor. It gave him the feeling that henceforth they were in the eye of the public, and they might not exchange their precious intimate thoughts, for which circumstances had given them so far little opportunity. The great separation had begun! Only the most impersonal matters might be discussed from

now on, and of course a little later he had no assurance
that he could write at all.

With all these things in mind he had made that letter a
kind of added farewell, a summing up of all the matters
they had not had time to discuss. So now as he thought
about it, he prepared to write even another letter. Just a
brief one now. One that he wouldn't mind having any
censor see. Blythe would understand, of course. It gave
him a kind of a hopeless feeling. War! *War!* Why was
it?

Yet he must not go out to a duty such as his with a
feeling like that in his heart. He must somehow find a
chaplain and get into conversation with him. Surely a man
who had come out to war on God's service would be able
clearly to point him the way to God. But though he
searched through the train several times he did not find a
man to whom he felt drawn enough to seek help from
him.

Just what was he looking for, he asked himself? A
saint? An angel? A man with a holy face? No, that wasn't
what he wanted. He tried as he stood at the front end of
the train where he had a good view of all the faces he
saw, to think what he was searching for, and he decided it
must be a man with a face of quiet wisdom and strength, a
man with a happy face, as if he were possessed of something which ordinary people lacked, yet wise and true and
tender, even when merry-hearted. Was there any man like
that in the train, or in the army anywhere? There ought to
be a great many. If there were any such men in the whole
wide world who had something real to impart to men who
were going out to die, they ought to be in the army.

He got to talking to another soldier, and they touched
on the topic that was in Charlie's mind.

"Yes, I've seen one or two like that," said the soldier
who was a private, and owned that he was scared—afraid
to die. "Of course there are a few great ones, like the man
we had at the first camp I was sent to. He was *swell*. He
really *believed* all he said, and he knew how to put it so
you found yourself believing it too. I wish I could have
stayed there long enough to have got all his dope. I heard
he was going out to visit different camps, and believe me he
was really popular with the fellows. He used to talk

about Jesus Christ as if he had really met him, as if he knew Him kind of intimately, you know; and when he preached you could see it all acted out there before you, like it was a play. You felt as if you had been there and seen the miracles done. I really was sore when we had to leave him. But I heard he was going around to other camps preaching. Perhaps we'll run on him yet somewhere. His name is Silverthorn. If you get a chance to hear him don't miss it. He gives you great stuff! You feel like you'd met God, after he gets through talking."

Charlie stood a long time talking to this young private, who had evidently been so deeply impressed by this preacher.

"I'll hunt him up," said Charlie, "if I ever get within hearing distance of him."

After that, because his heart was sick and sore with longing for the love he had found and lost so soon, Charlie went back to his belongings, hunted out pen and paper and wrote another brief note.

Dearest: I've just heard of a man who preaches real things and might tell one how to die courageously. I want to be more than just a conqueror. It's got to be something greater than courage, because I'm not afraid to die. Dying is nothing in itself. A little pain, a little oblivion. But then what? My mother wasn't afraid to die, and she was not physically so courageous. But she had something bigger, something that lifted her above any physical fear. It is not fear of the pain of death that makes people afraid to die, it is fear of what comes after. I am not afraid to die, but I wonder if I know much about what comes after. Do you? For after all, whether in war, or in peace, we all have to die, and we all need to understand and be ready for what comes after.

If you and I expect to spend eternity together, we should look into this and be ready, the way we used to have to prepare for a lesson or an examination that was coming. You and I always used to be prepared, didn't we? Perhaps you are ready for what may be ahead, but I don't feel that I have been, so I'm studying. Will you think about this? Because we don't want to take any chances of missing the great things that are ahead for us who love one another. Will you think about this too, so we shall be one in thought? We'll only be preparing for an eternal joy; and together, I trust, dear love. Don't let this make you sad. It was just something I felt ought to be said between us. You have all my love.

Yours, Charlie.

Afterward as he thought it over he wished he had not written that last letter. Would it seem desperately gloomy to her, put a damper on her ardent joy? Yet of course it was something he wanted her to know, his feelings on this great subject of death about which they had said so little. But it was too late to do anything about the letter now. He had put it in with the rest of the mail as soon as it was written, and he did not wish to go through the routine of trying to get it out again. No, he would write her another presently, in the morning perhaps. A happy letter, without a reference to death, and try to dispel the gloom.

So, he drifted off into sleep again, wondering what the future was about to hold for him, and for his beloved.

And the next morning, as soon as it was light enough to see, he wrote briefly:

Dearly Beloved:

I want you to be happy, bright and cheerful, and happy every hour of your days. Every day of your years. Do not grieve for me, for I shall be in the way of duty, and I shall be glad that I am counted worthy to serve my country, and the cause of right. And if letters cease, you will know that I am on my way. Trust God for the rest. Yours,

Charles.

And then, toward evening, the train drew into a camp, where he learned they were to spend the night, awaiting other men who were joining their company. And there in the darkening dusk a name sprang forth into the sky in brilliant lights! "SILVERTHORN," and below it flashing an instant later. "Hear him tonight!"

His pulse quickened. Could that be the same man the private had told him about? He would go and see.

Chapter 7

BLYTHE HAD COME down the next morning with dark rings under her eyes and a worried wrinkle on her brow. Her mother, looking up from the morning mail smiled at her cheerfully.

"How would you like to run down to Florida for a few weeks, dear?" she asked quite casually, and Blythe knew that the campaign was on.

Blythe tried to smile when she looked up, and shook her head.

"Oh, no, mother dear! I just couldn't spare the time. I'm so interested in the work I am doing. I wouldn't interrupt it for anything."

"But I know you are overworking, dear. I was talking to your father about it last night after you went to your room, and we decided you ought to get away from it all for a while at least and get toned up. You've got dark circles under your eyes, and we can't have you going into a decline, you know. Remember you've been working hard in college, and it's time you had a real rest."

"But I don't want a rest," said the girl earnestly. "I want to stay right here and do all the nice things that I am doing. I just love the babies I am working with in the day nursery, and the hospital class is so interesting. And besides I've undertaken a lot of things at the Red Cross class. No, I couldn't *think* of going away now. I'm having the time of my life!"

"Well, you certainly don't look it this morning," said her mother, scanning her face thoughtfully.

"But mother, don't you know what makes me look that

53

way this time? After you gave me a regular scolding for not going out with Dan Seavers you got me worried."

"For pity's sake, child! Why should that worry you?"

"Well, I just don't like going out with him any more the way I used to do. I don't like the crowd he goes with, and I don't like the way he talks and acts. I think you are all mistaken about my having a mission to change him. I know I *haven't*. Of course I'll be as nice to him as I can when we are thrown together, but I don't see that I should take him over to bring up."

A puckered frown came on her mother's forehead.

"Why no, of course not, dear. I didn't mean anything like that. But I can't see why you can't make it plain to him why you don't care to go with such people. Let him see that if he wants your company he'll have to choose a different group."

"Oh, yes, I suppose I can do that, if the occasion offers," sighed Blythe. "But I'm really not much interested. You see, mother, he doesn't want me to make him over. He's trying to make me over to suit his own plans. And I don't care to be made over."

"But Blythe, you don't want to be left without *any* escorts, do you? You know so many of your old friends have gone overseas or to the camps, and there aren't so many men that you can afford simply to turn a respectable one down. I wouldn't like the idea that you had *nobody* to take you out."

"Mother, if I were in the army, a Wac or a Wave or something, or if I were working in a defense plant like a lot of the other girls, I wouldn't have to have an escort. I'd be going places by myself."

"Blythe! My *child! You* working in a defense plant?"

"Well, why not? Of course I'd rather be doing what I'm doing, than trying to be a riveter, but that is a perfectly respectable job, and lots of nice girls are doing it. And in these war times girls haven't time to go around to parties and have escorts and be so formal. There isn't time for frivolity. And do you know, mother, somehow it doesn't seem good taste to be running around to parties and entertainments when so many of our friends and acquaintances are facing death to make our world safe for us."

"Why, Blythe, I didn't know you felt that way. You

never seemed particularly interested in the boys in the army or navy."

A flash of color went over Blythe's face.

"Oh, but I am *now*, mother! The more I see of those young boys going out from their homes before they are really half grown up, the more fine-looking older men in uniform I see, the more I feel what serious business this war is. It doesn't seem the thing for us older ones who stay so safely at home, to run around trying to amuse ourselves like a parcel of children."

"Blythe! What a strange thing to say! You don't want everybody to sit around and be gloomy, do you?"

"No, certainly not. I think we ought to be bright and cheerful for the sake of the young soldiers who are lonely and sad about giving up their lives at home, and looking forward into no one knows what terrible futures."

"But my dear! What a gloomy view to take. I shouldn't think you would be much help among the soldier boys if you talk as if they weren't any of them coming home."

"But I don't *talk* that way, mother. Of course a lot of them *are* coming home—I hope—and of course we must make it as cheerful as possible for them. I'm only saying that the ones who do not have to go, who have duties that keep them at home, ought to put aside any childish desires they may have to amuse themselves, and try to make the ones who have to go have a good time while they are waiting to be called."

"Well, I don't see your line of reason, but it does seem to me that the boys who are staying at home to do important work for the war have as good a right to have a good time now and then as the ones who are going over."

Blythe drew a long breath that had a little note of almost despair in it.

"Well, mother, perhaps you are right, but somehow I don't seem to have much respect for the boys at home who have to be babied, when a lot of their own age have set their lips, and their wills, and have gone out to face whatever comes, even death. It is like people trying to have a dance while they are waiting to find out how many of their friends have been killed in some great disaster."

"Well, my dear, it is sweet of you to be so sympathetic, and it shows a beautiful maturity and gravity of thought

in one so young, but I do think that everyone, both young
and old, ought to keep just as cheerful as possible. And
then of course there are boys at home who are not physically able to go and fight."

"Why, yes, of course," said Blythe, weighing each sylla-
ble carefully to be sure it was true in her own heart.

Yet there was a gravity in Blythe's face that made her
mother uneasy.

"Well, if you feel that way, we'll wait a little while and
see how you look. If you continue to have these dark
circles under your eyes something will have to be done
about it. But there is one thing I shall insist upon. I want
you to stop that work in the Red Cross class right away.
You can call up and tell them that you can't come any
more, and they will have to get someone else to take your
place, for I won't have you spending so much time in the
company of people who dare to talk about you."

Blythe laughed.

"Why, mother dear, you mustn't feel that way. Everybody talks about everybody else when they happen to
want to, and I can't get out of every place where they
talk. I'll just be careful not to give them anything to
criticize if I can help it."

Her mother looked troubled.

"I'm afraid you can't do that, Blythe. You know when
people get started talking they just make up things to say
without realizing it. I would rather you didn't go there
another time. Out of sight you'll perhaps be out of mind,
and so free from their gossiping tongues."

"No, mother, they'll just call me a quitter, and I'm not
going to have them say that. Besides, I've just undertaken
to make the buttonholes on a whole lot of the darlingest
little nightgowns for babies, and I can't leave till that's
done. You know I love to make buttonholes. No, mother
dear, I'll just stick by the work I've promised till something really worth-while needs me. I'm quite content with
what I'm doing for the present."

"But you really need some young company, and I can't
bear to have you forlorn and alone. If you are so determined that you can't go with Dan any more you'll just
drop out of everything, and have no friends at all."

"Oh no, I won't," said Blythe with a happy little smile.

"Don't you worry. I'll be all right. And please don't go and get up trips to Florida and things like that for me, for I really don't want to go anywhere just now. I would rather stay here and do just what I'm doing."

"Very well," said her mother with a sigh, "if you want it that way of course. But I hate to feel that you are holding aloof from everyone, all your young friends."

"Don't feel that way, mother. I'm quite happy with the friends I have, and there will be others, too, some day," and a sweet little fluttering smile flickered over her face.

And then, if Susan hadn't come into the room with a message from the grocery man, it is possible that Blythe might have started in to tell her mother about Charlie Montgomery, only that she still dreaded so her mother's worried look when she told her that a perfect stranger to them all had told her that he loved her. Had dared to tell her that and then go off to war. Her natural reaction would be to resent his daring, and Blythe felt that she could not quite bear that yet.

"Well," said her mother with a sigh, as she rose to answer Susan's questions, and get a list for the tradesman, "I suppose if you feel that way perhaps it's as well for you to go this once, but if I were you I would get out of that work just as fast as possible and let us find some more congenial work for you. And Blythe, I wish you wouldn't go today, at least. You look so very tired."

"No, I think I'd better go," said the girl. "And mother, the boys at the front don't wait for some more congenial work. This is war, you know, and we must work where we are bidden. You're doing it, and I must do it too. Don't worry about me. I'll be all right. And now I must go. I don't want to be late at the class again. Bye, mother dear!" and Blythe jumped up and gave her mother a soft little kiss and hurried away.

It was true that her heart was a bit heavy this morning, for she had just begun to realize that Charlie was going farther and farther away from her now, and into the dread possibility of death. Would he ever return? Would any earthly joy ahead come out of this beautiful sorrow that had come to her? And would she be able to go along and bear her cross all through the long uncertainty?

So, setting her thoughts on the fact that Charlie loved

her, and had told her about it before he went, she breezed into the Red Cross room with a fairly good imitation of happiness and greeted them all as if they were her dearest friends, and she had no idea that any one of them had ever dared to say unpleasant things about her.

"Good morning, everybody," she lilted out. "Isn't this a lovely day? I was afraid it was going to rain again, but it certainly has cleared off beautifully, hasn't it? Now, where are my buttonholes? How many of them ought I to get done this morning? I always like to set a goal for myself. It's so much more fun to try and finish what I plan."

Anne Houghton looked up astonished. She had taken pains to fnd out that Blythe had not gone out with Dan Seavers the night before, and she could not understand her being so joyous. What did she have up her sleeve now? Some new man who hadn't yet been seen in town?

"You seem to be very gay about it," she said contemptuously. "Almost as if you had private information that the war was over."

Blythe looked at her, a bright smile kindling on her lovely face.

"Wouldn't it be nice if I had?" she said with a twinkle in her eyes. "Wouldn't I just enjoy telling you all about it, bit by bit, and speculating about the difference it would make in our poor tired world. Why couldn't we pretend that it was so this morning? Wouldn't it seem a bit more cheerful? For some day, likely, that *may* happen you know. I always did like to play 'Let's pretend.' "

"I'm afraid I haven't that much imagination," said Anne Houghton coldly. "I never saw any advantage in kidding yourself along, because the truth always catches up with you sooner or later, and the let-down is too great!"

"Oh, do you think so?" said Blythe. "I can't help feeling that there is a decided advantage in keeping cheerful."

Some of the others cast significant glances at one another, and a few, of whom Mrs. Felton was the leader, gave her a commendatory smile.

There was a quiet little woman sitting at the far end of the line, sewing with all her might, swift firm stitches, neatness and precision in every angle of her trim slim

body, and the set of her fine thin lips—who took no part
in these pleasantries, and did not even cast an eye in her
direction, and Blythe took quiet note of her attitude. She
seemed to have no acquaintance with the other women,
did not speak, and was not spoken to. Her garments were
plain and her hands had the look of being workworn. Yet
there was about her an air of intense purpose, as if this
work she was doing meant something to her. Meant more,
perhaps, than it did to these other women, some of whom,
at least, were merely here because it was an easy way of
discharging a war duty and gave pleasant publicity to their
efforts. Not that it wasn't important enough, of course, but
most of them had the languid air of not caring much
about what they were doing. Blythe wondered what made
the difference, and when a little later the woman who had
been sitting next to the quiet one, vacated her chair to go
out on an errand, Blythe quietly went over and took it,
giving a bright little smile to the busy woman who barely
glanced up when the newcomer arrived next to her, as if it
made little difference to her who sat there.

A fleeting smile crossed the gravity of the silent woman,
and Blythe followed it up. Quietly, not so that the attention of the other women would be called to it.

"Mind if I sit by you?" she asked pleasantly. "I think
there is a little more light by this window, and I thought
you looked as if you would be a pleasant person to sit
beside."

The little woman looked up surprised.

"Why, you're quite welcome of course," she said cor-
dially. "But I'm only a very unimportant person. I'm just
Mrs. Blake, and I don't live in a very fashionable quarter
of the city. In fact I think my house is just over the edge
in this section and I don't really know these ladies. I've
thought perhaps they rather resented my being here. I
don't know. But this was where I was told to come, so I
came."

"Why, of course," said Blythe with a tone of merriness
in her voice, "and why should anybody resent anybody
else in the world, no matter on which side of an imaginary
line they live? We're in a war. We have no time for silly
trifles like that. Do you think we have?"

Mrs. Blake looked up astonished again.

"Why no, I don't suppose we have, but you can't change the way people think about such things just because there's a war, can you?"

"I don't know why not. It seems to me when almost everybody has some dear one in that war, either far away or on the way somewhere, that we all feel for one another, and love one another, at least a little bit more than we used to do. Isn't that the way it should be?"

And then Blythe lifted her eyes and Anne Houghton came into her range of vision, and it came to her suddenly that she didn't love Anne Houghton, or feel for her a bit more than she used to do. In fact she was in a fair way to hate her because of the way she was acting. Well, she'd got to check herself up on that. But she went on with her conversation with the quiet little woman by her side who somehow interested her greatly.

"Yes," said Mrs. Blake with a quick-drawn sigh, "I guess that's the way it ought to be, but I'm not sure it is always, even yet."

"Perhaps not," said Blythe thoughtfully. "But I think we *ought* to be that way. Now take yourself, I'll have a guess that you have somebody in the service. You seem so interested. You seem to work with some purpose, even just sewing."

Mrs. Blake was still for a minute, and then she said with another sigh, "Yes, I've got somebody in the war. I've got three somebodies in it. In fact there were four till my husband got hurt in the munitions plant where he was working, and that laid him aside in the hospital, but he still hopes to get well and get back to his job. You know, he thinks it was sabotage that caused the accident that put him on his back, and it's hard not to hate the people who would do a thing like that, isn't it?"

"Why of course," said Blythe. "I guess that's the kind of thing we were meant to hate, isn't it? That's devilish. That's just what the war's about."

"Yes, I feel that way," said little Mrs. Blake, snapping off her thread and putting a knot in the end for another seam.

"But you said you had four-bodies in the war. Who are the other three?" asked the girl, starting in on another buttonhole.

"Yes," sighed the mother. "There's Floyd. He's in Guadalcanal in the hospital. But they say he's getting better. He's hoping to get back into the service soon. I don't know where they'll send him next. And there's Johnny, he's in Africa; that is, he was the last time we heard. And there's Walter, he's in camp, getting ready to go somewhere. He thinks maybe it will be Iceland. But they're all fighting in the war, thank God, and so I come here the only free time I have to sew a little while. It's all the time I have free to give. You see I work in a munitions plant myself afternoons and evenings, and I have to take a little time to keep our two rooms tidy for me and my little girl who is in school yet. So when I come here I have to work hard and fast to get as much done as possible."

"My dear, I think you're wonderful!" said Blythe with true admiration in her eyes.

"Oh, no, I'm not wonderful! I'm just a common wife and mother doing her best to help her family keep right and brave and win the war. But tell me about you. They say you make wonderful buttonholes, but something tells me that's not all you do. Have you got somebody dear to you over in that war?"

Blythe's cheeks flamed rosy for an instant and a very sweet look came into her eyes as she lifted them to the new friend she had found in this unpopular corner of the room.

"Yes, I have," she said softly, "somebody *very* dear!"

She paused a minute, and then added in a still softer tone, "He's not a father or husband or son, nor even a brother. He's just a friend. A very dear friend."

"I see," said Mrs. Blake understandingly. "I used to feel that way about Jim, my husband, before he was my husband. When he went away to France in the last world war. I know just how it is. And—does he know you care? Or perhaps I ought not to ask that. Excuse me for being so forward."

"There's nothing to excuse," said Blythe gently. "Yes, he knows. And *he* cares—too!" she added softly.

"That makes it nice," said Mrs. Blake. "You've something to look forward to."

Blythe was silent a moment and then she lifted sad eyes.

"I'm—afraid not," she said sadly. "You see he's gone on some very special mission. And he thinks—it is pretty sure death! He seemed to think he might not come back. In fact he was sure there wasn't a chance. I don't know where he is. It's a military secret."

"Oh, *my dear!*" said the little woman sadly, with a great tenderness in her voice and eyes. "I'm sorry for you!"

"Thank you," said Blythe with a catch in her voice. "You're the only one I've told about this—but I knew you wouldn't say anything."

"No, of course not, child. But I'm greatly sorry for you, and—I'll be praying—for you—and him!"

"Oh, thank you!" said Blythe, brushing at a quick tear that was trying to get out. "I'll remember that—always!" and suddenly her lovely smile bloomed out like a rainbow in the rain.

The gathering broke up just then, everyone hurrying away to lunch.

"I must go," said Mrs. Blake. "I mustn't be late to my next job. But I'll not be forgetting to pray for you—and *him!*" and she hurried away.

Blythe smiled sweetly at her, and then looking up saw Anne Houghton's scornful glance upon her.

"Getting quite chummy with our slum-lady, aren't you?" she sneered. "Not trying to hire her for something, are you? I'm sure I don't see why they put a woman of that sort in with our crowd. She just doesn't belong, and she really lives out of the district. Somebody ought to write to headquarters and have her sent to another group."

"*Don't!*" said Blythe sharply. "She's very sweet, and Anne, she has three boys in the service."

"She would, of course, but they're just the common herd, children of a woman like that! But that's all those common boys would be fit for, anyway, to go out and fight."

Blythe looked at the other girl appalled and could not think of words to express her indignation, so she turned and walked away, wishing she knew how to make Anne understand what an utter snob she was! Realizing that utter silence was probably the best rebuke she could give her.

On her way home Blythe began to wonder at herself for telling this stranger woman about the sweetest thing in her life, her love for Charlie. How was it that she could tell this stranger, and she hadn't yet mustered courage to tell her own dear mother? Oh, if she could only be sure that her mother would take it in the sweet sympathetic way that the stranger woman had listened. What made the difference? Not just the fact that Mrs. Blake lived on the wrong side of the township line, or wore plain clothes and worked hard for her living. Was it because she had children in the war, and knew what war possibilities were? Oh, war did make a difference. And maybe her mother would begin to realize that soon, and she could bring her sweet secret and share it with her precious mother.

And then she went into the house and found there a letter from her beloved, the first one he had written and mailed just after talking to her on the telephone that first time. She was glad that there was no one about, not even Susan, and she might unquestioned steal up to her own room, and read her letter undisturbed. Her first wonderful letter!

Chapter 8

BLYTHE WAS TREMBLING as she settled down in her chair
to read her letter, grasping it tenderly as if it was something fragile, something almost elusive that might take
flight from her hand even yet.

Carefully she opened the envelope, studying the forma-
tion of her own name in Charlie's handwriting. It seemed
so much like a miracle that he should be writing to her.
She laid her face softly against the folded letter, and
closed her eyes an instant, with a soft little smile on her
lips. Then she unfolded the letter and began to read:

To the most wonderful girl in the world.

My dearly beloved:

I am filled with an almost heavenly joy to be writing
to you, with your permission, and to know that you are
letting me love you and take your own love with me as I
go out into a world of sin and death and uncertainty,
with practically no chance that I can ever return.

But I want this to be a happy letter because you have
given me so much joy by taking my intrusion into your
life in such a beautiful way. So, may I go back through
the years and tell you what you have meant to me?

The first day I went to school in your city I looked
around the room, and saw you almost at once. You
wore a yellow dress, and there was sunshine on your
curls that gave them a golden glow, and sunshine in
your happy smile. I thought you were the most beautiful
little girl I had ever seen. I went home and told my
mother that you looked just like an angel. If my dear
mother were living on earth now she would delight to
tell you about that.

It wasn't many days before I discovered that you were a very bright little girl who always knew your lessons and could answer the questions the teacher asked, quickly, as if you understood what she was talking about. It made me eager to study and do my best too. I didn't want you to think I was dumb. You see you were a great inspiration to me. Though I had no idea I would ever get to know you, or have opportunity to tell you these things of course. You were just like a beautiful angel living up near Heaven somewhere, out of my world.

I shall never forget the day when we were both sent to the blackboard to work out a problem in algebra, and stood side by side for a little while. We were told to compare our work, and explain it to one another. I was so thrilled at being so near to you that my brains would scarcely work, and to look into your beautiful eyes, and hear you talking to me with your sweet voice made my heart beat so that I had hard work to control my own voice to answer you. Just thinking this over afterward brought me great happiness.

And once when you stood near me in class you dropped your little scrap of handkerchief and I picked it up and handed it to you, and as you took it your fingers touched mine, and swept the most wonderful thrill of joy over my soul. You wouldn't have noticed that touch perhaps, but it meant a great deal to me, and I thought of your lovely hands with the utmost reverence. Your touch had seemed to me like the breath from an angel's wing.

Do you think all this language is silly? But I wanted to let you see once into my heart and know what you have been to me all these years, even from very early childhood. It sort of explains, and perhaps just a little excuses my temerity in coming to tell you of my love at this the last minute. My heart somehow ached to let you know.

For you see when high school days came, and you and I were even farther apart than we had been as children, there was less opportunity even to see you. For social life, in which I had no time to take any part, had come in to make a farther separation.

Though I can recall the lovely vision of you which I had in those days, brief glimpses. You wore enchanting garments and seemed a picture in each one. I used to rejoice that you were not all painted up with lipstick and rouge like so many other girls. You were just fine and different. So that was the background for my great love for you, which grew and grew through the years, even after I went away to college and didn't see you any more. Till one day it came to me that I loved you, with a great deep love that filled all my being.

Yet I never presumed even in my mind to look forward to having you for mine. Your people were cultured and wealthy, and mine were poor, and what culture they had was not from worldly advantages. I was a poor boy, and while if the war had not claimed my services, I might have tried to get up in the world and do something worth-while, I never dared to hope that I would be in a class where your people would like to have me for their daughter's intimate friend.

So that was how it all began for me, and I think you have a right to know. And to know that I have always thought of you as one for whom I was trying to keep myself fine and pure and true in my daily life; just that I might be worthy to love, even from afar, even though you might never know it.

I do not think this is much of a love letter, yet I felt you had a right to know all this.

And now, because this may be the last letter I can write that I am *sure* will go uncensored, I must tell you again of my great love for you, which has been growing and growing so long, that it finally drove me to find you and tell you about it before I go away.

I want you to know how your sweet presence is going with me, wherever I am, and the joy of your precious lips on mine will thrill me again and again when things grow hard and fearful. My hungry arms will remember how it felt to hold you close, with your dear face against mine, your lovely hair touching my cheek. It will be a precious memory which I shall hold reverently as long as I live. I have always looked upon you as very sacred, have always had the utmost reverence for you. My mother used to tell me when I was just a small kid that some day God might send a girl who would seem that way to me, and I must take care that I kept myself fine and clean for her in spirit as well as in body. Perhaps almost unconsciously I have remembered that, and kept it in mind definitely several times when you seemed to me to be high above all other girls.

Well, and that's what you seemed to me all through our school days. Do you wonder that I dared at the last minute before I said good-by to my native land, to come to you and lay my love at your feet, as a tribute to what you have been to me?

But there is one thing I want to make clear, and that is that I do not want my love to be a hindrance to you in your life in any way. And if I do not come back and the future should bring you another lover, do not feel you must send him away because you have told me that you love me. The joy of love is that the loved one shall be happy. Only so can I go contented to whatever my duty has in store for me. I am sure you will understand that I had to say this, even though for the time being it may sadden you. But don't be sad. Be glad that we had the joy of one another for at least a few hours.

If in any future letters I do not speak of my love so plainly, remember that I am conscious of censorship that seems to me a sort of desecration of our precious love. But you will understand.

So, to bring my letter to a finish I am closing my eyes, and feeling your lips upon mine, my arms about you, my darling!

Your lover, Charlie.

Blythe finished the letter slowly, and then buried her face in it for a moment or two. Such a precious, precious letter! Why, this was a letter that she could show to her mother and father. It was a real picture of the story of their love. It gave a true account of their first knowledge of each other, it showed what Charlie really was. Mother and father could not help understanding how fine he was from that letter. Oh, she was glad he had written it! Yet, would he like her to show it to even her nearest and dearest? He had written this because he knew that there was censorship ahead, and he wanted his letter to come to her before any other eye had seen it. Well, she had it now, as it came straight from himself, without any alien eyes between. Yes, it was hers to use as she felt was right. She was sure Charlie would agree with her. She would think about it. And she would read it over and over and get it into her heart. She would be able to tell in time whether she wanted to share that letter with her parents.

Happily she began to read the letter again, reveling in every word, following his memories and matching them with her own. How he had felt just as she had done again and again. It was almost like having him there. How she could vision his speaking face as she read! How she could thrill with the memory of his arms about her, the tenderness of his kiss!

She was just starting to read the letter over for the third time when she heard her mother's voice downstairs.

"Oh!" she caught her breath. She didn't want to be interrupted in this third reading of the letter, and she hadn't decided yet whether or not she was willing to show this letter to her mother. She listened for an instant and heard another voice. Ah! Then mother had brought someone home with her, and there would not be opportunity to talk with her alone at this time anyway. So with a quiet smile on her face she went on through her third reading of that precious first letter.

A little later she heard the summons to lunch, and she went down to find a friend of her mother's was a guest. So, her secret was her own for another little while at least, but she sat through the meal with such a happy smile on her face that the guest could but remark on how well Blythe was looking. But Blythe was hugging to herself the thought of this first letter of Charlie's. And already she was planning how she might answer it, and make plain to her lover how his words had rung bells of joy in her heart, even though the censor's eagle eye might keep him from writing another like it. Oh there would be ways to write that a mere censor would not understand, words that yet would convey a depth of love and trust each to the other.

And Mrs. Bonniwell, watching the happy face of her dear girl was relieved to see that the dark circles under her eyes were gone, and that there was a healthy flush on her cheeks. She must have been very tired the night before, or else upset about her words concerning Dan Seavers. Strange that young people took such queer notions about each other when they began to grow up. Dan had always been such a handsome well set-up boy, rightly born and rightly bred. His people were intimate friends of the Bonniwells and their children had been educated in much the same way. She could not think that Blythe was right in what she thought of the way Dan had changed. Very likely this was only a whim, and would pass. Dan and Blythe would presently be as good friends as ever, perhaps, and she wouldn't worry about it. There was one good thing about it. Blythe wasn't fond of any other young man, she was sure of that.

So she put away the worried thoughts she had had and quite entered into a discussion of the best way to conduct the new War Bond drive that they were planning. Soon after lunch Blythe escaped upstairs to write to Charlie, her first answer to his first love-letter to her.

Meantime downstairs in the library Blythe's mother, and her guest Mrs. Corwin, had settled down before the open fire to have a nice talk and plan the War Bond drive.

"What a charming daughter Blythe has become," said Mrs. Corwin. "She used to be so tall and gangling, but she seems to have filled out so beautifully, and is really lovely now. I'm so glad to have seen her again. And why did she go away? Wouldn't she like to sit in on this conference? I'm sure we could give her something to do. She is so ornamental she ought to be sitting in one of the best positions to reach the right people, say, in the bank, or one of the big department stores. Why don't you call her down?"

Mrs. Corwin was one of those who could always spoil any complimentary remark she tried to make by some unfortunate word like gangling, and as that word had never described Blythe's slim loveliness, it rather annoyed the mother. Blythe had always been lithe and graceful as soon as she got out of actual babyhood.

Mrs. Bonniwell looked up sharply.

"No," she said decidedly. "Blythe already has too much war work to do. She has no time to relax and have a little social life. I wouldn't think of letting her get into this."

"Oh, of course, if you feel that way, said the guest persuasively. "But she is so lovely, and would make a grand drawing card, I'm sure. But of course a young girl should have some amusement. I suppose she goes out evenings a good deal and stays up too late. I hear she's very popular."

"We haven't encouraged her going out too much," said Mrs. Bonniwell. "After all she's just got through her college course and the last year is always so strenuous. But

Blythe is doing some hospital work in the early evenings among little children, and other days she works in the baby day-nursery."

"How sweet of her!" said Mrs. Corwin, "so many girls wouldn't bother to do a thing like that. It's very strenuous."

"Blythe loves it," said Blythe's mother, bringing pencils and paper and settling down ready for work.

"Well, that's all very well for a little while," said the guest, "but I suppose her young friends will soon clamor for her release. I think you are so fortunate to have her at home again, and to have such a delightful companion for her in Dan Seavers. So many of the young men are gone overseas, she is fortunate to have one so good-looking and so devoted to stay near by. Has he received his commission yet? I understand he has been asked to take over some very important work for the government. Is it arranged yet where he will be stationed?"

"Why, I wouldn't know," said Mrs. Bonniwell coolly. "I haven't heard the matter discussed."

"Oh, *really?*" said the guest lifting her stylish eyebrows. "Why, I should think you would be one of the first to know. They're engaged, aren't they? I suppose if he is stationed near by they will be married before he goes and she will go with him."

"Engaged?" said Blythe's mother lifting a haughty chin. "Of whom are you speaking? Who are engaged?"

Mrs. Corwin rippled out a musical little laugh.

"Why, I'm speaking of Dan Seavers and your charming daughter, of course," she said with a daring little smile. "I understood the engagement was to be announced in a few days. Isn't that so?"

"Engagement?" said Mrs. Bonniwell severely. "Between my daughter and Daniel Seavers? Certainly not! They have no idea of being engaged, and never have had. Where in the world did you get that idea?"

"Why, my dear, I have heard it everywhere. Everybody has been saying what a delightful match it is, and how simply perfect for you to have your daughter marry a young man you have known so long and so well, and one who is such an admirable fellow. Simply everybody is saying that. You certainly surprise me."

"Indeed!" said Mrs. Bonniwell. "It is quite amusing how people can make up stories out of whole cloth with nothing to go on but a few scattered appearances in public together. They are good friends of course, have been for years, but nothing more. I am afraid Blythe would be quite annoyed if she knew that her world was parceling her off in this wholesale manner without even asking her if it is true."

"But Alice! You surprise me! I had no idea I was speaking of affairs that were not yet in the open. I do hope you will pardon my speaking beforehand. Of course I felt you were an old friend, and I would be expected to congratulate you. I didn't understand that something must have happened, and the engagement was off."

Mrs. Bonniwell gasped.

"But my dear, you don't understand yet! There *never* has been an engagement, and *nothing* has happened, and therefore there is nothing to 'be off,' as you say. Now, forget it please, and shall we get to work?"

"But my dear, I'm so embarrassed. I didn't think you'd be so secretive with me!"

"Why, Clarice, the idea! I'm not being secretive. I have nothing to be secretive about. There is *nothing* in all this at all. I can't understand who could have told you a thing like this. But please, *please* put the matter entirely out of your mind and let us plan this drive."

After much persuasion Mrs. Corwin stiffly agreed to drop the matter, but her manner retained its stiffness, and she had the air of having been deceived about something. Deceived and intentionally left out of something important.

So, amid an undertone of hurt and suspicion the two ladies went to work, and perhaps even more was actually accomplished than would have been if there hadn't been a dignified restraint in the atmosphere.

The work had progressed to the stage of two very neat complete lists of names, two sets of programs finished, and two note books with various items listed that must be attended to later. Suddenly they heard Blythe coming lightly down the stairs humming a gay little tune, and Blythe's mother rejoiced that her child sounded happy and lighthearted. Mrs. Corwin couldn't possibly go out and tell that Blythe was wasting away because Dan Seavers had jilted her. But there was no telling. Mrs. Corwin had certainly proved herself this afternoon to be capable of getting up almost any story out of nothing.

"Blythe, is that you, dear?" called her mother suddenly. "Are you going out this afternoon?"

Blythe appeared promptly at the door, her cheeks beautifully rosy, and what looked like star-dust in her eyes, a letter in her hand.

"Why, mother, I'm just running down to the post office with a letter I want to get off in a hurry. I think it will go more quickly if I take it down. Can I do anything for you?"

"Why no, dear, I think not. Will you be going out after dinner?"

"Yes, mother, I'm on the evening shift at the hospital tonight, but I shall be done by eleven. Would it be convenient to send the car, or are you using it somewhere else? I can come back on the bus if you are."

"Why no, dear. You don't need to do that. I have to run over to Mrs. Haskell's a little while to get her ideas about this War Bond drive, and suppose I stop at the hospital and pick you up. Eleven, you say? All right. Do I go to the side entrance? Very well, you can plan for that. Now run along with your letter, dear, and leave us to our work. We're almost done, and we simply must finish this and get the lists off to the printer."

"Well, I'll say good-by, Mrs. Corwin," said Blythe, pleasantly. "So nice to have seen you," and Blythe smiled on the lady and flitted away like a bright bird of passage.

"She certainly looks happy," said Mrs. Corwin provocatively.

"Yes, she's a very happy child," said Blythe's mother. "She seems so glad to be at home again. Her father asked her this morning if she wouldn't like to take a trip somewhere, but she said no, she wanted to stick by her war work. She is enjoying it very much, especially her work in the day nursery."

"Well, that's certainly commendatory," said the lady stiffly. "And now about the list of people who are to work the suburbs. Do you have Mrs. West's suggestions for the district around the northwestern part of the city?"

"Yes, here it is. I looked it over and it seemed very good to me. See what you think." And so the work went rapidly on to the finish, Mrs. Corwin presently went away and Blythe's mother drew a long breath of relief. Was this kind of thing what Blythe had meant? Well, it was most annoying. Nothing bad, nothing that would do any harm to her dear girl of course, and yet it was most trying. No girl liked to have her affairs settled by a committee of the town, nor pried into. And of course if Blythe stopped going with Dan abruptly everybody would say he had deserted her. But there, what was the use of worrying? So long as Blythe could bring such a happy face around, no amount of gossip could really hurt her. Her mother smiled indulgently and went slowly upstairs to her room to snatch a few minutes' rest.

What would she have thought or said if she had known about that first real love letter her daughter had received and answered that day? What would she have thought about Charlie Montgomery?

Blythe back in her own room was standing by her window staring out across the lawn with a look of distance in her dreamy eyes. She was feeling as if she had just been talking with Charlie, and was reflecting that it was only a few hours ago that he was actually with her and now he seemed so far away. She must not lose sight of that wonderful first visit of his. And now, as soon as her mother waked up she probably ought to go and talk it all over with her. She must not have the blight of any burden on the joy of her heart. It was burden enough that very soon Charlie was going into awful danger, and how she was going to bear that when the time came she did not know. But she simply must not let her present happiness be spoiled. It was something so perfect that it must not be touched by gloom.

And then, just a few hours apart, Charlie's other letters began to arrive, a dear procession of them, and she seemed to be living in his company, all the way of his journey, although of course she had no idea just where he was going.

Chapter 9

As Charlie Montgomery went from the train into the camp where he had been given to understand he was to await further orders, he looked about him at the men who stood watching the newcomers, and then suddenly he heard a voice calling out:

"Hello, Charlie Montgomery!"

He turned sharply and looked into a young face that seemed familiar even in the army outfit. Eager gray eyes searching his face, doubtful, hesitant voice:

"You *are* Charlie Montgomery, aren't you?"

"Sure!" said Montgomery, in turn searching the boy's face.

"Lieutenant, I mean," said the young soldier turning red and saluting apologetically.

"Why, sure, but—who are you?" said Charlie. Then his face broke into a grin. "Walter Blake, as I live! You don't mean to say you're in the army *already?*"

"Oh, sure," said the lad straightening up and trying to look old and experienced. "I've been in this camp two months already. I think they're sending me off somewhere worth-while pretty soon."

"You don't say!" said Charlie astonished. "But surely you are not old enough yet?"

"I was seventeen three months ago, and Mom signed up for me," said the lad. "She said there was no use trying to hold me in any longer, and both my brothers are in."

"Well, I am surprised. Why, kid, I don't see how the home ball teams are going to get along without you. You haven't finished high school yet, have you?"

"Sure!" said the lad. "I took summer school, and then

they gave some of us examinations, and allowed us to graduate. We could either go into college, engineering, or the service. I chose the army."

"Good work, kid. Do you like it?"

"Yes, it's swell! I like it a lot, but I'm about ready to get into some real work."

"I see," said Charlie, smiling. "Well, I suppose that's what we all feel."

Walter looked up wonderingly.

"But *you're* in!" he said with a glance at the insignia Charlie wore. "You're a lieutenant. Did you feel that way?"

"Sure I did," said Charlie. "What do you suppose I'm here for? Amusement?"

There was new respect, almost adoration in the lad's eyes.

"You are wearing—wings!"

Charlie smiled.

"Where are you going?" He breathed the words eagerly. "Or must I not ask?"

Montgomery smiled again.

"I wish I could tell you, but—"

"It is a military secret?" the boy asked, "It is then something quite important. I was sure you would have something of that sort. Oh, if it might be that I could go *with you*—!" The boy's words were almost like a prayer.

But when Charlie Montgomery spoke, his words were quite commonplace.

"I wish it might be, lad," said the former football star, smiling down on the younger man most kindly. "I would like nothing better than to have you for my companion. But I'm afraid that would be out of the question. Mine will probably be a solitary way. But I'll be thinking of you. I hope you'll have some great needful part in this war, and I'll be sure you'll do as good work, whatever it is, as you used to do on the field in the old days—"

The younger man flushed and there was a pleased light in his eyes, as he marched in step with Charlie.

"It seems to me I used to see you at some of our college games," said Charlie.

"You sure did!" said young Walter. "I used to come to all the games in our city whenever your college played the

University. I stuck by you and cheered you for all I was worth."

"Good work!" said Charlie Montgomery. "I guess that's why we won so often when we came to the home city. But it seems to me you came to one or two other places where we played, too. Wasn't that so?"

"I sure did. I used to work overtime to get money to follow you around wherever you were playing if it was at all possible. You were always my hero. That's why I'd like to get transferred to your outfit if I could." The boy's tone was wistful.

"Well I certainly appreciate that, Walt, and I wish it could be managed, but I don't see any chance at present. Maybe we'll run up against each other again."

"I sure hope we do!" said young Walter sadly. "Say, are you thinking of going over to the meeting tonight? Ever heard that Silverthorn? He's swell! All the fellows like him. I'd like to go with you if you do."

"Silverthorn! Why yes, I've heard *about* him. All right, I'd like to go with you if I find, after I check in, that I am free this evening. It's nice to see somebody from the home town, you know. Where shall I find you? What time?"

"Oh, I'll stick around and show up when you're ready."

The two parted and Charlie went in to make his arrangements and get his orders. A little later, after mess, he came out to find Walter Blake waiting for him shyly, and together they walked over to the auditorium that was already filling up fast.

The place was brilliantly lighted and a burst of song greeted them as they stepped inside and found seats.

There was something heartening and thrilling in the music from so many men's voices. For an instant it almost seemed to Charlie as if it might be a church service at home where he used to go with his mother when he was a youngster, and something constricted his throat, and brought a sudden mist to his eyes as he remembered the past. Only this singing had more volume and power, more enthusiasm than they ever had in those old days at home. He gave a quick look around and noticed with how much fervor most of the men sang, as if they loved it. As if they meant every word they were singing.

It was an old hymn they were singing, as they sat down, and presently Charlie, noticing that Walter was joining in with a clear voice, found himself singing too.

> Rock of Ages, cleft for me,
> Let me hide myself in Thee;

He could almost hear his mother's voice quavering through the words. Those last weeks when she was with him, after her long illness, when her voice was soft and unsteady. And sometimes she could not sing very loud, just a sweet little quaver, a tremble. She hadn't really been well enough to go to church, but she had insisted upon doing so. She said she needed the strength she drew from the service. He was glad that the last few times they went he had managed either to borrow a car to take her or to get a taxi. That was just a few weeks before her last illness and death, and as Charlie sat there with that old song his mother had loved surging about him, he felt the tears stinging into his eyes, and a great longing came into his heart that he might find his mother's refuge, which he was sure she had.

> Let the water and the blood,
>   From Thy riven side which flowed,
> Be of sin the double cure,
>   Save me from its guilt and power.

That part of the song didn't mean much to Charlie. He wasn't conscious of being a sinner. At least not much of a sinner. He had been taught to be clean and true by his wonderful mother, and had always been too busy to break laws and carry on the way most boys did, which was what sin meant to his mind. But this was the good old-fashioned gospel, of course, that his mother had taught him, and he had accepted it without a thought. So, it wasn't sin that was troubling Charlie. He wasn't exactly sure what it was that troubled him, only that he was presently going out alone to meet death, and he felt he needed *something*.

The singing went on. Many old hymns, new choruses too, in a little red book, and he enjoyed using his voice and being a part of the swelling melody that was filling the hall.

Then there came upon the platform, a young man in uniform walking easily, assuredly.

"That's him," murmured Walter in his ear. "That's Lincoln Silverthorn."

"But—he's in the *service?*"

"Sure! He's a chaplain, 'sposed to be! But he's different from a lot of them. He's real!"

And now Lincoln Silverthorn was speaking.

"Good evening, fellows," he said in his clear pleasant voice, that seemed to be speaking personally to each one in the room. "I've got a pleasant surprise for you. Just a few minutes ago a good friend of mine who has worked with me for several years, walked in on me. He has a great voice that can sing to your heart, and he's going to sing for you and strike a keynote for my message tonight. Fellows, this is my buddy, Lieutenant Luther Waite, and he's doing a very important work for our war. Go ahead, Lutie!"

And then a big redheaded fellow, also in uniform, came forward grinning.

"Glad to meet you, fellas," he said, and then began to sing.

It was a rich full voice and it held the audience from the start, every note clear, every word distinct:

> I was just a poor lost sinner,
>   Till Jesus came my way.
> He smiled into my eyes and said,
>   "Come walk with me today."

Probably some fellow who was reformed in some mission or other, thought Charlie, as he settled back under the spell of the song.

But as the song progressed the singer's eyes seemed to seek out Charlie, and be telling his story directly to him. There was something about the way those true fine eyes held his attention, and made him listen to every word, on through several verses, that made the singing a story of the man's life, the story of a testimony of what the Lord Jesus Christ had done for him.

But when he came to the last four lines those earnest eyes which seemed to have been piercing Charlie's soul, looked deep into Charlie's eyes again as if they were alone and were having a conversation:

> Me! A sinner! A poor lost sinner!
> I'm telling you it's true!

The singer's manner was most impressive:

> He died upon the cross for me
> He's done *the same* for *you!*

Charlie was startlingly aware of being charged with something that he had never before felt was true. "He's done the same for you!" seemed to be aimed directly at himself, as something that had been done for him, of which he had never been aware before, and for which he never made any acknowledgment to the Donor. He was filled with a sudden compunction, a kind of new shame.

And then at once his self-esteem began to assert itself, that he *wasn't* a sinner. Not a sinner like that, who needed *saving!*

It was strange that almost upon that thought came Link Silverthorn's words, announcing his theme.

"*All* have sinned and come short of the glory of God. ... The wages of sin is death."

There was a tense silence that gripped every listening heart. Even the protest that was beginning to form in Charlie Montgomery's heart, the outcry against being called a sinner, was silenced, as everyone waited for the next word about this hopeless situation in which they had all found themselves to be.

"The greatest sin, *all* sin, is not believing in Christ, Who took all our sin on Himself, and paid the price with His own blood. Unbelief is not accepting what He did, not appropriating it for ourselves."

The speaker was very still for a moment, letting them take that in. Then he went on.

"Some of you think you are not sinners, don't you? But you are. That's not my idea. You look pretty fine to me. But *God says* you are. Ever since Adam sinned we were all born sinners. God had told Adam that there was but one law to keep. He must keep that one law or death would come into the world. And Adam broke the law, took the forbidden fruit, and since then we were all born sinners, and are all under condemnation of death for our sin. But God loved us, and He made a way for condemned sinners to be saved through accepting what Christ His Son did for them.

"Did you ever think of Christ as having come voluntarily away from Heaven and glory to live down here and be crucified in your place, just as if He had been the sinner, not you? Have you ever considered Him there upon the cross in your place, where *you* belonged, bearing upon His sinless self every thought and word and action, and even that indifference of yours, just as if they had been His sins? And bearing it even unto death?"

As the young chaplain talked he seemed to be possessed of a supernatural power to create a picture of what he was saying, so that as he went on, with simple words like strokes of an artist's brush, there appeared a vision before the listeners' eyes, of the Christ, standing before his persecutors; standing before Pilate; and those unbelievers who would stone Him, kill Him, anything to get rid of Him. Somehow Charlie began to feel himself one of those unbelievers who had not accepted the Christ for what He was willing to be to him, and a great desire came into his heart to array himself with the followers of Jesus, and not with the unbelievers. He felt it so keenly that he longed to be able to go up to that silent figure standing alone, and tell Him he wanted to follow Him. It was not pity he felt, for somehow that quiet figure of the Saviour of the world who seemed to be standing up there on the platform alone, had a majesty about Him that defied pity.

And now came the cross, and Jesus, lifted up with all that sin—sin of the whole world—upon Him, and all the world's death punishment to bear! Never before had Charlie Montgomery felt that he himself had had aught to do with hanging the Son of God upon that cross. But now he suddenly saw it. Charlie Montgomery who had always been so proud of himself that he had gone through school and college against such great odds, always so smugly sure that he was doing the right thing, and always would do the right thing; and yet he had been one who had helped to crucify the Son of God, when He was dying for him!

It was very still in that big hall. The speaker had utmost attention. Perhaps all those young men were seeing that same vision of Jesus, up there suffering for their sins.

Once Charlie gave a quick glance around and saw the deep interest in all eyes. Even the boy by his side was all interest. Jesus, the Saviour of the world was holding them all, and Charlie Montgomery felt that he had found what he had been seeking—A Person. Jesus the crucified was what he sought. It was his mother's Christ. He had a strange feeling during the closing prayer that he wanted to slip up to that platform, and tell the Christ who had been dying there for him, that now he believed. That now henceforward through what days were left for him to live, he wanted to walk with Christ. He bowed his head quietly, and found there were tears on his face.

As the petition at the close of that wonderful message came to an end, the big man with the great voice and the red hair began to sing.

> I would love to tell you what I think of Jesus
> Since I found in Him a friend so strong and true,
> I would tell you how He changed my life completely,
> He did something that no other friend could do.

How that voice stirred the throng of young men! And then Charlie felt himself to be a part of a company of astonishingly saved people. There was no reasoning it out. Jesus Christ had been up there before them all dying for them, and he had found out he was a sinner, too, with all the rest of them. The singer went on giving his testimony.

> No one ever cared for me like Jesus,
> There's no other friend so kind as He;
> No one else could take the sin and darkness from me.
> O how much He cared for me!

When it was over they stood there looking toward the platform.

"Wantta go up and speak to him?" asked Walter shyly. "He don't mind. He likes the fellas to come up, and he's swell about explaining things he's said. The fellas all call him 'Link.'"

Charlie Montgomery gave a thoughtful look at his young companion.

"Have you been up before?" he asked.

"Sure, I been up a couppla times. I liketa hear him talk."

"All right! Come on!" said Charlie Montgomery, and followed his young guide up to the front, where Link Silverthorn was talking interestedly with a lot of the men, as if they were all intimate friends. So they drew nearer and nearer to the eager group around the speaker, until they could hear, and became a part of the innermost group. At last Charlie Montgomery came to be in the forefront, listening with keen eyes on Link Silverthorn.

And then suddenly Link's eyes caught Charlie's glance, and he came down the steps of the platform, and stood beside the young lieutenant, placing a kindly hand on Charlie's arm and reaching down to grasp his hand.

"Are you saved, brother?" asked the young chaplain.

Charlie looked steadily into Lincoln Silverthorn's eyes with no reserves in his own glance.

"I'm not sure," he said slowly. "I'd like to be. I'm going out in a few days on a commission where there is very little likelihood that I shall ever return to my own world. I've always believed in Christ and His dying for the world, but it never, somehow, seemed to have anything to do with me personally. Tonight you made me see Him. What do I have to do?"

The young chaplain smiled with a great light in his eyes.

" 'Believe on the Lord Jesus Christ and thou shalt be saved,' " he quoted, "but that means more than a mere intellectual belief. It means a real heart belief. It means accepting Him as your personal Saviour. Accepting what He has done for you. Are you willing to do that?"

"I am," said Charlie steadily.

"Then let's tell Him so," said Link, and the two slipped down on their knees beside the wooden bench, while Link prayed.

"Lord Jesus, here's a seeking soul who wants You. He says he is glad to accept what You did for him, in taking his sin upon Your sinless self, and suffering the penalty of death that was rightfully his. We're asking You now to fulfill Your promise when You said 'He that heareth my word, and believeth on Him that sent me, *hath* everlasting life, *and shall not* come into condemnation, but is passed from death unto life.' Take him now, dear Lord, and show him how to walk with Thee."

"And now, brother, will you tell Him, too?"

Charlie was still for a moment, and then he spoke, his eyes closed, his head bent low resting on his lifted hand:

"Lord, I believe. Forgive all the years of my indifference. Stay by me, and show me the way."

Neither Charlie nor Silverthorn had noticed young Walter kneeling down beside them, his head reverently bowed, his eyes closed.

The gathered groups around the platform had drifted a little farther away, talking in low tones, regardful of the ones who were kneeling, and as the two arose, Walter rose with them, stepping back shyly. It was only then that Silverthorn saw him and put out his hand to touch the lad.

"And how about you, buddy?" asked Link Silverthorn. "Don't you want to be saved, too?"

"Yes, sir," said Walter, his eyes lighting up. "I *was*. I did it yesterday."

Link's eyes shone.

"Are you glad you did it?"

Walter Blake flushed, and he lifted brightening eyes.

"Yes, sir, I am. A lot I am! It's easier to go on now, sir."

"That's right, fella," said Link, giving the boy a hearty grasp of his hand. "Are you two fellows—brothers?"

Walter shook his head.

"We're from the same home town," offered Charlie with a warm lovingness in his tone, that made Walter's face flush again and his eyes lighten.

"He's the best quarter-back in football you ever saw!" burst in Walter enthusiastically.

"Oh, so he's your football hero, is he? Well, that's great! And now, I hope you're both going to be the best Christians this army ever saw, and win souls for Christ wherever you go."

"Okay!" said Walter. "That's what we—that's what I want too!"

"Here too," said Charlie smiling. "I guess it was his doing that I came here tonight, and I'm glad I came. I thank you, sir, for the help *you've* given me. I think I can go out now without worrying."

"Oh, I'm glad to hear you say that. I certainly am, and I'm glad to have had a little hand in it. I'll remember you fellas, and I'll be praying. I'll be praying that if it's God's will He'll bring you both safe home again, alive and sound and well."

Then suddenly he motioned toward the big redhead who had sung.

"Here, Lute, I want you to meet these two fellows. They've just found Christ, and one of them's going out on a hard assignment that doesn't give much hope of returning. I want you to remember these fellows and pray for them, and when we pray together, remind me about them specially, will you, Lute!"

"That I will," said the big man with a wide genial smile. "Praise the Lord! He's able to keep you true all the way through, fellows, and able to bring you back again, too, no matter how great the odds. But if instead He calls you Home, why that will be all right, too, won't it?"

Charlie gave a grave sweet assent to that, and Walter nodded with a seraphic smile. Walter knew what he was doing and was content. And for the first time since Charlie had left Blythe, a great peace came to dwell in his heart.

They walked along together, with a ring to their footsteps, and finally separated.

"Isn't he swell?" said Walter at last, really thinking aloud.

"He certainly is," said Charlie. "I'm glad you took me there! And I'm glad you—*belong*—too. That makes us sort of buddies in a special sense, doesn't it?"

"It sure does! Good night, I never thought I'd ever have anything as grand as this in my life, not in the army anyway. Having you come to Christ along with me! I didn't think I'd ever be tied in any company as fine as you. And to have you find Him too at the same time! It'll be something to remember always. Gee, but mom'll be glad when I write her about this. You don't mind if I tell her about you too, do you? She knows who you are. She's always been glad to help me get away to one of your games, and she'll be awful pleased that you're a Christian."

"Mind?" said Charlie. "Why, no, I'm glad! I only wish my mother were at home now and I could write to her about it. She'd be glad too."

And then they parted for the night with a heartier handclasp than even football would have brought about.

Chapter 10

THE NEXT THREE days were a time of great strengthening for Charlie Montgomery in many ways. The morning found him summoned to an audience with an instructor in the special mission that was to be his in the near future, and his heart swelled with the tremendous import of what each move he was to make would mean toward victory in the great task he had undertaken.

Yet he found that the thought of it did not appall him as it might have done, now that he had taken the Lord Jesus Christ for his Saviour. When he had time to think of it all, it was as if he were going out hand in hand with God's Son, they were yoke-fellows in this work to put down evil that had a grip on the world. God *must* want it stopped, and had put it into the hearts of men to go out and stop it, to put an end to the selfish ambitions of men who did not consider God, men who were out to destroy all good thoughts and motives, and even to destroy the thought of God in the hearts of men, if they could. Somehow as he thought of it, it seemed to him that God was going to use him for His own purposes, and he was solemnly glad. And glad too with a light heart, because his heart was right with God. Whatever came now, whether life through a hard way, or the death which seemed to be the inevitable outcome of this undertaking, he was safe, a child of God! Saved through His blood!

As the day waned, and the time for the evening service drew on, Charlie's work with the instructor finished for the day, his thoughts went more and more to the decision he had made the night before, and he seemed to have a revelation of himself. Only a few hours ago he hadn't thought of himself as a sinner at all, or as one who needed saving. His only concern about this matter had been somewhat in the nature of going through a form of preparation for a change from life to death, as one would get a passport for a journey, or a reservation on a train, or register in the army.

What was it that had made the difference in him? Could it be that it was that one evening's glimpse of Christ, as the man Silverthorn had described Him, that had made the change in his whole point of view? He had *seen* Jesus with the eyes of his spirit. He felt as if he knew Him now. Was it possible that that one short view of Christ had acted as a measuring rod to show him wherein he himself was lacking? Had that brief transaction, on his knees, wherein he handed himself over to the Christ and took Him for his personal Saviour, shown him how mistaken he had always been when he thought of himself as no sinner?

Of course he had not been conceited about himself. He was sure of that, for his mother had dealt determinedly with every possible showing of conceit in his nature, but he had thought of himself as a pretty fairly good fellow. Oh, a few imperfections of course, as any one might have, but nothing to be alarmed about.

And now, why! Thoughts, feelings, even attitudes of mind, began to crop out, and take the form of sin when seen in the light of the eyes of God, and of His Son, Jesus Christ.

Why hadn't he known all this before, with a mother like his to teach him? A mother who loved God and lived her life as in His presence? And yet he had never taken more than the mere head knowledge of a few facts that he had accepted without thought! And that wasn't the way he had taken any other subjects that he had been taught. The difference must be that now he had seen Jesus, and before he had merely *heard* about Him, and swallowed the knowledge as a fact to which he need give but small concern.

There were two or three invitations to go places from other men, officers, and some men he had met before, old college mates, but he put them all aside and went to the meeting with Walter.

They sat up very near the front this time, and received welcoming glances from both Silverthorn, and Waite, who was still there, and it seemed sometimes to Charlie as if parts of the service were just arranged for his own help, though of course there must be others in the same situation as himself. But his soul was hungry for this knowledge of holy things that was being given out here, and he was drinking it in eagerly. And again the preacher brought the Christ in vision before them all, and Charlie seemed to look into His eyes, and get a recognition from those wise and loving glances, so that he came away from that meeting with a sweet assurance in his heart that he was Christ's, and nothing could harm him, even death could not take him out of the continual presence of his Saviour.

It was after Walter had left him for the night that it came to him to wonder if Blythe knew the Lord in this way?

Oh, she must be a Christian. He had seen her going to church several times. He knew which church her people attended. But did she know Jesus Christ as a Saviour? Had she ever felt her need of a Saviour, or was she just careless about it all, as he had been?

Quite early the next morning, before the day's routine called him, he wakened, and wrote a very brief letter to Blythe, telling her of his experience, and there came to his heart a solemn anxiety for her. Would she understand what he meant when he tried to tell her, or would she be hurt and think he was discounting her fineness and belovedness? He found himself shyly asking God to help him write that letter so she would understand, and so that no thought of any censorship could detract from its meaning.

Two days later Charlie got his orders to move on, and with a parting blessing from Link and Luther Waite, and attended to the train by Walter Blake, he took his way again into the unknown.

There was a few minutes' delay at the train, and the sorrowful Walter tried to think of all the things his bursting heart would like to say.

"I—wish I—was going—with you," he choked out,

blinking back the unbidden tears. "You—kinda—seem like—*home* folks!"

Charlie gave him a pitying glance, and owned that he felt that way too.

"I'll tell you, kid, you might get a furlough pretty soon. Do you suppose you might get home at all?"

"I can't tell," said the boy. "I might! Depends on where they're sending me. If I go overseas pretty soon they might let me stop off home for a day or so."

"Well, say, kid, if you do get home, and it doesn't take too much time from your family, I wonder if you'd deliver a greeting for me to a friend of mine?"

Charlie was merely figuring to take the lad's mind off from their parting, and he reckoned rightly for Walter's face brightened.

"Sure. I'd be proud to. Who is it? Your family?"

"No, they're all gone. It's—a friend—of mine. Did you ever hear of the Bonniwells?"

"Sure I did. I useta deliver papers there, and they always bought magazines from me."

"Then you know where they live?"

"Oh, sure! Big stone house on Wolverton Drive. Got a daughter named Blythe. Useta go to our school when you and she were in high. She the one?"

Charlie grinned.

"You're right, kid. How'd you know?"

"Oh, I've seen her around. Saw her at a couppla your football games. Saw her watching you play."

"Well, that's something!" said Charlie, realizing that that was something he and Blythe had not had time to talk about. Of course he had seen her there, but he had not been aware of her watching him. She hadn't been one of his crowd, and he hadn't even ventured a greeting to her at those games.

"Well, think you could give her a message? Here, I'll write just a line. Of course if you lose it before you get there it won't matter. You can read it and repeat it."

The engine screeched a warning, and Lieutenant Charles Montgomery standing on the bottom step of the car, seized his pen and notebook from his pocket and wrote.

"You'll havta make it speedy, pard," said Walter, forgetting his army manners, "she's about ta start."

"Beloved. I'm off. God bless you. Love, Charlie."

The engine gave a lurch and then a warning whistle.

"Make it snappy, Lieutenant," breathed Walter anxiously.

Charlie folded the paper and put it in the eager hand, even as the train began to move.

"Good-by, kid. Keep it safe, and if you have a chance to talk with her, tell her how we met and all about it. If you don't get home, well, never mind! Take care of your faith, kid, and don't forget to pray."

"Oh sure, you know I won't!" shouted the boy-soldier, as the train moved away beyond his following feet.

Two days later Walter was moved on, *without* his furlough home. He had wrapped the precious slip of paper in a bit of cellophane and fastened it between the flyleaves of the testament his mother had given him when he left home, which he always carried over his heart. That meant that Charlie's message would never get lost, and would *some*time be delivered, unless the young soldier was lost himself. This commission from his hero was his only consolation for the sorrow that he could not go with Charlie, through fire or death or whatever was to come to him. And his prayers every night for Charlie, yes and for the girl to whom he had sent his farewell, were most fervent, and never forgotten.

Two days more Walter had, following after Silverthorn and his friend Luther Waite, and then they went on to another location but the boy-soldier had learned much from sitting at the feet of these two servants of the Lord, and he carried a lighter heart as he went out into the great unknown future that was to be his. His hand was in God's hand, his strength was the joy of the Lord.

But as he went he thought often of his friend and hero Charlie Montgomery, and sent up a prayer for him. For though he had no idea what Charlie was going into, he was sure it was full of danger, more than most soldiers and fliers were destined for, and his heart would fail him sometimes as he thought that perhaps he would never see Charlie again on this earth, but he was glad, glad that he was sure of that meeting in Heaven. There would be no doubt nor anxiety about that.

And then, at his first opportunity Walter wrote a long letter to his mother.

"I met a fellow from home, mom. He was with me in camp for three days. He's the football guy I used to talk about so much, do you remember? His name's Montgomery, and he's a prince, he sure is. More of a prince even than he used to be. He's a lieutenant, but he wasn't a bit stuck up for his rank. He went around with me a lot, and we went to a wonderful meeting together. That chaplain named Silverthorn was here, and he preached swell, and we went to his meetings every night, and both of us took Christ as our Saviour. I thought you'd like to know that. And I *mean* it, mom! And I feel a lot better about going into war since I did it. So did Montgomery. He's something special, going out on a separate commission. Something pretty high up, and pretty dangerous. It's a military secret what it is, and of course he didn't tell me, but I judge from what he said he doesn't expect to come back. But I'm glad I met him. He's swell, and I guess we'll meet in Heaven anyway. I said I'd like to go with him, and if I get a chance to get transferred to his location I sure will accept. So, I'm telling you, mom, if anything happens to me you can know it's all right with me, and Christ is my Saviour. So, mom, don't you feel bad. And tell my sister Peggy I've sent her a little pin like the one I wear."

Mrs. Blake cried tears of joy over that letter, and prayed for the two who had gone their separate ways, and in due time went to her Red Cross sewing class, from which she had been absent for a couple of weeks on account of extra time at the plant where she worked, and when she came into the room Blythe noticed that there was a look of peace on her face, and a light in her eyes that she had not seen before.

As usual the other ladies paid little attention to her, except to nod a cold good morning. Only Anne Houghton, who remarked hatefully:

"Oh, *you're* back, are you? I thought they'd got you transferred."

But even that didn't disturb the calm of Mrs. Blake's tired little face.

Blythe had been sitting at the other end of the room

when Mrs. Blake entered, and had distinctly heard the disagreeable greeting. She made an excuse, presently, to change her seat and take the one beside Mrs. Blake.

"I've been missing you from the class," she said sweetly, and quite distinctly, so that everyone could hear. "Have you been ill?"

"Oh no," answered the little woman pleasantly, in a very quiet refined tone, "I had extra work at the plant and couldn't get away, but I came back as soon as I could."

"Oh, I'm glad you weren't sick," said Blythe, beginning on another buttonhole. "So many people have had colds this time of year. And then I thought of your little girl, and wondered if she were sick. All the children in our neighborhood have had the measles."

"No, Peggy's quite well," said her mother. "She's been joining that Junior Red Cross group they've started at school, and she heard me telling what wonderful buttonholes you make, so she wants to learn how, and I told her I'd watch you if I got the chance and see if I could give her some help. I never was very good at buttonholes myself, but maybe if I watch you I could teach her."

"Oh, let me teach her, Mrs. Blake! I'd love to. That would be fun."

"Why, would you be willing to? That would be wonderful. But I'm afraid that would be a lot of trouble for you."

"No, I'd love it. What time does she get home from school? Could she stop at my house on her way home a few times? We'll make a fine little buttonhole maker of her."

Mrs. Blake fairly beamed.

"Well, I'm sure I never can thank you enough for being so kind. It's just beautiful of you to offer."

"Oh, please don't get the idea I'm doing anything great," smiled Blythe. "We're in a war, you know, and everybody is supposed to do everything they can to help along. I'm sure if I succeed in making Peggy a good buttonhole maker, why then she can help to finish more garments, and so we'll be doubling our output. Isn't that good reasoning?"

So they laughed about it, and little Mrs. Blake's face took on a very sweet look. If Charlie Montgomery could have seen Mrs. Blake he might have said she looked like her youngest son, Walter. But Charlie Montgomery was not there, except in the thought of one dear girl whose mind was always hovering about his memory.

"This is a happy day for me," said Mrs. Blake, "you offering to do this for Peggy, and I know she'll be so happy about it. And then I had a letter from my Walter this morning. I was almost late getting here, stopping to read it. In fact I haven't read it all yet, but I just read one sentence near the end where it was folded that said he had met with somebody from home and it made him very glad. He went around with him for a couple of days, and it's evidently braced him up a lot."

"Oh, that is nice! Poor boys. It must be very hard for them to be torn away from their homes and families this way and compelled to grow up suddenly and go out and fight! It's hard enough for the older ones, but for the very young ones it must be terrible. Didn't you tell me he was only seventeen?"

"Yes, just turned seventeen," said the mother sighing.

"Oh, why did you let him go yet? Couldn't you have kept him at home for one more year?"

"Well, yes, I suppose I could, but it would have been like holding wild horses in. He was just raring to go, and he really felt kind of ashamed, his two brothers both gone already. You know the boys feel it."

"Yes, I suppose they do! Poor kiddies! They don't realize what it is, but I suppose there are some good things about it."

"Yes, perhaps," sighed the mother. "Well, one thing in Walter's letter made me real glad anyway. He says he's been getting to know the Lord." She said it shyly, with almost a hush of shamedness in her voice as if she wasn't used to talking of such things, and she didn't know how this girl from the aristocracy would take it.

"Oh," said Blythe embarrassedly. "Why, that's kind of wonderful, isn't it? I suppose war does make the boys thoughtful. They aren't always sure how they are coming through."

"Yes," said Mrs. Blake, "I suppose it does. Though before they went that was one thing I worried about. I was afraid they would get into bad company, and get to cursing and swearing and doing all sorts of dreadful things. You see I always tried to bring my children up to be Christians, though to tell the truth when they went out from home and were with other children they kind of got away from it. They'd make any excuse to stay away from church, you know. But now Walter says he and this fellow from home went to a meeting every night. Some chaplain that's very interesting has got them to thinking real seriously."

"Well, I guess you ought to be very glad over that," said Blythe. "Maybe there are going to be some good things come out of this war after all. Of course it's going to be awfully hard for their families, a lot of sorrow having them gone, and not knowing if they'll come home safe, but it's good there is a brighter side."

"Yes," said Mrs. Blake. "If I thought my boys would get to be good Christians and be right ready if they had to die, I wouldn't worry so much. And that's why I'm so glad over Walter's letter."

And then suddenly the sewing class broke up, and they all went home. Blythe and Mrs. Blake lingered just long enough to make arrangements about Peggy's coming for her buttonhole lesson, and then Blythe hurried away, for somehow Mrs. Blake's telling of the letter from her son made her eager to get home and see if there might be another letter from Charlie.

And sure enough there was, the letter he had written that early morning after he had given himself to the Lord the night before.

Chapter 11

MR. BONNIWELL, busy in his office that morning, had received a telephone call from Dan Seavers, asking urgently to be allowed to see him at once, and Blythe's father had annoyedly put aside some very important telephone calls that he had planned to make right away, and told him he might come, if he would make his business brief, as he had but ten minutes to spare. Young Seavers agreed, and presently presented himself at the office.

There was no humility in the bearing of the gay young man as he entered the Bonniwell office smiling, almost condescendingly.

He was in officer's uniform, and looked very handsome and dominant. Mr. Bonniwell suppressed a definite dislike that he always of late had experienced, whenever he saw this young man. Even the stunning new uniform did not dispel this feeling and the older man struggled against it and tried to be decently cordial. Of course his own prejudice dated back to when Dan was ten years younger and he saw him do a very unfair thing to a schoolmate who was even younger, and definitely not as well dressed as himself. But of course, he tried to tell himself, the fellow was grown up now, and had likely got over those snobbish tendencies. Anyway he would give him the benefit of the doubt. He was Blythe's friend of course, and she must see something good in him or she wouldn't be off with him so much.

"Good morning, Dan," he said, trying not to be stiff in his manner. "Won't you sit down? Sorry to have to hurry you about time, but I am a good deal rushed this morning. Now, what's on your mind? I see you're in uniform. Does that mean you are going to leave our town soon?"

Daniel smiled proudly.

"Yes, I suppose so. I just got my commission, and I'm getting matters arranged for my departure. And that's why I wanted to see you without delay so I can begin to get everything shaped up. You see it is not quite settled yet where I am to be stationed, but the order may come through in a few days, and I don't want to have a lot of things to attend to at the last minute, and have to rush, you know."

"Yes?" said Mr. Bonniwell lifting puzzled eyes to the young man, and trying to understand what his glib speech could presage. "And how do I come in on that?"

The young man gave a self-conscious laugh.

"It's about Blythe, sir. My mother brought me up to feel that it was the proper thing always to ask permission of the father before one formally asked a girl to marry him, and I came this morning to get that over with. I know it's rather old-fashioned to assume that the parents have anything at all to do with the modern marriage, and it isn't done much any more, but I know that both my mother and Blythe's mother are rather sticklers for the old time formalities, so, as I want to do everything up right and please everybody, I came this morning to formally ask you for your daughter's hand in marriage."

Mr. Bonniwell sat there and stared at the young man, suffering a distinct inner revulsion, and he stared so long at Dan that he grew slightly impatient. Dan had expected a smiling acquiescence, at the very least. Was he not honoring this man's daughter? The man ought to be very grateful that he had even troubled to ask his permission. Most fellows wouldn't think of stooping to do that nowadays.

"You see," he said uneasily, to bring the matter to a head, "if I should have to go suddenly it would be well to have the wedding over with, and not have to be rushing through everything. One has to prepare in plenty of time to avoid confusion at the end, you know, and I hate above all things to be rushed. Half the beauty of a stately and magnificent wedding is to have it without any appearance of hurry, just calm and perfect. Don't you think so, sir?"

But Mr. Bonniwell was not considering the stateliness and perfection of wedding ceremonies. Instead he was looking sharply at the young man who was talking, wondering if it was just his prejudice and imagination that made him suddenly feel that there was a great weakness in Dan's chin. A weak chin! And that man with a weak, selfish chin and conceited eyes wanted to marry his little girl!

When he noticed that the lazy affected voice had ceased for a moment, he spoke. His voice was husky, as if he had received a shock:

"Have you talked this over with my daughter?"

"Well, no," drawled the lazy voice. "I was trying to do the proper thing according to the old-fashioned acceptation of that term. That is why I came to you first. That, and because I felt that I would be in a stronger position with your daughter if I brought your O.K. with me; and also thus save much trying discussion of a matter which I have already worked out to perfection. I didn't want to run the risk of having to wait around for formalities, so I'm taking them ahead of time and arranging things for myself. That is why I came to you to get your consent right from the start."

Mr. Bonniwell continued to look the young man over carefully, sadly. And at last he said:

"Why do you want to marry my daughter?"

"*Why?* Well, that's some question. You act as if it was a surprise to you. Surely you've seen us going together for years. I've been coming to your house in and out since I was a child. Everybody has always known we were meant for each other, Blythe and I have gone together so long. We're pretty well used to one another. It's rather late for you to be asking *why* I want to marry her, isn't it?"

"Perhaps so. Nevertheless I'm asking you. Just why do you want to marry my daughter?"

Mr. Bonniwell looked keenly into the young man's eyes. His own mouth was very firm and it was evident he wanted an answer.

"Well," laughed Dan, "if you insist, of course. Why, I decided she was the one best suited to my needs in a wife.

She's good-looking and graceful, and well-bred. She has an easy manner and will make an excellent hostess. I would never need to be ashamed of her when I chose to entertain, even royalty. She knows how to dress well. Her education is all right, and she's very adaptable. Besides she isn't set in her way. She wouldn't be always insisting on having her own way. And then, she has—we both have—plenty of money. We wouldn't be troubled financially. I could always be proud of her in any situation. Say! Isn't that enough reasons why I want to marry her?"

"No!" said the father, suddenly straightening up and turning his eyes to the window, looking off as if he were seeing a vision of other days. "No, that isn't enough! You've left out the main thing. You talk of her looks and her education and her money, and her position and breeding, you talk of her ability to exercise social duties, and to yield her own wishes to yours, and you think on the strength of just that that a marriage can be made! No sir, young man, you are all wrong. I'm older than you are, and I've lived through a good many years of marriage, and if I had had only what you have named it would have been a mighty poor chance of happiness I'd have had. You've got to have more than that, boy, before I'll ever endorse your marriage with my daughter. She's worth more than that. This isn't a mere commercial transaction, you know. No true marriage is. There's got to be something more than that, or you'll go on the rocks for sure before many years."

Dan looked at the man whom he desired to make his father-in-law haughtily and in some perplexity.

"I don't understand you," he said in a tone of annoyance. "Is there something more that you require?"

"Yes, there is," said the father shutting his firm lips with decision. "You haven't said anything about your personal feeling for my daughter; and true love is the only foundation for a successful marriage. No father would be willing to see a beloved child go into a loveless marriage. Dan, do you love my daughter?"

"Oh! *That!* Why of course, that goes without saying," said Dan amusedly. "I've always been nuts about Blythe, and I'm sure she's crazy about me. But that is entirely a matter between Blythe and myself, isn't it? At least she's always seemed very happy in my company. I don't think you need have any hesitation on that score. Of course I'm very fond of her."

"That isn't enough," said the father decidedly. "No boy, just being fond, or even 'being nuts' isn't enough. It's got to be more than that. It's got to be something that will stand when trouble comes; tribulation and poverty, and death."

"Poverty!" laughed Dan contemptuously. "I guess there's no danger of that!" and he lifted his patrician chin haughtily.

"It's quite possible to have poverty come to anyone," said Mr. Bonniwell soberly. "Things happen in this world, and you can't ever be sure any of them won't come to you. And when they come I'd want to be sure that there was gentleness and loving kindness, and tenderness, and a world of protection for my girl. Sickness and suffering, too, may be anybody's lot."

"Oh, I'll take the chance," said Dan with a shrug and a laugh.

"But that isn't enough. You've got to be sure you will be all that my girl needs to help her weather these things, if, or when, they come. I don't want my girl to take a chance."

Dan smiled in a superior way.

"Oh, don't be a pessimist!" he said. "You don't need to worry about that. I'll look after her. She'll be all right. Come Mr. Bonniwell, don't let's draw this thing out. You know you can bank on me all right. Give me your O.K. now, and I won't bother you any longer."

Mr. Bonniwell straightened up with that firm set of his lips that his business associates knew meant serious disagreement, and shook his head.

"Sorry, Dan, I can't comply at present. I've got to have time to think this thing over, so you needn't go any farther in your plans until you hear from me, and that's final. I'll bid you good morning now, for I've got to get back to my work."

"But—Mr. Bonniwell—" began Dan leaning forward with a wheedling manner.

"No buts, Dan Seavers! I meant what I said."

"Mr. Bonniwell, you wouldn't like it very well if Blythe and I *eloped,* would you?" asked the young man, flashing his eyes with a look which he meant to convey dangerous threats.

"No," said Blythe's father, "but my daughter would never do that."

"I wouldn't be so sure of that if I were you. Your daughter might do just that thing if the right arguments were brought to bear upon her. If I know her at all I'm sure she would if you made it necessary by withholding your consent."

"If my daughter did that, young man, she would have to take the consequences. Now, I will bid you good morning again, and this is final."

While he was speaking he pressed the buzzer on his desk, and his secretary promptly appeared at the door, pencil and pad in hand, ready to take dictation. She took her regular seat near Mr. Bonniwell's desk, and the business magnate swung around, reached for a letter tray and began to dictate a letter, so Dan Seavers perceived that the interview was ended, at least for the present. He arose and stood hesitantly a moment, but perceiving no further notice was to be taken of him he spoke again, in a quiet, rather haughty tone:

"When can I hope to have that answer from you, Mr. Bonniwell?"

The father finished the sentence he was dictating and then said, lifting his eyes briefly to his persistent caller:

"I will let you know when I have had sufficient time to think the matter over." And then he went on with the letter he was dictating.

Dan Seavers turned angrily toward the door, and then with his hand on the doorknob he flung back:

"I think you will be sorry, Mr. Bonniwell, that you have taken this attitude."

This time Mr. Bonniwell did not even lift his eyes as he answered almost meditatively:

"It may be so. And then again I might be even more sorry if I should take any other."

Furious at the failure of what he considered a stroke of genius, calculated to put his future father-in-law forever in his debt, Dan Seavers stalked from the room and closed the door forcefully. Mr. Bonniwell went calmly on with his dictation, though he was by no means calm within himself. This idea of his little girl grown up and somebody trying to marry her in a hurry and take her away, was entirely a new thought to him, and that somebody a young snob with a weak chin and a way of trying to act superior! What did it matter that he was handsome and had a lot of money in his own right? The young scoundrel hadn't even had the grace to say that he loved her! Bah! Was it possible that Blythe had had so little insight into character as to fall in love with that poor excuse of a man? Well, if she had he probably would have to give in, but *poor child!* Wasn't there some way to save her from a future like that? And so he went on thinking, and trying to dictate with the other half of his brain. It was well he had a smart secretary, who knew his ways, and framed her sentences with a view to his usual habits of diction.

But as the morning went on he grew more and more opposed to the plans which Dan Seavers had outlined to him, and less and less able to concentrate on his business. And at last about lunch time he called up his wife and asked her what time she was going to be at the house, saying he had something important he wanted to talk over with her. But when he found that she was not to be back from a committee meeting until late in the afternoon, he settled back grimly to work again, getting a lot of important trifles out of the way and giving definite orders about matters of business to his efficient secretary, planning the morrow's work pretty fully for her, with the idea in mind that he simply couldn't do any real work down here at the office himself until this matter of Dan's proposition was settled one way or the other.

As the day wore on he felt much as if there were a sudden and calamitous illness in the house, the outcome of which could not yet be foretold.

He tried to tell himself that this was ridiculous. That he simply must not get so upset at the idea of Blythe's belonging to anybody else but her parents, tried to tell himself that probably all loving parents felt the same way when called upon to give up a beloved daughter and let her go away to make a new home of her own. And of course it was right that she should. He wasn't a fool, and he had

always counted on such a possibility. But somehow it
seemed too soon. Why, she was just home from college,
and they had so counted on her coming back to them!
And then to have her marrying this unsatisfactory playmate of her childhood, this Seavers fellow he had never
quite liked. It was unthinkable! It was unbearable! He
couldn't *stand* it!

Over and over the changes rang on his troubles, winding in and out of the business he was forcing upon
himself. He would resolutely put all thoughts of this fan-
tastic proposition of Dan's out of his mind; and then the
next moment it would come blasting back into the depths
of his soul again, threatening to disarm him utterly.

And then that phase of having a wedding almost immediately! Why, it was preposterous! A war wedding! *His*
daughter. A wedding was a sacred thing that should be
approached deliberately and with solemnity, and consider-
ation. Not rushed into in a frenzy of enthusiasm to keep
up with the times. It certainly was not going to help the
war to be won to have a host of young people mating off
in droves, merely because everybody else was doing it.
Even if a man were going out to die it would not help him
any better to die to have gone through a hasty wedding
ceremony. But this young man was not even going off to
die. He was taking over a comfortable berth in an office,
and there was no rush about it. There was plenty of time
for Blythe to be sure what she was doing. No marrying in
haste to repent at leisure for *his* daughter. She must be
sure she had the right man, and be sure there was mutual
love. Not just fondness!

Again and again he would come back to that unfortunate word "nuts" and his lip would curl with distaste at the
thought of the way Dan had said it, with a casual
tolerance in his attitude. Oh, he couldn't stand it to have
Blythe go off with that young man! He would never be
able to trust her with him.

Then he would get up and prance across his office, back
and forth, and dictate with all the feverishness that a most
momentous business proposition might have caused, out
of all proportion to the importance of the letter he happened to be dictating.

He sent his secretary out to her lunch early, and had a

cup of coffee sent up from the restaurant for himself; but still his unhappy musings continued. The situation seemed to grow more and more impossible as the day went by.

When the late afternoon drew on he began to wonder about his wife. Did Alice know about this? Had Dan talked to her? Had she talked with Blythe about it? Did Blythe have any inkling of Dan Seavers' feeling for her?

Fondness, indeed! You needn't tell him that even the modern young people had got to the place where they were contemplating an immediate and hasty marriage without some preliminary love making? The world couldn't have changed that much since he and Alice were courting. But then the thought of love making between his daughter and a man who merely professed a "fondness" for her, became so obnoxious to him that he could scarcely contain himself, and though it was a full half-hour before the time that he had promised himself he might with self-respect go home and go into this matter most thoroughly, he finally told his secretary that she had wrought well, and might go home and finish the last few letters that he had dictated in the morning. She had worked hard and must be tired.

The secretary gave him a puzzled, half worried look, but thanked him and departed, and eagerly he got into his overcoat, took his hat and brief case and started on his way, the same old thoughts thrashing themselves out in his weary brain.

When he reached home he found that neither his wife nor daughter had as yet arrived, and in despair he put on his dressing gown and slippers and went and lay down on his couch and went to sleep!

Chapter 12

WHEN MRS. BONNIWELL came in half an hour later, she saw her husband asleep, and tiptoed around, not to waken him. Poor father! He was working so hard these days, he must be all worn out, or perhaps he was sick. She found a light shawl and softly spread it over him, drew the shades down so that the light would be dim, preparing to get quietly out of the room and keep the house still. But Bonniwell wasn't so sound asleep but that he heard her, and felt her ministrations, and his spirit underneath the light sleep was still so troubled that he came sharply awake and sat up.

"Alice!" he said blinking at his wife. "Is that you? I thought you would never get here. What's kept you so long?"

"Why, I came as soon as I could after you called," she said. "There were some matters in the committee that I had to settle first, and then I had to wait for a bus. But I'm here now. What is the matter? Are you sick? I never saw you lie down in the daytime. Have you a fever?

"No, I haven't any fever, except inside. I'm just worried. Alice, has our little girl been falling in love with that nincompoop, Dan Seavers? Because if she has I won't have it! I tell you I *won't have it!* He has a weak chin, and shifty eyes. I know you women think he's handsome, but if you like that sissyfied beauty in a man, I *don't*. I tell you he's no man for our girl. But if she thinks she's in love we've got to deal with it carefully, for I won't have her hurt. But I want to know the *truth,* the *whole* truth about it, and *right away!* It's important, I tell you."

"The truth about what, daddy," chirped Blythe, suddenly arriving from the side door and coming into the room rosy and radiant.

Mr. Bonniwell gasped and then faced the issue.

"The truth about you, child. Are you in love with anybody? I want to know the whole truth. Are you planning to run off and get married without our knowledge? Tell me at once!"

For answer Blythe laughed merrily.

"Why daddy! Where did you get that idea? Of course not. You didn't think I'd ever *elope*, did you?"

"Well, I didn't *think* you would, but you haven't answered my question. Are you in love with anybody?"

Then the mother put in.

"Now daddy, aren't you being awfully abrupt with your only child?"

The father glared at his wife.

"You keep out of this, Alice. I want my question answered."

Blythe flushed, and then looked up with wheedling glance, perceiving in her heart that the time for confession might be near at hand.

"Daddy! And suppose I was, do you think I would like to have the fact drawn out of me like a sore tooth?"

"You haven't answered me! *Are* you in love?"

Blythe's cheeks got rosier, and she gave one swift glance at her mother, then lifted her eyes bravely to her father's face.

"Well, daddy, I might be," she said sweetly. "What of it?"

Her father came up standing.

"With that nincompoop, Dan Seavers?" he thundered.

Then Blythe laughed out merrily again.

"*Daddy! Where* did you get that idea? Who ever could have told you that?"

Mr. Bonniwell watched his daughter sharply, grimly, his jaw set, his brows drawn, his gaze steady.

At last he spoke.

"Blythe, I *insist* on being answered. Are you in love with someone?"

"Well, daddy, I've always been in love with *you*—and *mother*," she added mischievously. She gave a whimsical little giggle. Was this the time for her to tell about Charlie?

"Blythe! I *mean* it! I am asking you seriously, I want an answer at once and no more nonsense!"

Blythe grew serious at once.

"Well, daddy, yes, I am in love with somebody, and I have just been waiting from day to day to have a good opportunity to tell you and mother about it. I guess this is as good a time as any. Let's go into the library where we won't be interrupted and sit down. And don't look so blank over it, it's nothing to feel bad about. Dad, you look as white as if you were going to fall over in a faint. Shall I help you to a chair?"

"Child, it can't be *possible* that you are wanting to marry that lazy good-for-nothing Dan Seavers?"

But Blythe only laughed.

"No, daddy, certainly *not!*" she said with a happy little lilt to her voice. "It is somebody a great deal finer than Dan. Dan's just an old childhood friend, but I *never* was in love with him."

"Oh, my child!" said her father with a relieved sigh, sinking down in a nearby chair.

"But my dear," spoke up Blythe's mother, "what is this you are saying? Somebody *else?* Oh, my dear! You've never said anything about somebody else to me."

"No, mother, I haven't. There hasn't been any chance since it happened. You were always going somewhere, or things were sort of strenuous, and I was waiting until I could tell you calmly."

Mrs. Bonniwell's face was white now and her eyes full of anguish. It might be bad enough to have her fall in love with somebody who wasn't just perfection, whom they had known from childhood; but this person that Blythe was talking about was as yet an unknown quantity, and the very thought of it made Mrs. Bonniwell weak. She sank down in another chair and looked wildly at her child, who suddenly seemed to have grown up away beyond her.

"Who is it, Blythe?" she asked in almost a whisper, unable to speak clearly with her shaken voice.

"Why, mother, you wouldn't know him. At least I may have spoken of him sometimes, but you wouldn't remember, I'm afraid."

"But my dear! You wouldn't certainly engage yourself to a stranger we didn't know without at least telling us of it."

"Wait, mother. Let me begin at the beginning and explain. Father asked me if I *loved* anybody and I have answered him truly, yes, I love somebody. Now, let me tell you all about it. Do you remember, mother, I used to tell you about one of the boys in our high school who was very bright, and always at the head of the class?"

"Why, yes, I do recall something like that, Blythe, but that was a long time ago and he was only a young boy. Surely you wouldn't mean that you have stuck to an ideal of your high school days, and fancy yourself in love with him! Why, child, you haven't had any opportunity to really get acquainted with him. It seems to me you never spoke of meeting him socially. Who is he? Who are his people? Are they all right? You know we couldn't ever consent to letting you marry into a questionable family."

"Let her tell, mother," interrupted the father. "Let her tell it in her own way."

"All right, Blythe, but tell quickly. I feel as if I could scarcely breathe."

"Don't feel that way, mother. I'll tell it as quickly as I can. Please calm down and don't take it for granted that it is bad. I think it is very beautiful."

"Oh, *Blythe!*" cried her mother, almost in tears. "To *think* it should have gone *so far,* and we didn't know anything about it!"

"Keep still, Alice. Reserve your judgment till you hear the whole story," said Mr. Bonniwell. "Go on, Blythe. What is his name?"

"His name is Charlie Montgomery," said Blythe calmly, lifting her head proudly. "They're not important people, not *now,* if that's what you mean. Charlie's father died about the time he entered high school. His mother is gone too, now. But he's a wonderful person, and if you could know him I'm sure you would say so."

"But Blythe, when did this all happen? How is it that we have not heard anything about it before?" asked her mother in a troubled voice. "It isn't like you to make a mystery of anything you are doing."

"Nothing has *happened,* mother," said Blythe cheerfully. "Charlie and I were in classes together four years. I knew that he was a boy with a lot of courage and principle, honest and fine, and a good student. He hadn't much time to get acquainted with anybody in high school, for he was working after school hours, and sometimes evenings. He took care of his mother, and I guess he had a rather wonderful mother from little things he has told me. But that doesn't matter now anyway except that she has been a great influence for good in his life, I am sure."

"But how do you *know* all this, Blythe, if you didn't have much to do with him in school?"

Blythe gave her mother a clear straight glance, and smiled.

"I'm not sure *how* I know it, mother," she said thoughtfully. I just *know* it. I think I have sort of grown into the knowledge of all that during our years of school together, not so much from anything he said about it, for he never said much to me about anything except our studies, until a few days ago."

"A *few days* ago!" exclaimed her father. "Do you mean that this is something *new,* Blythe? I don't understand it. Where has the young man been that we haven't seen him about at all."

"He's been away to college, as I was, of course," answered Blythe.

"Well, but—have you been corresponding?" This from her mother.

"No, mother. Never. But one day—just a few days ago—you were busy with your War Bond drive, you know and I couldn't interrupt you. But Charlie came one morning to see me, and told me that he was being sent on a special mission by the government into enemy territory, under circumstances which made it very unlikely that he would ever return alive."

She hesitated an instant and her voice trembled, her eyes cast down. Then she caught her breath and went on.

"He said he wasn't even sure whether I would remember who he was, but he had felt he wanted to let me know before he went away that he loved me. That he had been loving me all the years through high school, and afterward when we didn't even see each other; and he wanted me to have the knowledge of his love before he went away. He wanted to say good-by. His mother is gone now, and he hasn't any other near relatives. He thought, since he was not expecting ever to return, I wouldn't mind if he laid his love at my feet as a sort of tribute to what he felt I had meant to him all these years." Blythe paused an instant and her mother saw that her eyes were full of happy tears, and a smile, like a rainbow was over her face.

"Well, that is certainly the strangest love story I ever heard," said her father. "Is that all? Wasn't there more? And when are we to see him? Surely he is coming to see me, isn't he?"

"No, that's about all, father. He had only a very short time. He said that he had waited till the last minute so that he would not embarrass me. He was very humble. He considered it a tribute to what I had meant to him during the years. He said he would not presume to think I cared for him. He had no wealth, nor social prominence."

She paused again.

"Well, what happened then?" asked her father impatiently. "Is that all?"

"No, I suddenly knew that I loved him, that I too had been admiring him for a long time, and I told him so. And then—" Blythe lowered her voice gently as if she were speaking of what was very sacred to herself—"then he put his arms very gently around me and held me close, and kissed me most reverently. It seems rather awful to tell it all out this way to you in words, something that has come to be a very precious experience to me, but I thought you had a right to know. And since father has asked me I *want* you to know what he is. He is really *very wonderful,* mother dear!" and Blythe lifted a face glowing with a great deep joy.

"But—why isn't he here?" said her father. "Can't he come over this evening and let us talk with him? I certainly would like to have some idea what he is like. Go to the telephone and call him, Blythe!"

Blythe's eyes grew sorrowful.

"He has gone, daddy. By this time he is far away. And he couldn't tell me where he was going. I'm not sure that he knew where the army was sending him. It's a military secret. A very special one. And it was really a good-by, I am afraid. He seemed to be very sure of that. It was something he volunteered to do, *knowing* there was probably death in it." Suddenly Blythe's face went down into her lifted hands and the tears flowed.

"I think that was a terrible thing to do. It was *cruel!*" said Blythe's mother, "To come here and make you suffer this way! It was *cowardly*—it was—!"

Blythe's head came up with a flash, and more rainbow-shining in her eyes.

"No, no! Mother don't say that! You don't understand! It was the most lovely thing that ever came into my life! I would not be without the memory of it, not for everything that life can offer! Even if he never comes back—and he was very sure it would not be possible—it will be my joy all my life to know he loved me that way. I am glad, *glad,* that he came and told me of his love! But I'm sorry if you don't understand. I was afraid perhaps you wouldn't, and that's another reason why I didn't tell you right away, although there really wasn't any time when it seemed we wouldn't be interrupted."

"Yes, I see," said Mrs. Bonniwell thoughtfully. "But, my dear, you surely must realize that this thing is all very much out of order, quite unique, and even interesting perhaps, but surely you wouldn't think of taking it seriously? You certainly did not go so far as to engage yourself to this young man on the spur of the moment as it were!"

"No, of course not, mother," said Blythe with an anguished voice, "does one get engaged to a man who is on his way to his death?"

Her mother gave her a startled look.

"Oh! Of course, I didn't realize. But my dear that was most wise of you. I'm sure you can always be counted on to do the wise right thing. I have always felt that you could be trusted with anybody, and you would not go beyond convention, no matter who urged you to do so."

A flash of almost anger, and then despair went over Blythe's speaking face.

"But mother, there never was any question of an engagement. He wouldn't have thought of suggesting it. He felt that he was on his way to his death, and we were not

considering life on this earth. We were facing separation.
It was enough for us that we loved one another. We had
no right to consider—afterwards—!"

There was a distinct silence, and the father and mother
were evidently impressed. It was a unique situation, and
they marveled that their daughter whom they had until
this time considered barely out of little-girlhood, had so far
matured as to be able to utter such thoughts as she had
just voiced, with such sweet poise and assurance. There
was something almost ideal about her attitude they felt.
Was it possible that a girl could love as she had asserted
she loved, and yet talk so coolly about the likelihood of
her lover's death?

The mother shivered at the thought, and said in her
heart: "She can't possibly understand what it means. She
couldn't really care, and yet take it this way!"

And yet when she looked into her child's eyes, and saw
that exalted look, as if she had somehow had a vision
from Heaven, and was still under its spell, she knew that
her conclusion was wrong.

"But Blythe," began her mother with a troubled hesi-
tance, "you have left us so without anything to go on. Just
your word that you admired this young person when he
was a mere boy in school. We haven't even an idea how
he looks. If we only had something tangible by which we
could judge him."

A swift look of decision passed over the girl's face.

"I have, mother! Just wait a minute and I'll get it."

Blythe jumped up and hurried out of the room and
lightly up the stairs. Now was the time to show them
Charlie's letter!

While she was gone the mother looked hopelessly across
the room into her husband's eyes.

"Isn't it *terrible*, father? It seems to have taken such
hold on her. Do you think she'll ever get over it?"

"Of course," said the troubled man. "Such things don't
last and she's young, you know. They get over it.
Unless—"

"Unless what, dear?"

"Unless it's *real*," said her husband thoughtfully. "And
it certainly looks as if she thinks she has something
there."

But now they could hear Blythe coming down, breathlessly, a soft flush on her cheeks, a couple of small photographs and a folded letter in her hands.

"This is the way he looked in high school," she said excitely, handing out a photograph. Her father got up, came over to stand behind his wife's chair and look over her shoulder at the picture.

"Why, yes, he is very good-looking for a young boy," said her mother leniently studying the picture. "I'm not surprised that you admired him. He looks like a smart boy too. You say he was a scholar. The head of the class, you said?"

"Yes," said Blythe gently, with a kind of reserve in her voice as if she were a bit disappointed at her mother's reaction.

The father reached down and took the picture, studying it carefully for an instant.

"Well, I like his appearance," he said, as he handed the picture over to Blythe. "At least he doesn't have a weak chin."

"He must have been a handsome lad, dear. Of course I can see how you admired him. But young boys often lose their good looks as they grow older, and coarsen up. And you are apt to idealize people and stick to what they appeared to be at first. Of course you must take that into account."

There was gentleness and indulgence in Mrs. Bonniwell's voice.

For answer Blythe handed out the other picture, Charlie in his officer's uniform, handsome and manly and assured.

"This is the way he looks now, mother," said Blythe quietly.

"Oh!" said Mrs. Bonniwell. *"Indeed!* Well he certainly has fulfilled the promise of his youth. He is *very* good-looking. I don't wonder you fell for him, Blythe. But you know appearances are sometimes deceitful. You cannot always be sure just by the looks of a person. And a uniform certainly does a lot for anybody."

But Mr. Bonniwell reached for the second picture and studied it carefully, and then, holding it off he looked again.

"Well, daughter," he said. "I am bound to say you have chosen well, if one may judge from appearance. That young man looks as if he had character, and a lot of it. So far as I am concerned I think you are to be congratulated, child. At least he hasn't a weak chin, and that's a great relief to me. I never could endure having a son-in-law with a weak chin!"

"Son-in-law!" exclaimed Blythe's mother in horror. "But John, as I understand it they have no idea of that. They are merely admiring friends."

"No, mother," said Blythe decidedly. "we are lovers. It may never be anything else, because Charlie is going out to meet death, but please don't speak as if that would be such a dreadful thing if it could never be a closer relationship."

"But Blythe, dear, after all, while he makes a very good appearance, and as your father suggests he does look as if he had some character, still you must remember that you know him very little, and we, your parents, do not know him at all. I think you should not expect us to judge him and rejoice in your new pleasure, until we know him better. Remember we have never talked with him, we have never heard him talk, and we shall certainly have to reserve our judgment until such a time, if there ever be such a time, when we can meet him, and get really acquainted—find out if he be suited to our beloved child."

"Yes, I know mother. I knew that you would feel that way, and so I have brought down a couple of his letters that you may read his own words and know just what he felt. At first I thought they were too sacred to show to even you, but after I had thought it over I felt that it was only fair that you might know how he looks on this thing that has come to us. And I am sure he would be entirely willing that I should show you his letters. You have a right as my parents, to judge him from his own lips. Here, daddy, read this one first. This was his first letter after he went away. It came a few hours after he had gone."

Mrs. Bonniwell was still studying the picture, taking in little details that even Blythe had not had time yet to analyze.

"I like the way he holds his head," she commended

pleasantly, as if it were going to be her policy not to antagonize her daughter.

Blythe's anxious eyes watched her mother. She was going to be fair, that was plain, but she was not so overwhelmingly carried away with the young man as Blythe had hoped. Though it was a hope against hope, for Blythe had rightly judged that it would take a great deal to carry her mother away at first sight, with any unknown quantity.

But it was her father's attitude that was giving Blythe her great hope. For Mr. Bonniwell was carefully, earnestly reading the letter she had given him and did not try to hide the fact that he was greatly pleased with it.

At last he folded the letter carefully and handed it back to her.

"Well," he said heartily. "That's a fine letter. I can see no fault in that at all. I think it shows unusual character, and you certainly are to be congratulated on having such a friend, even if he were only a friend. As for the lover-part, I cannot conceive of more delicacy of feeling, discerning appreciation, and restrained tenderness. I think you would be most fortunate indeed to be loved by such a man, and I for one can give my hearty endorsement to *that* young man. I certainly hope he comes back. I wouldn't mind having him for a son-in-law."

"John!" reproved his wife in a startled voice. "But it seems so cruel in him to have forced himself upon her this way, and *compelled* her to recognize his love when he says he has no hope of returning. I cannot see anything fine and delicate in such actions."

"Read it, Alice, read it! You can't help seeing how really superior that letter is."

"But John, you can't mean that you think a man who was expecting confidently to die in a few days, had any right to dare to offer his love to a decent girl."

"Why not, Alice? It seems to me that that very fact shows a fineness of soul, and an unselfishness that is exceptional. It sets his love in a class all by itself. It puts love on a higher plane than merely fleshly pleasure, and worldly advantage. And I cannot see that even a jealous mother can object to a lover who puts his hopes on a plane that only looks for consummation in Heaven."

"John! How can you talk so? I can't see any reference to Heaven in this letter. In fact it doesn't seem to be in the least *religious*. And that's it. What do we know about him? What church did his people attend? You can't be sure that he even believes there is a God."

"Oh, but mother, there is another letter I want you to see. It just came this morning."

"Well, I haven't finished this one yet. Wait. But I will say this in favor of the young man, he certainly writes a handsome hand, very clear and readable. You seldom see such chirography."

But Blythe, light-footed, was already on her way upstairs for the letter that had been written that early morning after Charlie had given himself to Christ in Lincoln Silverthorn's meeting. In a moment she was down again and put the letter in her father's hand that was held out for it.

Then Blythe went and sat down in a shadowed corner where the window draperies half hid her face, and watched her father's expression. She had been loth to show this almost sacred letter to anyone, dreading sneers and misunderstanding, but the look on her father's face fully justified her having shown it. She felt sure in her heart Charlie would be glad to have that letter especially, shown to anyone.

Chapter 13

AS SHE WATCHED her father read the letter, her mind was going over it sentence by sentence as it seemed to be graven on her heart.

Dearly beloved:

I have arisen early that I may talk a little while with you alone, before the rest of the camp is astir. For I want to tell you of something extraordinary that befell me last evening. It seems to me that my eyes have been opened to the greatest thing in the world, or in the whole universe, and I want you to see it too, my dearest.

I have told you of a man I have heard of, a chaplain, going about from camp to camp, bringing cheer and salvation and hope to men who are going out presently to die. I had heard that his preaching was wonderful, and when I found myself dropped here for a brief stay on my way, and saw his name in shining letters over the hall where he was to speak, I was glad; for I knew that I needed something more before my life went out.

A boy from our home town, Walter Blake, hailed me, when I arrived, and went with me to the meeting. The name of the speaker was Silverthorn.

At first when we entered they were singing. All the men in the place singing with mighty power, and we presently began to sing. And the prayer that followed stirred my heart to its depths.

But when this Silverthorn began to speak, it was not as if a man was talking. It was as if a thing were being enacted there before us on the platform. For I presently saw Jesus Christ standing there alone being tried for my sins. Sins He had never committed.

I have never considered myself much of a sinner, but

as Christ stood there alone, with the shadow of a great cross beginning to appear in the dim offing, I began to realize that He was a sinless one, and as I looked at Him, I saw myself in contrast, as most sinful. I learned a great Truth right then and there, as I looked at the Jesus who was ready to die for me, and that was that one does not fully recognize sin in one's self until one has looked into the face of Jesus.

So, as I sat there and watched Him, looked into His eyes, He turned and looked into mine and I realized that He had been loving me all the blank years of my life. I had been trying to cultivate the brains He had given me, and get a great education, and He had been loving me, and had died in my place, and I hadn't been thinking at all about Him! Then I was made to see that *that* was sin, the greatest of all sin, unbelief and indifference.

It does not sound so great as it really was when it is merely written down, but I want you to know that before the evening was finished I went down on my knees with Silverthorn and gave myself to my Lord who died for me. Or, as they say it here, I accepted Christ as my personal Saviour.

Perhaps *you* did this long ago, but if you did not then I hope you will right away.

And now I am sure that whatever comes, I shall be safe in the hands of my Lord, and life or death I shall be sure of Heaven. I wanted you to know this.

You will perhaps be interested to know that the lad, Walter, belongs to the Lord also. We knelt together with the same prayer.

There used to be an old hymn my mother sang, something about Christians meeting around the mercy seat. It went something like this:

> There is a place where spirits blend,
> Where friend holds fellowship with friend,
> Though sundered far, by faith they meet,
> Around one common mercy seat.

And it has come to me that so you and I may hope to meet, at the feet of our Lord Jesus, and talk to Him about one another, and of our love for Him. Will you meet me in prayer at the mercy seat, my precious friend?

Now the camp is astir and I must close.

But I want you to know that I am very glad in the

knowledge of the Lord Jesus, and filled with a great peace.

May He be with you.

I love you.

                                                    Charlie.

As Mr. Bonniwell read this letter a mist stole out on his lashes, and tears rolled unnoticed down his cheeks. As he finished and handed the letter to his wife he commented:

"A beautiful letter! A most extraordinary setting forth of sacred things. My dear daughter, I congratulate you."

"It seems to me it must be a very gloomy letter," commented Mrs. Bonniwell as she took the letter, "you are both crying!"

"Oh, no, not gloomy!" said her husband. "It is full of peace."

Blythe and her father were very quiet while the mother read that letter, and she held it thoughtfully in her hand for a full minute after finishing before she spoke in a reserved husky voice:

"Very—commendable—I'm sure."

Then she handed the letter to Blythe and the three, without further talk, went quietly up to their rooms.

When the father and mother had silently prepared for sleep, and all sounds had ceased from behind Blythe's closed door, her parents, now lying in their beds, staring wide awake in the dark room, stirred uneasily. At last the mother began in a fearsome whisper:

"John, she'll soon forget him, don't you think so? She's so young! You think so, don't you?"

There was another silence for a moment and then the father replied:

"I trust not! No, certainly not! If I thought that Blythe was vapid enough to forget a man like that I should be in despair about her."

"But John! You certainly don't want your little girl to go mourning all her days for a dream-man! A person she doesn't really know, and never has. You can't possibly think she won't forget him after a little while!"

"Suppose an angel from Heaven should come down and talk with you for an hour? Would you forget that in a little while?" asked her husband.

"Oh—well, an angel—of course. I wouldn't *forget* it exactly. It would be a kind of a pleasant memory, but it wouldn't hinder my going right on living a normal life, John! Clubs and war work, and things like that."

"No, I suppose not," said the man thoughtfully. "Bridge clubs, and dinners and the latest fashions of course."

"Now, John, you're being sarcastic. I know you don't care for bridge, but is that any reason why I shouldn't play once in a while? I don't really spend much time at it. Especially now since there is so much war work to be done."

"Yes, I suppose so," said the disinterested voice of the man.

"John, you're not listening to me."

"Oh yes, I am."

"John, what are you thinking about? You act so absorbed, just as you do when you've brought business home with you. John, are you worried about Blythe and that strange boy who dared to upset her before he went away to war?"

"No," said John thoughtfully, "I'm less worried about Blythe than I have been for a long time. I'm delighted that she's interested in such a young man. A fellow with real thoughts in his head, and a sane way of expressing them. I tell you that young man has got hold of something we all need, in these times especially, a real hold on God, a knowledge of God. And he's got the kind of courage that won't fail at anything he has to do. I wish I felt as sure of Heaven as he does."

"Why, *John!* How ridiculous! *You* to talk that way! Why, you've been a Christian man for years. You've been a trustee of the Presbyterian Church. Of *course* you're sure of Heaven."

"No, Alice, I don't think being a trustee of any church makes you sure of Heaven. It takes more than that, and I never thought about it before. If you want to know what I'm thinking about, that's it. I was wondering, if I had to go to war, in some job from which I was pretty sure I wouldn't ever return, I was wondering if I had enough faith in God to take along with me and protect me in danger. Alice, I don't believe I have."

"Nonsense, John! You're all unstrung by this queer thing that has happened to Blythe. You always did take things that happened to Blythe so terribly to heart. You'll snap out of it and be your normal self in the morning. I believe you ought to have some vitamins. I'll get you some in the morning, and see that you take them too! And now for pity's sake let's get some sleep. I have an early committee meeting in the morning. Don't worry about Blythe. She'll be all right when she wakes up. She's just excited over this unusual happening, and I don't blame her a bit. I think it was a perfectly awful thing for that fellow to do, when he had never paid any attention to her before. Don't you really think so, John?"

"No!" said John shortly. "I think it was a beautiful thing to do, and I wish I might have had a little chance to know a fellow like that. I admire him greatly. I'd like him for a son-in-law, and I hope somehow his God keeps him alive and brings him back to our little girl."

"John! How perfectly terrible! I never heard you talk like this before. It seems to me you've taken leave of your senses."

"On the contrary I've been wondering if I've ever had any before. You see, Alice, we've been walking by the pattern of all our neighbors, and I think the time has come to stop and get a pattern of our own. I'd like to know God better. I think perhaps that's why war came, to teach us that it was God we needed. Come now Alice, don't you honestly feel that it is reassuring for Blythe to have a friend who is religiously inclined instead of wanting to go to night clubs all the time?"

"Well, I'm not so sure," sighed Mrs. Bonniwell. "It's easy to go too far religiously of course. I shouldn't like Blythe to get tied up with a fanatic, would you? And when people talk like that last letter she showed us, they are apt to go too far and become fanatics."

"Yes? And just what is a fanatic? Would you define it as being one who knows God too well?"

"John! Why, you actually sound irreverent, speaking of God in that light familiar way. I never heard you talk so before."

"Well, I'm not sure that I've ever been stirred so deeply before as I was by that letter. A young man who is consciously going out to die, with very little hope of returning, to surrender his whole self to the God who made him, and who is really his only hope of eternal life! And he not only has done that, but he has been able to put the thing he has done into clear logical words that have come back to his girl's father and convinced him that he too needs such a Saviour."

"But John, I don't like you to talk as if you didn't have all you need in a Christian way."

"Nevertheless it's true, Alice, and I'm not going to drop it at this. I'm going to make it my business to find out what that young man says he has found."

"Well, all right, John, only please do drop the subject now. I'm very weary. This has been a long hard day, and the evening was most exciting. I really must get some sleep if I am to run that committee meeting in the morning, and it's going to take some maneuvering to get everything through, and keep every woman satisfied, and not at sword's points with all the rest."

"Yes, go to sleep Alice. We'll talk of this another time. Good night."

There was silence in the room after that, but it was a long time before the master of the house slept.

And over across the hall Blythe was down upon her knees beside her bed, praying a real prayer, perhaps her first real prayer since her little childhood's believing days. For she too was seeking the Christ that her lover had found.

"Dear God," she prayed, "won't you show me the way to see your Son, Jesus Christ, the way my Charlie has found Him?"

But the sweet and loving mother slept the sleep of the just to get ready for her strenuous committee on the morrow, serene in the knowledge that she was a good Christian woman, and did not need to have keen sight into spiritual things. Resting in the firm belief that her precious daughter would soon recover from this imagined obsession that she was in love with an unknown stranger, who couldn't possibly be the type of boy that would be suited to a girl as cultured as her daughter.

And all the while out in the night world, Daniel Seavers

and Anne Houghton with whom he had happened to be thrown that evening, were seeing life together.

Anne hadn't been at all the companion Dan would have chosen to help him forget his annoyance at Mr. Bonniwell's reception of his gracious propositions. But he had to get through the evening somehow, since his plans were being held in abeyance for a brief space, and perhaps it would be as well to let his future father-in-law see that his daughter wasn't the only pebble on the beach, the only girl in the city. Just give him a day to himself and he would come around. If he didn't, then he would wait no longer. He would collect Blythe and they would carry out the threat of an elopement. Of course that would be one way to get the high hand with a father-in-law. Let him see that he meant what he said and would take no orders from anybody from henceforth. He had obeyed the conventions and asked permission to address Blythe, but if it didn't bring prompt action, then Dan would just forget the conventions and do as he pleased. He was very sure he could bring Blythe to his way of thinking, if he went about it in the right way, for he had had plenty of years in which to study Blythe and know the best ways to get around her, to bend her to his will. Of course he wasn't taking into account the years in which they had been separated by college life, and the expulsive power of a new affection that had come into this girl's life. He was a young bully who had always been accustomed to having his own way, and he intended to have it now without delay.

So, he took the first girl that came along and it happened to be Anne Houghton. He didn't particularly admire her, but he knew her to be a good sport on occasion, and she was handy to his need, so he asked her to have dinner with him, and take in some night clubs afterward. Daring and reckless, Anne was, and she fitted in with his disgruntled mood, so they went from one gay spot to another, till they had reached a place where their jaded sensibilities were ready for anything.

Driving home in the small hours their way led over Wolverton Drive, and Anne indulged in a few sharp pleasantries about Dan's erstwhile playmate, Blythe Bonniwell.

The Bonniwell house sitting quietly back among its

beautiful trees, sheltering its sleeping family with strong comforting walls of stone, looked impregnable under the shadowed waning moon and it somehow angered both the young people.

"Poor Blythe," babbled the spiteful Anne, with a tongue let loose by the many drinks she had taken, "she thinks she owns the earth with a gold fence around it, doesn't she? I'm glad you took a night off from letting her wind you around her pretty little finger, and are showing her that you can have a good time with some other girl now and then. It will do her good. She really is getting insufferable."

"Oh, I don't know," drawled Dan lazily. "I never have any trouble bringing her to terms if I want to bad enough. The trouble is she's too much under the dominance of a puritanical father and has prudish ideas of what she wants to do. But of course, if I chose, I could take that out of her. If I thought it were worth the trouble. But it's been good sport to go out with a girl who knows her way about in the world. I don't know when I've had such a good time. We'll have to try it again sometime. How about it, Anne?"

"That will be all right with me," said Anne with a triumphant ring to her voice. "I like to step out with you, and anytime you want to show that demure little mouse where to get off, you can count on me to help you out. But frankly, I should think you'd be terribly bored with her. I tried to talk with her in the Red Cross class the other day, but we really haven't two ideas in common. I finally gave it up. And she has such common tastes. She's always taking up with some poor little scrap of humanity who doesn't really belong in our crowd. I think it's a pose, showing how kind and benevolent she can be, you know. But of course she's very young."

"Yes, quite," said the young man drowsily. "I think she'll grow out of it. I've known Blythe since we were children, you know. I guess she'd be all right if she could get away from her family. They dominate her entirely too much."

They were driving past the Bonniwell place now, and Anne cast baleful glances at the peaceful house in the moonlight. She would show that Bonniwell girl just how much hold she had on Dan Seavers! Just give her two or three more nights like this one, and she would soon have him where she wanted him, and then Blythe might smile her prettiest, but she would have lost her Dan.

They drew up in front of the Houghton residence, and Dan took care to find the deepest shade, not directly in front of the house, where thick shrubbery hid the car completely.

"Now," he said, "we've had a good evening. Suppose we rest a bit just to say good night." He reached his arm and drew her close within his clasp. He put her head down on his shoulder, and looking into her face he slowly stooped and brought his lips to hers, in a hard passionate kiss, to which Anne responded fervently, her warm soft lips lingering tenderly on his own.

"That was good," said Dan settling down beside her and drawing her closer. "This is cosy, isn't it? Why didn't we ever do this before? Boy, I believe I'm tired. It feels good to rest, and you're a pleasant little body to have around." Then he laid his lips on hers again.

Yes, Anne was pretty and responsive, but she hadn't any money, though she did have "family." But she lived with a stingy married brother who had a number of children to get his money.

And down the Drive a few blocks away, in a quiet house where dawn was beginning to bring out its protective lines, slept the girl whom Dan had decided to marry because forsooth she had plenty of money. The girl of whom he had said he was "fond." The girl who had a wonderful lover gone to war, and who had just been dedicating her life to finding his Christ.

On his way home at last, with the streaks of dawn more distinct in the sky now, Dan's thoughts reverted to Blythe. Blythe had always been shy of any suggestion of love making. She held herself aloof. But what would Blythe be like if she were married to him, and felt it the conventional thing to let herself go? Or would she ever be demonstrative? Boy! Anne Houghton certainly had it over Blythe when it came to showing a man how she felt about him. The touch of her lips was still upon his, and he certainly had had one night to remember. But tomorrow morning he must go to Mr. Bonniwell and deliver an ultimatum. Now or never. Permission for his whole plan, wedding and all with a hint of a big settlement; or, an elopement! Let him have his choice.

Chapter 14

DAN PRESENTED HIMSELF at Mr. Bonniwell's office very soon after the work of the day had begun, and Mr. Bonniwell was deep into the morning mail.

When the young man went blustering into the outer office he told the assistant who met him that he wanted to see Mr. Bonniwell at once. It was very important, and he hadn't any time to spare.

Word came back over the telephone to the clerk at the desk that Mr. Bonniwell was very much engaged at present, but though he had not yet sent for Mr. Seavers, it would be all right. He would see him as soon as he could finish his present interview, if he cared to wait. Or if not Dan might return that afternoon any time after two o'clock.

Dan frowned.

"I'll *wait!*" he said shortly. "But tell him to make it snappy!" he added.

The young man at the desk did not, however, transfer this latter sentence over the telephone, and Dan sat down and glowered at the young official. Well, perhaps it was as well to bide his time and get these preliminaries over, but when he was finally married he certainly would pay his father-in-law back in full for all he had cost him.

It was almost an hour before a man and a secretary emerged from the inner office and Dan was told that Mr. Bonniwell would see him now. During this time Dan had sighed and writhed, and wriggled, and drummed on the table with his fingers, and in every way manifested his impatience. So he was on his feet at once and pranced into the audience chamber with an arrogant manner.

"Well, you certainly took your time," he announced impudently to the man he expected to make his father-in-law.

"Yes?" said Mr. Bonniwell, with an amused lifting of his eyebrows. "And now you are taking mine. Well, sit down."

Dan dropped into the most comfortable chair in view and frowned again.

"Well?" he said sharply. "Let's get this over with. I've waited too long already."

"Yes," said the business man with a twinkle, "perhaps you have. So, what I have to say is that you have my permission to talk this matter of marriage over with my daughter. Is that what you want?"

"Why, yes, of course," snapped Dan, utterly flabbergasted. He had been much wrought up by the night's delay he had endured, and had fully expected some kind of a long argument before he got any satisfaction out of the man. He was actually embarrassed to get what he had asked without question.

"Oh—why, yes," he began awkwardly. "Well, now, that's very kind of you, and I appreciate it of course, though I do wish you could have said yes at the beginning without all this forethought. However, what's done's done, and I'll get to work and carry out my plans as fast as possible. I hope you told your wife what is going to happen so she'll be ready to co-operate with us without holding up the affair any longer. But then women, I will say, are usually all in favor of anything like a wedding."

"But aren't you forgetting a little matter?" asked the father, watching the young man still amusedly.

"Forgetting?" said Dan. "Why, no, I'm not forgetting anything. What was it you refer to?"

"Why, I only gave you permission to talk this matter of a marriage over with my daughter, and you are assuming that the arrangements are as good as settled."

"Oh," said Dan with a sudden sharp look at the elder man. "Have you then laid your commands upon your daughter? Is that your way of answering me?"

"No," said the father. "I haven't even talked it over with her. Blythe is fully able to settle her own affairs, I feel. I think she will tell you what she wants. You merely have my permission to address her. There is however one question I would like to ask you before you leave."

"Yes?" said the young man, alert at once.

"I would like to know, just as a matter of personal interest, what you think of God? How well do you know Him?"

"God!" exclaimed Dan, a kind of shiver of horror going over him. "What in heck has God got to do with it?"

"Well, when you have lived as long as I have lived, young man, you will find that God has to do with almost everything more or less. You can't get away from that. I was just interested to know what you thought of Him."

"Well, if you want to know, I never thought anything about Him. It wasn't in my line, and what's more I never saw any indication that it was in yours either."

"That is quite possible," said Mr. Bonniwell. "I'll have to own that it hasn't been. But I've come to see that it should make a difference in a man's life and in his relations with his family and friends. That is all, young man. I'll have to go back to my work now, but I certainly hope that you may learn a great deal about the best things of life before you are done. Good morning!" and Mr. Bonniwell buzzed for his secretary. She appeared promptly, and held the door open for the exit of the somewhat bewildered caller.

As Dan went his way he was saying to himself: "Now what in heck did he mean by all that gaff? I wonder, has he got something up his sleeve? I just can't figure that he would give up as easily as this after all that bologny about taking time to think, unless he talked it over with Blythe and told her where to get off. But maybe after all he is really pleased at the arrangement, or perhaps his wife has taken a hand at the argument. I can't help feeling she rather likes me. At least she's a good friend of my mother's of course."

So Dan went on his way and tried at once to call up Blythe to make a date for a good talk to get things settled.

But Blythe was off to her day nursery, and he had to wait again. However, he was fairly comfortable in his mind about her, for he felt sure he could handle Blythe, and get her to see eye to eye with him about their marriage.

And in the meantime he called up a few friends whom he would like to have figure in the wedding party, not telling too much about his plans, but enough to give them an idea of what to expect. And while he was about it, perhaps it would also be a good idea to find out if the church the Bonniwells attended, and the pastor who officiated there, were available on the day he had fixed his mind upon as the suitable time for this hasty marriage. And so the hours marched on with a fair amount of interest and excitement for the would-be bridegroom, and Anne Houghton never once entered his thoughts, except as a pleasant background for a dull evening that hadn't turned out so badly after all.

But when the day drew toward evening, and, having failed to find Blythe anywhere in his goings, and having called up twice at her home to locate her and found her still away, he called up again at dinner time.

"Hi, Beautiful!" he said when he heard her voice answering. "I've been hunting you all day and couldn't get a trace. What's been doing that has kept you so busy?"

"Oh, Dan! Good evening! Sorry I have been so elusive, but you see I went to one of the centers for soldiers and got so interested I stayed all the afternoon."

"For sweet pity's sake! What could you possibly find interesting in a lot of half-baked boys in uniform? I should think you'd be good and sick of that war stuff by this time. Why don't you cut it out and give a little attention to your friends? What's the idea? Do you think you can fight the whole war alone? I don't like women doing war work. I think you ought to let the men fight the war, and the women ought to stay home and be feminine."

"Oh!" said Blythe with a catch in her breath, "is that the way you feel about it? But—Dan, you're a man. What are you doing about the war?"

"Me? Oh, I'm right in it with both feet. Haven't you heard? I've got my commission now," said Dan with a satisfied smirk that almost could be heard over the wire. "You haven't been in evidence yet to be told about it, but it's come, and I've some interesting things to tell you about what is going to happen. I'll be over this evening to tell you all about it."

"Oh, I'm sorry Dan, but I guess your news will have to wait. I have an engagement this evening."

There was a displeased silence on the wire, and then a question snapped out:

"Beginning when?"

"Beginning now," said Blythe firmly. "I am leaving in half an hour."

"Break it!" ordered the young man with a voice equally firm.

"Oh, but I couldn't possibly," said Blythe. "It's something I couldn't miss. It means a great deal to me."

"Oh, is that so? And I and my wishes don't mean anything. Is that the way you feel?"

"Why no, Dan, if there was something I could do for you at a time when I am free I'd be glad to do it. But this is something that I cannot cancel."

Another instant's silence and then the spoiled arrogant voice of Dan came sternly over the telephone.

"Well, I'm coming over there right away, and I think you'll change your mind after you hear what I have to say! Good-by!" and the telephone was slammed up.

Blythe hung up quietly and turned away with a sinking of her heart. Oh dear! Was she going to have trouble getting rid of Dan? If she only could get away before he arrived. Would it be possible? She glanced at the clock. No, there was no time. She knew too well how quickly Dan could get to their house when he was anxious to get there in a hurry. He had so often done it in his childhood. He knew every inch of the way, every stick and stone and pebble to cross, every flowerbed to circle. No, she could never get away before he arrived, and she must not stay, for she would miss the meeting that she was so anxious to attend, a meeting which the wonderful Silverthorn that Charlie had written about was to address. She was taking Mrs. Blake. She was meeting her at a certain spot in the city station, and it was but a short ride to the camp where he was to be. She would not disappoint Mrs. Blake for all the Dan Seavers in the world.

Rapidly she finished the hasty toilet, hat, coat, gloves. She was ready and on her way downstairs when Dan walked in from the back door and met her at the foot of the stairs.

"Yes, I thought I'd find you running away from me," he declared offendedly, "but you're not getting away this time, lady. I got here just in time. Come into the reception room and sit down. I've something important to tell you, and something important to give you also."

"But I can't, Dan. It's impossible! I'm meeting somebody at the station and taking her to camp."

"Listen, Beautiful! I'm sure what I have to tell you will stop all that. You see, it's very important. You and I are going to be married one week from today, and going on our honeymoon right away. And does that make you open your eyes and take notice?"

For answer Blythe suddenly broke into peals of merry laughter.

"Oh, Dan!" she said, and dropped down into a chair and put her laughing face down in her hands. "You certainly are a scream. Am I to understand that this is the most modern form of a proposal, or is it just a joke?"

Dan stood gazing sternly down at her, displeased, indignant, puzzled.

"Well, I like that!" he said, a furious note in his voice. "Here I'm offering you the greatest honor a man can give a woman, and you ask if it's a joke! Really, Blythe, this is serious business, and I haven't a whole lot of time to waste. I've got my list of ushers made out. I've enquired tentatively if your church will be free at the hour I've selected for the ceremony, and did a little feeling out to see if your pastor will be at liberty. I've got as many things in train as I could before I got your word that the time suited you, and now I've come for that. If you're so busy as you claim all you've got to do is say the arrangements suit you and I'll go ahead, so that you won't have a whole lot to do, and can concentrate on your trousseau. Any little details you care to add to my arrangements we can talk over, but in the meantime, I want your formal consent of course. And I might add, in case you are still a stickler for conventions, I have your father's permission to address you formally. Now, will you stop that silly giggling and sit up and take notice? I don't see what's funny about this, anyway. Come, I want *action,* I tell you."

Blythe suddenly straightened up, wiped the laughter tears from her eyes, and drawing a deep breath, looked straight at her angry would-be lover.

"Excuse me, Dan," she said, her voice growing steadier as she spoke, "I'm sorry I misunderstood you. I didn't, of course, realize that you had any such serious intention in mind. I didn't know what you meant. But no, Dan, I couldn't marry you, either now or next week or *any*time. I don't think we have enough in common for marriage. I don't love you and I don't think you love me. We've been good friends for a long time, but that was all, and I have never thought of marriage with you, nor wanted it. I wouldn't want to be unpleasant about it of course, but I certainly can't marry you, and we might as well settle it now as later. Perhaps I should thank you for the honor you have done me, and of course I hope you'll understand that it is nothing against you that I do not want to marry you. You have been a long-time friend, and I certainly wish you well, and I hope in good time that you will find somebody a great deal better for you than I could possibly be, but definitely it never could be myself."

Dan regarded her with disgust.

"Yes, I thought so. Your father said he hadn't talked it over with you, but I can see quite plainly that he laid his commands upon you all right, and it is up to me to overcome those commands, so we better get at it at once, for I haven't much time to spare, and I want the invitations to get into the hands of the engraver at once. I've already arranged that he will attend to them very swiftly, but he wants the wording at once, so we'll have to work fast. Come, we're going to take dinner in a quiet place where we will have opportunity to talk and a place to write our lists. My car is outside. Are you ready? Is this the handbag you are taking? Come, don't keep me waiting."

Blythe took the handbag from him and tucked it under her arm, looking up at him with her pleasant lips firmly set.

"You are mistaken, Dan. My father has laid no commands upon me on this subject or any other. And I am sorry to disappoint you, but I cannot possibly take dinner with you tonight. But even if I did not have another engagement, I would not want to go anywhere with you to discuss this matter, either now or at any other time. Definitely, Dan. I will not marry you, and you will have to reconsider, and cancel your plans without further discussion. It is utterly out of the question. Now, I must go at once. I have a definite appointment with someone, and a train to catch, so good-by, and I'm sure you'll soon get over this notion and find the right person to marry. Goodby!" Blythe smiled and turned and suddenly flashed out of the room and the house and hurried down the walk to the taxi that was waiting at the side door for her. She vanished out of his sight while Dan stood astonished and indignant, unable to believe his senses.

Chapter 15

DAN SEAVERS seldom wasted much time even in being angry. He could almost always think up something else to do that would be more interesting, and yet be in a fair way to help carry his point, and it wasn't long before he reflected he could still make progress in some other line to further his determined plans. So, he cast about him for some other line to follow, and presently thought of Blythe's mother. She was a good friend of his. A pretty good sport at times. He would go and talk to her. She would lay down the law to Blythe and then he would have smooth sailing.

So he went back to the Bonniwell house, and discovered that Mrs. Bonniwell had just come in from a full day among her committees and was very tired, but she welcomed Dan pleasantly, though her manner was a bit abstracted. She had always liked the handsome Dan. Moreover, there was still hovering in the back of her mind, a wistfulness about her daughter's old playmate. He had seemed so altogether desirable to Blythe's mother.

"Mother Bonniwell," he said with a smoothly flattering tone, "I think I need your help and counsel."

Now Mrs. Bonniwell always liked to give counsel to anyone, particularly to a pleasing young man, and she beamed on him and settled down to hear what he had to say.

"You see," he said. "Blythe and I want to be married next week, and I've come to you to help me get things straight. I've got this thing beautifully planned out, thought of simply everything, I'm sure, and even got reservations in some things, and priorities. And now, Blythe is trying to hold things up. And I thought you would know how to go about this thing with more finesse than I evidently have, smooth down Blythe's ruffled feathers, and set her ideas straight. Will you understand and help us out?"

Mrs. Bonniwell gave the young man a startled look, lifted her well-groomed eyebrows, and said:

"*Married!* You say you are planning to be *married?* Since when did this happen? Blythe has said nothing to me about it, and she always tells me everything. How long has this been going on?"

"Why, surely, you've understood we've had that in mind for several years past. Everybody else has, I know. I find it has been sort of taken for granted for a long time. And now that I have my commission and am very likely to be sent to a location very soon I thought it would be best for us to get married at once, and be ready to go together. So I've set the day, and I want your help in bringing Blythe to see that it is the wisest and best thing for us to do."

"But I don't understand, Dan. What does Blythe say about it?"

"Well, she doesn't say much, only that she doesn't want to get married now. She's too busy with war work and the like, and she thinks it's too soon to get her trousseau ready and all that, but good night, the stores will still be here after we are married and she can pick out her togs at her leisure. I thought you could make her see that. And lots of girls are hurrying their marriages now before their men go overseas. It's quite the swagger thing to do. And I thought if you would just advise her about this, Mother Bonniwell, and get her to see the thing straight it would be a great convenience to me. You see I don't want to be rushed at the last minute, and if Blythe would only co-operate everything would go smoothly. You'll help me, won't you?"

"But Dan, this is utterly new to me. I didn't dream you had any such move in mind. In fact—well—I would have to talk with Blythe before I made any promises."

"Now look here, Bonny! You might as well own up at the start. You and Papa Bonny have been hashing this thing over and agreed on what you'll say, haven't you?

That's the same kind of hooey stuff he gave me last night. Now own up."

Mrs. Bonniwell raised an offended chin and looked the young man in the eye.

"Certainly not, Dan! I don't know what you mean. I don't consider that is a very respectable way to speak to me."

"There, there, Bonny, now don't get your ire up! I just thought it was funny you and your man had the identical same reply ready."

"There is nothing strange about wanting to think over as serious a thing as marriage," said Mrs. Bonniwell, "and I couldn't possibly agree to further your plans without being sure that my family were agreed. However, why don't you tell me your plan in detail and then I can think advisedly."

So Dan adroitly painted the picture of his proposed marriage, wedding ceremony, invitations, trousseau and honeymoon, as fully as he had done it for Mr. Bonniwell, except that he went still further into details. Gradually, as he named prominent people who were to have part, the good lady was half intrigued, and sat nodding acquiescence, as she in her mind's eye saw the wedding procession marching up the aisle of the most aristocratic church in the community, and visioned the number of full dress uniforms that would be a part of the picture.

"It sounds all very lovely, Dan, and you seem to have planned a beautiful order of things, though I'm afraid perhaps it sounds a trifle too elaborate for war times. However, Dan, I would have to talk with Blythe and find out just what her objections are, before I could promise anything. Just what objections has she given you?"

"Well, you see, she won't really settle down and talk it over. She says she has engagements, and I haven't been able to get her to discuss it with me. She hasn't comprehended that haste is a necessary factor in the whole arrangement and there's where I thought you would be able to help me. You know Blythe, and you know how to make her listen. So, will you talk it over with her, and call me up either early this evening or tomorrow morning at the latest? It really ought to be tonight to make things work smoothly. Will you do that, Bonny?"

"Well, I'll see what I can do, Dan, but I'm not at all sure that I can make Blythe see things as you do. However, I will endeavor to get her to give you an immediate opportunity to talk with her, and you will have to do the rest. Blythe won't be home till late this evening. And if she's not too tired perhaps I can say a few words to her then, and phone you at once. Will you be home all the evening? Or at the latest the first thing in the morning? I'll let you know what to expect. But remember Dan, I'm not promising anything. It's all got to depend on Blythe."

Dan arose with a bitter dissatisfied look on his face, almost a sneer.

"Same old bunk!" he muttered. "You needn't tell me that you and the old man haven't talked it over. But I can tell you, Mamma Bonniwell, if you go against me, Blythe and I are going to elope and make a pretty scandal in the town for you and Papa Bonniwell to swallow, so keep that in the back of your mind while you think it over!"

"Well, really, Dan! I'm not accustomed to such talk. If you feel that way I certainly don't think you are a fit man to marry my daughter."

"Oh, now, Bonny, don't get excited. You know I'm all right. I just want to get things going in a hurry. These are war times, you know, and you can't afford to loiter, it's so hard to get anybody to do anything these days."

"Very well, Daniel, I'll see what can be done, and let you know, but I'm not promising anything. I feel that Blythe's life is her own and she must plan it the way she wants it, but I'll endeavor to put before her what you are suggesting, and then I will let you know, or ask her to let you know when you can see her. And now, Dan, I'm afraid I'll have to ask you to excuse me. I have to meet a delegation of women at quarter to eight and I simply must snatch a few minutes of rest before they come, for I am all but worn out."

So Dan, inwardly cursing his ill luck, yet priding himself that he had got Mamma Bonny pretty well on his side, took his way home, to await the message.

Mrs. Bonniwell went to her room and composed herself to rest, hoping still to snatch a few minutes of actual sleep, but her mind was in a turmoil, and though she closed her eyes and lay very still she could not keep her mind off the problems that were thickening around her.

To begin with, there was Blythe and that alarming and absurd obsession she had that she was in love with an absolute stranger.

Of course it was quite possible that this proposition of Dan's might be a very good thing to come just now, and help Blythe to forget the abrupt and fanatically inclined unknown. On the other hand, might it not be too soon to hope to have that romantic happening offset by a sensible marriage into her own set? It would be comfortable, too, to think of Blythe with a husband who was wealthy in his own right, and not dependent upon her fortune. Also, Mrs. Seavers was her friend, and she certainly would like to use her influence to help on what Dan's mother wanted, the assurance that Dan could be saved from questionable girls, girls who were beautiful perhaps, but absolutely nothing else, just gold-diggers, wasn't that what they called such girls, always out to lure some rich young man?

On the other hand Blythe was happy and bright just now, and they certainly were enjoying her presence in the home after her long absence at college. And it would be truly beautiful to have her with them now, with that almost unnatural glow of joy in her eyes, a real lovelight, and it was utterly useless to hope that it could change into such a glow for Dan. He wasn't the kind that could bring romance in such an enchanted form to a girl. He was solid and gay and good, maybe even dependable, but not one who could easily turn Blythe's fancied romance into love for himself. It really would be wiser in him to delay this marriage business a while until Blythe had forgotten the boy Charlie, or perhaps till word had come that Charlie was "missing in action," or something, as it likely would pretty soon, unless he had gotten up a cock-and-bull story to storm his girl's heart. Though somehow the letters hadn't seemed to make him that kind of a lad either. Rather too solemn perhaps. Strange that her girl would be interested in a staid young man like that. Stranger still that she had never said much about him before, even when she was a child in school. Well, she must talk with Blythe as soon as she returned, and she must prepare her approach and not antagonize her. She simply must find out just how her daughter felt about this marriage. It wouldn't do for her girl to miss the chance of a happy marriage with a finely set-up young man like Dan, just because of some silly romance between herself and a young man who was confessedly going out to die.

So Mrs. Bonniwell thrashed the matter over carefully, and did not get her much-needed nap. She studied over what she would say to Blythe as carefully as if it were one of her popular addresses to women's clubs, or a speech to mould the pliable opinions of her committee. And when the duties yet before her called her from her couch she went with half her mind occupied still with what she was going to say to Blythe that evening when they got together. All through the rest of the hours as she went from one appointment to another, the arguments were growing stronger by which she intended to lead Blythe on to see that she had no right to fill her mind with a stranger when her life-long playmate was needing her. And then, when the late evening hour came and Blythe arrived, her face shining with a wonderful light, and real joy in her eyes, the mother began hastily to consider whether she had any argument in her whole list that could combat a joy like this. At least while it lasted it was going to be hard to turn her girl aside from the ideas that seemed to possess her.

"Oh, mother," she said as she came in, "it was really wonderful! It was just as Charlie said in his letter. That Mr. Silverthorn spoke right to the men's souls. They sat and listened as if they were spellbound, and I listened too, and found more wonderful help than I have ever heard in any sermon I listened to in church."

"Well, now, dear, that is going pretty far. I am glad you enjoyed your evening instead of being bored as I was afraid you would be, but when you go to discounting the orthodox churches I really can't agree with you."

"Oh, mother, I wasn't discounting churches, not the real kind, but this talk tonight was something that seemed to help me so much. It made God and Christ so real, that you felt as if you never could doubt Him again. And you got that feeling, just as Charlie said, that Jesus Christ was right up there on the platform beside him. You saw Him being tried, you saw His eyes, so full of love and pity and suffering for a world that was sinning against Him, and *enjoying* the sinning, while He was getting ready to die for that sin as if it had been his own."

"He must be a very magnetic speaker," said Mrs. Bonniwell, trying to explain to herself the effect of the speaker on her daughter, forgetting for the moment the subject that had filled her mind the last half of the day. "There are not many speakers who have that dramatic power to make their audience see those about whom they are speaking. It is a wonderful gift, and would be just the way to influence young men who were hungry for something different."

"Oh, mother, it wasn't just that," said Blythe, struggling eagerly for words to convey the wonderful message that had reached her own heart that night. "It was like a real message sent from Heaven, just as Charlie said. He made you see yourself, and how sinful you were to have ignored a love like His."

All unseen Mr. Bonniwell had come softly into the front door and now was standing in the hall, listening as his daughter went on, but Mrs. Bonniwell had reverted to her promise of the afternoon for which she had been preparing for several hours, and smoothly she assented to what her daughter was saying, and then skillfully slid into a different note.

"Well, that sounds very beautiful, dear," she said graciously. "Perhaps sometime we can all go somewhere and hear this wonderful man. Such orators are always worth studying, no matter what subjects they specialize in. I'd really like to hear him myself. But in the meantime, dear, I have been staying awake to tell you something that is quite as important, and must have an immediate decision."

"Oh! Yes?" said Blythe with a quick flash of anxiety. What was coming now? Her mother's voice was definitely antagonistic, somehow not in sympathy with the wonderful things she had been telling about the meeting she had been attending. She dropped into a chair, yet alertly, and fixed her eyes on her mother's.

"Dan Seavers has been over here—" began her mother, floundering around in her mind for the careful approach she had planned to this interview. But Blythe put a sudden quietus on the subject by the finality of the tone in which she answered:

"Oh! He *has!* I thought he wouldn't be suppressed very easily. So he has appealed to you also, has he, as well as to dad? Well, mother, you can just tell him nothing doing. I do not intend to marry him—*ever*—and I told him so decidedly. I will not be inveigled into talking it over any more. If worst comes to worst you can tell him I love someone else. Although I don't really think it is any of his business until I get ready to tell it myself."

"No! Of course not," the mother hastened to say. The thing she really wanted least was to have anybody else know anything about this absurd obsession of her daughter's. Let it rest in quietness until it died away of its own accord. Have no publicity about it, not even to save Dan's feelings. That was much the best policy.

"But really, Blythe. I think you owe it to Dan as an old friend, to listen to what he has to say, the plans he has made. You gain nothing by running away from anything. It is always better to face a matter clearly, politely and in a way that you won't regret later when you think it over."

Blythe looked at her mother thoughtfully an instant, and then she said:

"All right, mother dear. When and where do you want me to see him? Was there any special time stipulated?"

"Why no, dear, only that he wants to see you at the first possible moment because he has several plans he is trying to arrange that depend upon your answer, and I think just in courtesy you owe him that."

"Very well, mother, I'll go to the telephone and arrange to see him at once. It's best to get this thing over. Best for us both!" and she turned to go out the door.

"Wait a minute, daughter," said Mrs. Bonniwell.

Blythe paused and looked at her mother inquiringly.

"I want to suggest that you be very sure of yourself before you go into this interview. You should consider just what you would be giving up if you turn this offer down. And you can't tell just what reaction you may bring about in Dan. He is very impulsive you know."

"Yes, mother, I'll remember. But I can't marry a man just to keep him from marrying a chorus girl or jumping in the river. You wouldn't have me do that, would you mother?" There was a merry twinkle in Blythe's eyes as she said it, the kind of twinkle that always brought an answering smile from her mother, no matter how much she had frustrated her motherly plans, and Mrs. Bonniwell gave the smile, and said, "Why no, of course not, dear," and Blythe turned with a laughing "thank you," and went to the telephone.

It was not until she was gone that the mother discovered her husband standing in the shadow out in the hall by the door, and she smiled at him.

"What a child she is!" said the mother, half worried, half pleased. "She doesn't grow up very fast, does she?"

"Well, I'm not sure but she's more grown-up than her parents," said Mr. Bonniwell, coming in and sitting down. "Personally I think she has more sense than either of us in more ways than one. I certainly am glad she is turning that Seavers kid down. I never liked him. He isn't even intellectually on a par with our girl."

"Now John, don't be too sure of what she is going to do. Dan had some very pleasant plans for their wedding and you can't tell what he may persuade her to do when she once gives him a chance to talk it over."

"I'll bank on our girl every time," said her father. "If she lets that ninny wheedle her into marrying him in a hurry to repent at her leisure, I shall be dreadfully disappointed in her. Especially since she has somebody real in her heart."

"Oh, *John?* I think you are foolish to put so much faith in a couple of snapshots and a letter or two. You might not like this old schoolmate of hers any better than you like Dan."

"Well, we'll just let it rest at that and see what Blythe does," said her father.

And then Blythe came back smiling, as if from an unpleasant duty well done.

"When is he coming?" asked her mother.

"Right away," said Blythe.

"Well, don't worry about how long he stays. I'll have your dinner saved for you if he is very long."

"He won't be," said Blythe cheerfully, "I told him I

could spare him only ten minutes and he had to make it snappy."

"Blythe!" reproached her mother, "don't you think that was a bit rude?"

"No, mother. It's the language all young people are using today, and I've already told him once before today that I didn't want to talk about this subject any more."

"Oh, my dear! But look here. Don't you think you should get into a fresher dress? You look a bit dreary and shopworn in that dark one. At least you can do Dan the courtesy of looking fresh and neat."

"No, mother, I'm not holding this matter up to make myself charming. I want to get it over with. There he is now," as the bell sounded through the house, and Blythe jumped up and ran down to the door herself instead of waiting for the servant to admit her caller.

The father, sitting in a shadowed corner of the room, smiled to himself at the summary way in which his daughter was handling this matter.

"She's a great girl!" he said aloud, with satisfaction in his face.

The mother cast a troubled glance at him.

"Yes, but I'm afraid she is acting in haste and will do something that she will regret all her life," she said, with a deep sigh.

"She won't!" said her father with confidence. "You'll see."

They sat in silence, listening as they heard low voices murmuring in the room below. Then suddenly they heard the man's voice rise. They heard his footsteps tramping back and forth in the library, and the mother cast an anxious glance toward her husband, but he sat quietly amused and waiting.

Low voices again, quiet, gentle murmur. That would be Blythe. Then a deep angry growl, more tramping, more growl, then loud angry words, and suddenly the tramping of an angry young man's feet as he went out of the house and slammed the door furiously behind him.

"There! John! I was afraid she would offend him, and she must have done it. I just knew she ought not to have gone at this thing in such a hurry."

"Alice, look here, don't you know enough about that

young man yet after all these years, to understand that he
would be offended of course at anybody who refused to
fall in with his plans? He wants to be *it,* and he won't
stand for anybody who hinders him."

"Oh, well, perhaps," sighed the mother, "but I'm not at
all sure but she is making a grave mistake."

"Well, I don't feel that she is," said her father. "And if
what she told you last night means anything at all to her,
you ought to feel that she has done the only right thing in
making it plain to Dan that she can't marry him."

"It's very strange, John, that you should so easily be
won over to someone you don't know at all."

"No, it's not strange, Alice. Blythe's Charlie is *real,* and
this Dan isn't. And some day you'll see it yourself, and be
glad you had a daughter with a lot of common sense."

Then they heard Blythe's light step coming up the
stairs, and Blythe's voice singing softly a hymn she had
heard at the meeting.

> Keep me in the shadow of the cross,
>   Purge my weary soul of its dross,
> Fill me with Thy spirit till the whole world may see
> The Light that shone from Calvary,
> Shining out through me.

A soft light came into her father's eyes as he caught the
words.

"She seems to be pretty happy, whatever it is," he said
gently.

"Oh, John, do you think so," said the mother sadly,
"such gloomy pathetic words. She's just the type that can
be made into a fanatic so easily. Talking about purging
her soul of dross! As if that child ever had a grain of dross
in her. You know yourself she's always been the sweetest,
most reasonable child. I almost never had to punish her,
even when she was very little. Talk about dross in *her,* it's
ridiculous! I tell you that boy she thinks she's in love with
is the wrong type for her. He'll just lead her into being a
whining old woman before her time."

"Perhaps he won't," said the father with a twinkle in his
eyes. "Perhaps he'll die, as he told her he was likely to. I
suppose you'd be glad if he would."

"Now John, you know I never was so awful as that I

would want anyone to die before his time. But I certainly don't see that he's good for Blythe."

"No," sighed the father, "you'd rather see her tied to that weak-chinned Dan, who will go on all his life getting drunk whenever he wants to, and going wild over first one night-club dancer or singer and then another, after he's taken his wife safely home and got her to bed out of the way. That's the way you want it, isn't it?"

"John! You know Dan isn't that kind of a fellow! You know he's fine and clean and self-respecting."

"*Self*-respecting, yes, but I'm afraid not fine nor clean. My dear you have lived a fairly sheltered life, and you don't know all I know about the ways of the world today. But I can vouch for it that Dan Seavers is well started on the way to such a life as I just described, and I should never be willing to consent to his marrying my daughter, no, not even if he professed a thousand times to reform."

Then Blythe came into the room and her father looked up.

"Well, you did that in fairly good time. How did you come off?"

"Why, daddy, I just told him I didn't want to marry him, now or ever, and that was all. Of course he was pretty haughty and pretty mad, but he went away."

"But didn't you let him tell you all his lovely plans for the wedding?"

"Oh yes, mother, he began before I was fairly seated, and he told everything, even to how the wedding invitations were to be worded, and what kind of trousseau he wanted me to have. The next applicant won't have very much to do to prepare," and she gave a funny little wry smile. "That's Dan all over. He always planned out everything for the whole crowd and *made* them do it, whether they wanted to or not. However, he's good at that sort of thing, and if I had been in for a big show-off he might have tempted me. But it all seemed so vapid and utterly out of keeping with the times to get up a big showy wedding, when a lot of the boys, our old friends, are across the seas somewhere dying for our country. However, when he had finished and asked me if I didn't think it was a lovely plan I said, yes, it would make a beautiful wedding. But that I did not want to be the bride. That he would always be my old friend and playmate, but marriage on those terms was impossible for me. I wished him well, said I was glad he had his commission and such fine prospects, and I hoped he would soon find the right girl to share it with him. And that made him *very* angry. So he said he had no doubt but that he would, and he made quick work of getting away."

"Well, that's good!" said her father. "And now, Blythe, I wish you'd go on and finish telling about that meeting you attended. I was interested to hear just what that Silverthorn speaker said."

"Oh, yes, dad, I'll love to tell you."

Then the mother arose.

"I do hope you'll excuse me," she said wearily. "This isn't anything really important, and I feel I must get some rest if I am to go on with those convention plans tomorrow. Good night."

Chapter 16

ON THE HIGH SEAS, Charlie Montgomery found himself at last, on his way to an enemy-infested land, going on a mission of extreme danger every step of which was fraught with peril, and knowing that one false move would bring forfeit of his life, or worse.

Charlie himself did not know how his going had been arranged, nor by what various routes he was to travel, save that the final stage of his journey would be by plane. He would receive his last orders before he set out for his final goal, and he did not yet know the exact location of that goal. But his real business when located would be to discover what was going on among the enemy, what was planned; and to send out alarms by well-planned and efficient means: by underground, by hidden radio in code, by trusted trusty messengers, by any way that could get the information back to Allied lines in time to frustrate what the enemy had planned. Sooner or later of course he knew he would likely be discovered, and shot, or imprisoned, or buried in an internment camp to waste away, or maybe even be beheaded, or tortured. But he had come, knowing all this, and ready to lay down his life for the great cause of freedom and righteousness, for putting down the tyrants, and setting oppressed peoples free. And he was going *now* in the strength of the Lord. For he firmly believed that God had called him to this work; and he was ready to sacrifice his life.

Two great joys he carried with him in his heart that gave him strength to go forward, unswerving; that gave him calmness, even peace in the midst of conflict, and alien surroundings. One was the love of God and the nearness of Christ, his newfound Saviour. The other was the knowledge that the sweet girl whom he had watched and loved from afar, had given him her love and trust, and that if he were never able to come back to her in this life they would surely meet in Heaven; and she would understand through it all. On these two facts his soul rested hard and took comfort.

For it was not an easy task he had set himself, to go among men who did not believe as he did, whose sympathies, if they had any at all, were in opposition to all his opinions, and yet he must act and be as one of them, in order to accomplish the purpose for which he had come.

Sometimes he stood on deck and looked off to sea, wondering if he would ever sail back again alive, and he thought of the girl he loved and what it would be like if he were free to go back to her and take her on a wonderful trip, seeing strange lands, exploring beautiful and wonderful places that both of them had studied about. Then something would grip his heart with an almost unbearable longing to take her in his arms again and set his lips upon hers.

And at other times he would stand on deck looking up at God's stars. They were *God's* stars even if he should happen to be looking at them from the deck of an enemy's ship, and God was as able to care for him there as if he were at home. God did love him. He believed it with all his heart, and he felt he could trust and not be afraid of anything that might come.

He spent much time studying his Bible, the Bible that Silverthorn had been delighted to give him before he left him. Much of it he could remember repeated by his mother's gentle voice. But it had never meant anything personal to him before. Now, however, it was everything. It seemed to be the very air he breathed that made him live, the hope of life forever.

"What is it you find to read that seems to be so interesting?" asked a uniformed man pausing beside his deck chair as he sat reading one day.

Charlie looked up with a smile.

"Orders!" he said tersely.

"Orders?" asked the surprised officer. "Do you mean

Naval Aviation orders? I never saw any bound that way before. May I see them?"

For answer Charlie held out the small Testament he always carried with him.

"No," he said, "Not Naval Aviation orders, captain. It deals with still higher orders than Naval Aviation. These orders come straight from God."

"From *God?*" asked the wondering captain, looking down at the small pliable book in his hands, admiring the feel of its binding, and turning the pages perplexedly. "But —isn't this a Bible? Just where do you get orders from that? What does it order you to do? Do you mean you really find orders here? And are they at variance with Naval Aviation orders?"

"Yes, I find orders here. And no, so far they have not been at variance with my service orders."

"But—I don't understand. What for instance do you find yourself ordered to do? I mean your God's orders? Is there a definite order?"

"Oh yes," said Charlie, "I find myself ordered to witness. That really is the gist of all orders. Witnessing. I find that's really why I am on this earth."

"But—I don't understand! What are you witnessing of? Is it in the nature of a testimony."

"Yes," said Charlie, "that's the idea. And I have to testify of what the Lord Jesus Christ has done for me since I took Him for my personal Saviour."

The officer looked at him steadily, studying him, still holding the little soft book in his hand, as if the very feel of it held charm for him.

"Well, go on," said the officer. "Testify! What has He done for you?"

Charlie's face lighted. He answered quickly, eagerly.

"He took all my sins away, and bore the punishment that was my due. And He's made me happy in Him. Even in the face of war! And He'll do the *same for you!*"

"How do you know that?"

"Because He says so in His word. He says, 'He that heareth my word, and believeth on Him that sent me, hath everlasting life, and shall not come into condemnation, but is passed from death unto life.' "

There was silence for a moment while the officer looked thoughtfully out to sea, and then Charlie spoke again.

"Are you saved, Captain?"

There was another silence while the older man seemed to study the question, and at last he lifted his eyes to Charlie's:

"I never gave any attention to a subject like that," he said slowly, "I don't suppose I am. It has never seemed important to me."

"But you'll find it is," said Charlie. "You can't be saved just on the glory of bravery in winning a battle. It takes believing in what Christ did for you, and making it *yours*."

The other man studied Charlie's face again. At last he said. "Perhaps I'll think about it. Do you mind if I borrow your book a little while? I'd like to look it over."

"Yes, take it," said Charlie with an eager smile. "You'll find it's all I said; for *I* did."

The officer walked away with the little book in his hand, and Charlie sat for a long time with his eyes closed, and prayed for that man who was reading his Testament. And later he went to his quarters and wrote a few brief words to Blythe to tell her how he had had an opportunity to witness for his Lord. Just a few lines, out of the depths of his heart, because he was longing to speak to her. And yet he was not at all sure that he would ever be able to send them to her, not till the war was over, for he had been told that where he was going there would be no opportunity for him to communicate with the outside world, except in so far as was arranged for his duty in his special war service.

It came to Charlie as a surprise that "witnessing" was a thing that brought returns of great joy, instead of being a task.

But Charlie was not reading his Bible all the free time. He was in demand for sports. Somebody recognized him as a former football hero and broadcast it, and the other fellows flocked around him, always wanting him to join in anything they had on hand in their leisure time. So Charlie was popular, and had ample opportunity to use his commission to "witness."

He did not go around preaching. He seldom talked of

his newfound joy. He simply lived it. His face radiated peace. The men talked about him now and then.

"Didn't some of you say that guy was going out on a special mission without much chance of returning?" asked one.

"They sure did. I heard his captain telling another man. They say there isn't a chance in a thousand he'll ever come back. And they say he *volunteered*. He wasn't just asked to do it, he volunteered."

"But say, I don't understand," said another fellow. "Hasn't he a girl back home?"

"Yes, Jack, I asked him the other day if he had one and he said he had. I judge she's a pretty swell one, too, from the way he spoke."

"Well, say, I don't get it. How comes it he always looks so happy? He's as cocky every day as if he was on his way home to get married or something, instead of going as fast as he can to his death. I don't see how he can look that way."

"I'll tell you what it is," said another quiet fellow, who didn't often take part in their discussions. "It's his faith."

"How *faith?*" exclaimed another. "So what? What's faith got to do with it? Faith in *what?* Do you mean he's superstitious?"

"Not on your life," said the quiet fellow. "It's his faith in God. He thinks God knows all about this war and is using it for the good of the world, or something of that sort, and he thinks God is guiding everybody that believes in Him, and takes care of them or something like that. And he believes that things will come out for us the way God wants them to, for our best good, or something of that sort. He just *trusts,* and that's what gives him that sort of look of glory on his face."

"Well, I should say that might be a good thing to have, a faith like that, only how would one go about to get it?" asked another man."

"Oh, he'll tell you how to get it," said the quiet one. "That guy has it all down fine. He knows all the whys and wherefores, and he likes to tell you if you really want to hear, only he'll never force it on you."

And it was so that during that long voyage Charlie

carried out his new "orders," and became a daily testimony to his companions, so that in the fearful months that were before them all, his testimony came back to many in their hour of need, when grasping for any help in the dark was all that they could do.

But there came quiet times when he could be by himself for a little while, and in these he wrote precious messages to Blythe, told her of the loveliness of sky and sea and stars, told bits of anecdotes about his companions.

But there came a day when he was to be parted from all these companions who had grown so near to him, and was to go out on his own, into that vast unknown which was to be his destiny.

And before he left he was told that if he had letters to write before he went into that great necessary silence he might write them now, and they would be sent in due time back to the loved ones, yet there was to be no mark about them to show where they were written, nor from what port sent, they were to be brief and simple personalities. Like a message from the dead.

Charlie was one of seven who were to go on like missions, though they were not going together, nor to the same destinations.

And so he wrote that night:

My darling:

My orders have come and I am to go in an hour. This may be the last letter I can send to you on earth, but if so, there is always Heaven, and I shall be waiting for you there. Keep on praying for me till you get word I am gone, and after that look up and think of me with my Saviour.

But if God in His goodness shall will that I can come back, there were such things as miracles, and God *can* bring one for us, but I can truly say that I am willing He shall do His will with me.

Beloved, I pray much joy for you, even though it may have to be mingled with sorrow. But He knows best.

Yours,
Charlie.

And then, into a starless night he set sail toward a

battlefield, his instructions written in his heart, his instruments of service well hidden, his plans well laid. And if he came not back, so be it! He was satisfied. He was going in the strength of the Lord, though his sponsors were not aware of that. They only knew that he was an unusual young man, and it was a pity that such a man had to die. Yet no other man they knew could do the work he was going over to do, as well as he could. That was why he had been chosen for the job.

So at last Charlie Montgomery was on his way to his meeting with death.

Meantime, back in his own land, Charlie's first good-by message entrusted to Walter Blake, had just reached Blythe.

It came about in this way. Walter, when he found that he was not to have the hoped-for few days furlough before he went overseas, had kept the little message wrapped, still in his Testament, with the faint hope that somehow there might happen to be a brief stop at his home town, even if only for a few hours, and he could still have time to take it around to the Bonniwell house himself and present it, perhaps to the lady herself, for he much craved to see how she looked, this ladylove of his beloved hero.

But at the last minute Walter's orders were changed, and he was slipped into the place of another fellow who had been taken ill and had to go to the hospital. So Walter Blake did not get home as he had hoped, and the tiny scribbled message was carried overseas with him. It often troubled Walter, but things had been so hurried at the end. What else could he have done?

In due time Walter arrived in a semi-stationary place overseas, and one day in going over his effects he came on the little wrapped message, and decided that he ought to do something about it.

So he sat him down to write home to his mother and put the note in her care. If she thought it wasn't too late she would be able to give it to Miss Bonniwell.

So he wrote his letter.

Dear Mom:
    By this time you know I didn't get home when I

thought I would, and now I've come across the great water, and I'm safe across, and ready to pitch in and do my part. But somehow it doesn't seem real, being over here. Of course I can't tell you where I am, but anyhow I'm HERE.

The last few days up in camp were kind of slow, after my pal, Montgomery, left. You see we got pretty close even in those few days we had, and so it went hard having him get his orders so quick. For he is real, mom, and no mistake about it. He's the kind you like, mom, and so when he got his orders I was just all worked up, almost as bad as when I left home, for you see he was from our home town, and it sort of seemed as if we belonged to each other. The worst of it, is, too, mom, he was going out on a very dangerous assignment, and they didn't give him any hope he would ever come back, so it was really good-by when he went.

I went with him to his train, and while we waited for the train to leave he was talking. He knew I was expecting to get leave home for a few days before I went over, and he asked me would I deliver a good-by word to his girl. Of course I said sure, so he stood on the bottom step of the car when the train began to move, and wrote this scrawl, and swung out holding to the rail as the train got under way, and put it in my hand. So I did it up carefully, mom, and now I'm located for a few days, and they tell me I can send a letter back too so I'm putting the message in for you, mom, to deliver, and will you please look up Miss Blythe Bonniwell, and tell her how this was written. If she's the right kind, same as he thinks she is, she'll be glad to get it. And maybe you can send me word what she says, so if I ever see him again I can tell him I delivered it anyway. Will you, mom?

So now, mom, don't you worry about me. I'm in God's hands, and I'm not afraid anymore, even if I have to die. I learned that from Charlie, and from his Mr. Silverthorn. So, good-by mom, and keep on praying for your boy. Walter.

So, the next day after Mrs. Blake received this was Red Cross class day, and Blythe Bonniwell would likely be there. She hunted out a clean envelope and put the soiled worn little cellophane packet in it, put it in her handbag and started happily on her way.

Blythe was a bit late that morning. There was a dressmaker at the house doing a little altering, shortening skirts, and the like, and she had been in demand for trying on and being measured. So she came in a little late and went to her usual seat beside Mrs. Blake, which was always carefully left for her now, and was greeted by a radiant smile from the grateful woman who basked quietly in her lovely presence.

"I've a bit letter for you," she said in a low tone, after they were seated and the work of the day mapped out.

"A letter for me," said Blythe happily, "Why how lovely!"

"Yes," said the other woman shyly. "It's me boy Walter has sent it. Maybe he was a bit presuming, but he asked me to pass it on to you, and I guess it'll be all right."

"But—a letter for me—from your son?" asked Blythe interestedly. "That is nice. But how did he come to write to me?"

"Why, you see, it isn't from Walter, strictly speaking, but he's sending it on to you from a young man who says he is a friend of yours. He's someone Walter met at the camp on the way, and he's a young man Walter always admired. You see he was a football hero, and Walter was just that crazy about him during his school days I could scarcely get him home in time to do his evenng work. He was always going to those games. And when he got out to this camp here comes this young man walking off the train and smiling at Walter, like home folks, and he was that glad to see him that he stuck by him whenever he had the chance. His name is Charlie Montgomery. Will you be remembering anybody by that name?" Mrs. Blake studied the girl's face anxiously to see how she reacted to the name, and when the rosy color flew into her cheeks she had no more fear.

"Charlie Montgomery! I should say I do! Do you say your boy has sent me a message from Charlie?"

"Yes, that'll be it," said Mrs. Blake, and she opened her purse and took out the small envelope that contained the battered note Walter had sent.

Blythe took it in eager trembling fingers, unwrapped it carefully, and read with a radiant glow on her face. Mrs. Blake watched until she was satisfied that the girl was pleased and then she fumbled in her bag and got out Walter's letter and presented it.

"That's me boy's letter, telling about how he met Mr. Montgomery," she said shyly. "I brought it along. I thought perhaps you'd like to read it. Of course it's not much of a letter. He's only a little over seventeen you know, and not yet through high school, but I had to sign up for him he felt so left out when his brothers went to war and left him behind."

"Oh, yes, I'd love to read it," said Blythe, accepting the young soldier's letter as if it were a privilege to see it, and the look on her face as she read it made more than one woman in the class look at the girl enviously and admiringly.

"What in the world is that woman showing Blythe Bonniwell that she's making such a fuss over!" asked Anne Houghton contemptuously. "Probably some petition she wants signed, or some contribution for her church or something. Blythe doesn't seem to realize she's just simply spoiling that woman. She'll be after us all probably, and get to be unbearable. I declare I think somebody ought to warn Blythe not to be so horribly chummy with a woman like that. It just reacts on the rest of us."

"How you must hate that girl," said Mrs. Felton, who happened to be sitting next to Anne. "What's the idea? Are you jealous of her, or something?"

A great smoldering anger burned up into Anne's face, as she flashed her eyes at Mrs. Felton, "I, *jealous?* What an idea! What has she got for me to be jealous of I'd like to know?" she asked with contempt.

"I'm sure I wouldn't know," said Mrs. Felton amusedly, "but it looks as if there must be something, for you never lose an opportunity to say something mean about her, and I wonder why?"

Anne tossed her head and shrugged her shoulders indifferently.

"Oh, you don't understand," said Anne. "I don't think she's of enough importance for that, but it amuses me the airs she takes on with people she must see the rest of us haven't taken up yet. I suppose she's trying to reprove us, she thinks she's so superior and so righteous. She makes me tired. Well, it doesn't matter," and Anne yawned daintily, behind a jeweled hand. "I suppose there will always be all kinds of people in the world, and we just have to put up with them."

"We certainly *do*," said Mrs. Felton pointedly.

But Blythe was reading Walter's letter, and seeing Charlie as he stood on the step of the car and wrote that precious tiny message to her. Her face was radiant, and her eyes bright.

"Just look at her," said Anne with a sneer, "you know she's not that interested in any papers that woman can bring. Not *that* interested anyway."

And then Mrs. Felton was prompted to put this to a test. She turned quickly toward Blythe.

"What is it, Blythe, that interests you so? Read it out and let us all enjoy it."

Then Blythe looked up and smiled, her eyes alight. She wasn't embarrassed, not even a little bit, for Blythe had poise, lovely poise.

"Oh," she said pleasantly, just as if she thought they were all her dear friends. "Why, you see, it's a letter from Mrs. Blake's boy Walter, and he's been meeting an old friend of mine who sent me a message. Wasn't that great? They're somewhere on the other side. Of course we don't know just where, but it's wonderful to get word from people who have been gone so long, after the great silence that envelopes them once they are doing anything important."

"Oh," said Mrs. Felton interestedly, "Have you a son in the service, Mrs. Blake? I didn't know that before."

"Yes," said little Mrs. Blake quietly, a soft flush spreading over her cheeks, "I have three sons in service."

"Why, Mrs. Blake! How wonderful!" burst forth several women in chorus. "How was it we never knew that before? We certainly ought to honor you. You're one of our war mothers."

Mrs. Blake looked uncomfortable. She did not desire this publicity.

"I'll tell you what we ought to do," said one of the younger married women. "We'll give her a tea. I'll make the cookies and maybe some darling little sandwiches. I suggest we have it Thursday afternoon. Will that be a good day for you all? Can you come then, Mrs. Blake?"

"I'm sorry, no. I couldn't come any afternoon. I work in a war plant afternoons. And please don't give me any tea. I couldn't take time to come at any time, and it really wouldn't be right in these war times. Send the cookies to your own boys at the front, and forget about me, please. And now, if you'll excuse me, I must go or I shall be late at my job. Good-by," and Mrs. Blake picked up her coat and hat from the hook on the wall near by and slipped quietly out of the room. But Mrs. Felton gave an amused withering look toward Anne Houghton before she folded her work and went to get her own wraps. Anne Houghton was wearing an inscrutable look, with her haughty chin in the air, and Blythe was stepping out the door like one who walked on wings. There must have been something in that Blake boy's letter beyond a mere hello from some soldier boy to make Blythe's eyes shine like that. Mrs. Felton was a wise woman, and a good reader of faces. Moreover she liked Blythe and she did not like Anne Houghton.

But it turned out after that that everybody in the class became kind and gracious toward Mrs. Blake. All but Anne Houghton. They smiled at her when she came in, and asked after her boys at the front, and made little pleasant remarks to her just as they did to the other women, and Mrs. Blake began presently to feel like one of the crowd. Not that she had minded their distant attitude so very much. She was very humble-minded, but it was nice not to have that chilly feeling around her heart whenever she entered the Red Cross room. So she was grateful.

But she was glad most of all about the look in that sweet Blythe's eyes when she gave her the bit of paper her Walter had sent. To think that it should be Walter's adored friend who was *her* friend!

Chapter 17

WALTER BLAKE was really only a kid when he went into the army, but he went with his whole heart, determined to give his all if need be to help win the war.

But when Walter met his old admiration, Charlie Montgomery, and went through those three days with him in that training camp on the way "somewhere," and what is still more, after Walter had gone with Charlie to those three wonderful meetings under the leadership of Lieutenant Silverthorn, there was a great difference. He would never forget those meetings nor the truths he learned there. He had that feeling of constant companionship, now, with God, that gave him strength and courage, and had taken away the fear he used to have sometimes when he thought about going out to face the fire of the enemy.

So Walter began to grow in spirit as he grew in stature, and others began to notice it, and to take account of him. His officers began to see, and now and again to favor him.

One day he was on duty near his captain's quarters, and the captain, as he had been doing lately, fell into casual converse with him, asking a few questions about his home, just a friendly gesture with a soldier to whom he had taken a great liking.

Then suddenly Walter asked a question:

"Captain, there's something I would like to ask you, if it's all right with you. If it's something you oughtn't to answer, why that's all right by me. I'll understand. But it's something I'd like very much to know."

The captain looked up surprised.

"Why, of course, son, go ahead," and the captain spoke like a man, a father, rather than a captain, with a gleam of sympathy in his eye.

"Well, sir, how would one go to work to get transferred to another line of service? Is that possible when one has got so far?"

"What's the matter, son? Don't you like your outfit? Don't you like your officers?"

"Oh, yes, sir! Sure I like 'em all right. But you see sir I always wanted to get right into the thick of things. Real fighting you know. Real danger. You see I've got two brothers in this thing, and I want to do my share."

"Oh, you needn't worry about that, kid," said the captain. "You'll get all the fighting and danger you'll want to see pretty soon. I mean it, for a fact, soldier boy. Doesn't that make you feel any better?"

"Yes, sorta." But Walter's face did not brighten to suit his professed zeal.

"What is it, kid? What's on your mind? It won't do any harm to own up. I may be able to straighten it out for you."

Walter was still for a minute and then he said, lifting a grave face.

"Well, you see, Captain, I got a buddy. Or maybe he was more of a pal, though he was older than I. But he comes from our home town, and he's a swell fellow. He was tops in football when he was in college and I've followed him around and watched his games for years, even when I was just a little kid in grammar school. And now he's gone out on one of those special assignments where they never expect to come back, you know. I don't know where he's gone. He didn't know himself the last I saw him before we left the states, and I'd have given a good deal if I could have gone with him. But of course that wasn't possible. His was a solo assignment. But I've been thinking a lot about him lately. If I could just get exchanged to be somewhere near him I'd like it a lot. You see I feel he might need someone to help him out, help him mebbe to get back home to his girl, if he was to get wounded or be taken prisoner or something. I'd like to get near where he was so I'd be there to help if he needed me. Of course I know everyone can't be near the ones they think the most of, but since he's gone to a post of great danger, if there was any way to get near him I'd like to try for it."

"I see," said the captain thoughtfully. "And you've carried this on your mind for some time, haven't you?"

"Yes sir."

"Well, what makes you so anxious about it just now? Got any idea where he might be?"

"No sir, only I was hearing the radio telling about the enemy offensive, and if he should be one of the men to go into danger after information about what's going to happen, I should think that would be perhaps about where he would be. I just thought he might not be so far off."

"Well, that sounds like reasonable thinking," said the captain looking thoughtful. "Do you care to tell the soldier's name? Or is that a military secret also?"

The boy lifted troubled eyes.

"His name's Charlie Montgomery," said Walter lifting his head proudly, "and he's a swell guy. But of course he may be killed by this time. He fully expected that. Only I can't rest easy till I'm sure he wouldn't need me."

"I see," said the officer. "Well, lad, I'll look into this, and make the inquiries about transfers and so forth, but I'm pretty sure of course that the place where you belong is the place where you are. If you're needed elsewhere that might come later. Just do your duty day by day, and if greater tasks are ahead, wait till they catch up with you. Still, I might be able to look up some records and find out if your friend is still alive. Give me his rating, and I'll try and find out. Would that help any?"

"It sure would help a lot," said Walter.

"Only, how about it? If he isn't living would that upset you so you couldn't be as good a soldier?"

"No sir, I'd want to be a better soldier, to sort of make up for his going, for he's an all right guy and no mistake. I know I couldn't ever make up for him, but I'd do the best I could."

The captain winked back a mist that came to his eyes as he watched Walter march tall and straight and proudly away when he was relieved from guard, and he marveled again at the mere boys who were showing such mature degrees of bravery. He would do his best to find out about

Montgomery now, he told himself, and he sincerely hoped that he was still alive.

That was the beginning of a closer relationship between Walter and his captain, and many a brief talk they had on one subject or another, till the captain came to respect the lad who seemed to have such a firm faith in God even in the midst of war, and to wonder over the influence that the other young man seemed to have acquired over him, even though he was older, and had not been closely associated with him during the years, and then only a few days at the end. But the captain took the pains to have the records looked up, and after a time he took the trouble to hunt Walter up and tell him that so far there had been no report of Charlie's being killed, or even that he was missing in action, so that he must still be "somewhere" on his important and secret mission.

That was a comfort to Walter, although it did not prevent him from constant watching for word from his friend. And when there had been a battle near by, and it was at all possible for him to get permission to help with the group who went out to rescue and bring back their wounded and dead, Walter was always a volunteer.

From one huddled still form to another he would go, give a keen glance into the dead face, and pass on, or offer a drink of water from his canteen to the parched lips of a dying man, or a kindly word. And sometimes he would kneel and pray for a soul that was going out into darkness alone, and wanted a prayer. There were many such opportunities. And although Walter wasn't a chaplain, and made no pretensions religiously before the men, he came to be known as one who was good to send to a dying man, a "guy who knew just the right thing to say," and his own heart life grew richer as he was able to help others. So with days of drill and nights of grave searching among the dead, the lines of Walter's young face which had been almost childlike when he first joined the army became more deeply graven, and a great gentleness and peace came into his eyes that made his superiors wonder as they observed him from day to day.

It was about this time that he wrote in a letter to his mother,

Dear Mom:

It beats all how these fellows came out here to fight, and never seemed to think to get ready themselves to die. I guess they thought it was such a great thing they were doing, killing enemies, that their own lives would be spared all right, but when they find themselves wounded, or just about to die, or even some of them when they are starting into a battle they get scared. They're afraid to die. They train 'em to shoot, and to obey orders, and to keep their uniforms clean and their buttons bright, but they don't seem to think about train- ing 'em to die. Oh, they talk about being brave and all that, but a lot of them don't know anything about Christ, and that He died for them, and that they can take hold of that when they get to the end and just trust. Why, mom, it seems they don't really know any- thing about God or the Bible. I don't see why their mothers didn't teach them that. You taught me. Maybe you think I didn't pay any attention to it at home, and I don't know as I did then, much, but I'm sure you taught me enough even if I was indifferent, so that I would have cried out to God for help. Even if I hadn't met Charlie Montgomery and heard Lieutenant Silverthorn preach and got to know the Lord sort of personally, I would have known He was a Saviour, and the only One to help me die, just from what you taught me. But I guess mostly their mothers didn't know those things, or else they would have taught their boys and not let them come off here as dumb and scared as they are. My! but I'm grateful to you that you weren't that kind. And I'm glad I know the Lord, and can tell some of these scared dying fellows how to be saved. Say, mom, you better be praying a lot. There are so many people going out without God, and then they need Him a lot. They certainly do.

Now I got to go on duty, so good night dear mom.

Your boy, Walter.

That was one of the letters that Mrs. Blake passed on to Blythe to read, one of the letters that Anne Houghton wondered about as they enviously noticed the happy look on the faces of the woman and the young girl.

Anne Houghton studied Blythe's face and tried to figure her out. Blythe wasn't in evidence at the parties any more, and she didn't seem to go with Dan Seavers, at least they were never together any more. Yet Dan was not coming to

ask Anne to go places with him. Had he found another
girl? She must do something about this herself, she decided. It must be that Blythe had found another soldier
boy and had turned Dan down, but she had fully hoped
and expected that such a move on Blythe's part would
send Dan to find her. Something must have happened.
And yet Blythe seemed perfectly content.

And then the next thing that happened they heard that
Blythe was taking a nurse's course, and perhaps going into
the army herself. Anne wasn't interested in taking up a
gesture like that on her own part so she put on her war
paint and began to call up Dan Seavers.

But Dan was sulky. He had been out for several wild
nights on his own, and was not in a mood to take on Anne
at present. He was still angry at Blythe and determined
not to give in to her refusal. She must marry him of
course. He had always intended that. So he went on
indulging his lower nature with the idea of getting it back
on Blythe to show her she couldn't treat him that way.

But Blythe did not even know of his drinking and
carousing, for she was engaged in more serious matters and
went out socially not at all. She had entered an entirely
new world, that centered around human woes, and the old
social group was not even in her thoughts any more.

But Anne got in touch with Dan at last and proposed
another "evening," said she was about fed up on war work
and wanted to get out and have a good time again, and
she couldn't think of anybody that could show it to her
better than Dan.

But Dan had other ideas in mind for that evening. He
had been intending to call up Blythe and have it out with
her, take another line of reasoning with her and see what
he could do. So he hesitated. He felt he would rather get
Blythe in line than to go dancing with Anne. If he failed
with Blythe it would be time enough for Anne. He felt
that there would always be Anne, and Anne didn't have
any money in her own right. So he hesitated.

"Well, I'm sorry, Anne, I'm not sure I can make it
tonight. There's something else I ought to do. But wait,
suppose I call you up in an hour and let you know if I can
make it or not? Will that upset your plans very much?"

Anne wasn't altogether pleased, and she let it be known

as she hesitated, and said, "Well, no, I guess not. But let me know as soon as you can, Dannie dear. If you can't go there's a soldier in town tonight. I might be able to get, although of course I'd rather have you."

That was Anne's method. Show that he wasn't the only chance of a good time she had. And it usually worked pretty well with this lad.

He paused thoughtfully, waited a moment, half resolved to call her back and say he would go with her, but then he realized that the time was getting short to carry out his original plans, and so he called up the Bonniwell house and asked for Blythe.

"Why, Miss Blythe isn't here now. She's in training," said Susan importantly.

"In *training?*" exclaimed Dan indignantly. "What do you mean?"

"Why, didn't you know she's begun training in the hospital? This is her first week, and she won't be home tonight at all."

"My *word!*" said Dan furiously. "Let me speak to Mrs. Bonniwell."

"I'm sorry, but Mrs. Bonniwell is lying down. She came in tonight and didn't feel able to eat her dinner. She's been overdoing on that war chest drive. You know she always will work so hard."

"Well, I'm sorry, but I've absolutely got to see her at once, Susan. You tell her I said it was important. Important for both hers and Blythe's sake."

At last he convinced Susan that his business was important enough to wake Mrs. Bonniwell, and presently Blythe's mother's voice sounded faintly at the other end of the wire. "Yes?"

"That you, Bonny? This is Dan. I'm sorry you're sick and I wouldn't have disturbed you but I simply *had* to find out what is all this about Blythe and the hospital. You don't mean she's taking on more hospital work?"

"Why, yes, Dan. She's gone into training, regularly. She's quite enthusiastic about it."

"But now Bonny, you know that's absurd! How can she keep that up if we're going to be married soon? You know she'll have to give it up. It's much too far to commute for a morning's work, even if this is war, where I'm going, and besides I won't have my wife looking after other people. Doing loathsome services for them, and being at the beck and call of every doctor in the place. I should have thought you would have known that. Gone in training as a nurse and going to be married very soon! What's she trying to be? Sensational? She'll make the front page of the paper all right if she keeps this up."

"But Dan," said the quiet voice of Blythe's mother, "I understood my daughter to say that she had told you quite definitely that she was not going to marry you either next week or any other time."

"Oh, but Bonny, you know she didn't mean that!"

"I'm sure she did, Dan, and you might as well accept it and get used to it at once, and not carry on this way."

"Now look here, Bonny. I want you to call Blythe up and tell her to come home at once, and then I'll come over and get this thing amicably settled between us, Mamma Bonny. Now please do that for Dannie boy, won't you?"

But Mrs. Bonniwell was not to be wheedled.

"No, Dan, I can't do that. It's against the rules of the hospital to call a nurse out from duty, and it would be quite impossible for me to do it. And even if we could do it, Dan, I'm quite sure what Blythe's answer would be. She does not want to marry you, and she does not want to marry anyone at present; and no amount of wheedling, even by you, will change her mind. Now, you'll have to excuse me Dan. I'm not feeling well, and I've got to go and lie down. Good night." And the lady hung up and blank silence was all that answered Dan's continued insistent ringing.

So at last he called Anne Houghton back and told her he would be around after her in a few minutes, and to be sure to wear her prettiest outfit. And that was the way that Anne won out.

Quite triumphantly she put on her most ravishing garments, and went down to meet Dan at the door, holding her head high and resolved to get away with something very definite before this night was over, for she felt it would not be good to dally too long and give Blythe a chance to change her mind. If Dan was in a mood to marry before he left for his war job, whatever that was, she hadn't as yet heard, she was ready to marry him at a moment's notice. She would show Blythe Bonniwell that she couldn't dally too long with a soldier's feelings. She must take him when he wanted to be taken, or he wouldn't hang around and wait. So Anne was blythe and gay and eager for the evening, and it wasn't long before she had definitely banished the gloom that Dan brought on his face when he arrived.

Pretty? Why, yes, he hadn't noticed before how very pretty she was. Twice as vivid and dashing as Blythe could ever be. Perhaps this was going to be the solution of all his difficulties after all. And maybe it would be a good thing not to have any bothersome father-in-law to deal with, always asking annoying questions and insisting on conventionalities, and demanding deference to himself and his family.

So quite happily Dan went out with Anne, resolved at least to make the most of the evening.

Chapter 18

DAN SEAVERS and Anne Houghton were married two weeks later in a great rush of furbelows and uniforms. It was only a little later than the date that Dan had originally set for his wedding with Blythe, for Anne said she simply could not get ready a suitable trousseau any sooner. Besides her favorite cousin was on furlough at the later date, and that would make another uniform. Anne was keen on uniforms.

Mrs. Seavers shed a great many tears for she didn't like Anne, and neither did Anne like her, and she sent for Mrs. Bonniwell and stayed in bed to talk with her, and complained about Blythe not marrying Dan as if it were Mrs. Bonniwell's fault.

Mrs. Bonniwell was not feeling well herself that morning, and she stood it as long as she could and then she said:

"But my dear! I couldn't possibly help it that my child did not want to marry your son. Of course I've always been fond of him, the way he has run in and out of my house, and been a good friend to Blythe, but young people have their own ideas today whom they wish to marry, or whether they wish to marry at all, and I don't really think it makes for happiness to try and bend them to your wishes, do you?"

"But my dear Mrs. Bonniwell," said the aggrieved Mrs. Seavers, "surely you can't contemplate with any sort of comfort having your child become an *old maid?*"

"Why, I don't think it is absolutely necessary that she become an old maid because she doesn't choose to marry your son, do you? After all you married the man you wanted to, and she has the same right. But even if she should become an old maid, what's so bad about that? I know a lot of elderly women who have never married, who have lived very happy contented lives, don't you? Could anybody be happier than Sylvia Comfort, or the Gracewell sisters, or Mary Hamilton? Yet they have never married, and I never heard anybody call them old maids, either."

"But you certainly wouldn't want that fate for your daughter!" declared the mother of the unwanted son. "Come now, be honest. Would you?"

"Well, I certainly would rather have my daughter have a fate like that than to marry somebody she doesn't love, and doesn't want to marry."

"Well, I don't think you're stating that in the right way. I don't think you have any right to say that your daughter doesn't want to marry my son, or doesn't love him either. You know perfectly well that you and John influenced Blythe, put the screws on her, and made her think she didn't want him. Blythe wasn't acting from her own free will. In fact you've always influenced her about everything, until she has no will of her own." Then the handkerchief came into play, with more tears. Suddenly Mrs. Bonniwell began to feel inexpressibly weary, as if she couldn't stand another bit of such talk. She looked at her erstwhile-friend with a kind of desperate determination.

"Matilda," she said, "I won't stand another word like that. Neither John nor I had anything to do with Blythe's decision. In fact we didn't talk the matter over with her at all. She made her own decision, and insisted upon it. And now, if you persist in saying such things I really am done with our friendship. I'm sorry you are disappointed, but I could not think of influencing Blythe on a matter like this, and after all Dan seems to be fairly well satisfied. He's marrying a nice girl, and will have a very pretty wedding."

"But I don't *like* her," sobbed the mother-in-law-to-be. "I never did like her, she isn't pretty like Blythe, and she's awfully modern. I just won't stand it, that's all!"

"But what can you do about it, my dear?" said Mrs. Bonniwell. "It's your son's life, not yours."

"Yes, that's it! I can't do a thing about it. Dan has just

practically told me it's none of my business, after I've loved him and slaved for him, and now he brings a girl I don't like and practically forces me to accept her."

"Listen, my friend. You oughtn't to talk that way. You won't want to remember some of these things you are saying to me. She's a nice girl well brought up, has been in our social set all her life. It won't be like some of those dance-hall girls you were afraid of. Anne will know how to do the proper thing, and you won't have to be ashamed of her. If I were you I would just make up my mind from the start to accept her, and make the best of it. Then there won't be anything on your part to repent."

"Oh, yes, it sounds well for you to talk that way, but it isn't *your* child! If your girl had accepted my son everything would have been all right. He had the plans made for a lovely wedding and he wouldn't have stopped at giving her anything she wanted. Oh, why did she have to be so stubborn? I believe it's your fault! I believe you influenced her! Yes! Yes, I *do*! *You* influenced!" and then the poor lady burst into another flood of weeping.

"But my dear," Mrs. Bonniwell began in an attempt to stop the tirade, "I tell you I had nothing whatever to do with this."

"Oh yes, you did! No matter what you say. You *did*! It was all your fault. Your fault and that nosy fanatical husband of yours. You thought your girl was too good for any man that ever walked the earth. Too good for my angel child who had been her playmate practically all her life. You stopped it, and I shall *never* forgive you!"

Broken and weary at last Mrs. Bonniwell abandoned her old friend to her tears and laments, and went home, too worn out to think of going anywhere else that day. Even Red Cross and War Drives had to be abandoned while the good lady took a real rest, and went to bed.

It was so that Blythe found her mother, when, an hour later, she ran home to get a few of her belongings that she found she needed.

"But mother, this isn't like you, going to bed in the daytime. Lying here by yourself and *crying*! Mother, what *is* the matter? Are you sick?"

"No, I'm not sick," protested her mother. "I'm just worn out with Mrs. Seavers' whinings and crying. An hour and a half, Blythe, and she blames *you* for all her trouble. And then she blames *me,* and says your father and I influenced you, and she'll never forgive us!"

"Oh, well, mother, don't worry about her. She always was dramatic! She'll get over it. And anyway, why should you care? I certainly am glad I don't ever have to call her mother. She is a pain in the neck, and what do you worry about her for anyway? She never was worthy of being your friend. She's a selfish woman who doesn't care what she does to her friends if she can only manage to get what she wants for herself."

"There, there, Blythe! Don't be hard on her. I really feel sorry for her, and it must be pretty hard on her to have to give you up and get Anne Houghton in your place."

"Oh, mother, you're the limit!" laughed Blythe. "First you take to your bed because your neighbor has worn you out weeping and wailing, and then you begin to weep for her because she can't get the daughter-in-law she wants. Well, you'll have to excuse me. I can't find any cure for your ailment but to go to sleep and wake up in the morning to find something more interesting to think about. No, I'm tucking you up the way I do my patients, and I want you to go to sleep at once. I'll be telephoning Susan after a while to find out if you are better, and if you're not I'm telephoning dad. Understand?"

But Blythe went back to her hospital with a worry on her mind. After all there had been dark circles under her mother's eyes, and surely they were not there because she too was troubled that her daughter was not going to be married to Dan Seavers. Well, so that was that, but definitely Blythe felt that her mother had been overworking. For Blythe had been in the hospital long enough now to recognize that look of pallor, that tiredness in the face she loved, and tonight she must call up and talk to dad about it. Dad would do something. He would perhaps take mother away for a rest or something, and let her have a good time. Although there weren't so many good times to be had in these war times. Also a woman who was used to organizing committees, and carrying on successful drives could not easily switch to just good times either. Dinner parties and clubs and such things would be a let-down after the hard work her mother had been doing.

That evening the invitations to Dan's wedding arrived, and there was another complication. Mother would say that of course they must all go to that wedding. It would be just too conspicuous if they stayed away, and everybody would say that Blythe was jealous if she wasn't there. Blythe had been so much with Dan.

Not that Blythe minded going to the wedding, but she knew her mother would mind it keenly if they did not go, and she and Dan's mother would sit glumly and let their eyes say to one another what they could not let their lips say. It certainly would be good if her mother could be away at the time of that wedding. But she didn't see how it could possibly be managed. The wedding was so soon. Of course her mother would overrule them all and they would go, with satisfied smiles on their faces, and well-bred gestures. And there would be at least two of those smiles that would be *real,* hers, and her father's. For she was sure dad hadn't ever wanted her to marry Dan, and certainly, she never had desired it.

So Blythe called up her father and urged him to get mother to rest, and then the next day when she had time off she went to the store and bought the most expensive, most exquisite piece of table decoration for a wedding present that she had seen in these war times. It was a centerpiece of crystal in the form of a beautiful ship, delicate in its workmanship as a crystal cobweb, yet perfect in all its details, standing on a mirrored sea, and arranged for lighting. There could not have been anything more lovely, and Blythe was pleased that she could find something that was so beautiful, and so seasonable, and yet had no possible connection with anything that she and Dan had ever done together. He couldn't possibly torture his mind into a sentimental meaning that she might have had in mind in sending it. She arranged for it to be sent at once, and then with a great sigh of relief put Dan and his bride out of her mind. If her mother decided later that they should go to the wedding, why that was all right with her, of course if her duties at the hospital didn't prevent, but that would be to be discussed the next time she went home.

So instead of bringing depression to Blythe by marrying Dan Seavers, as Anne had hoped it would, the wedding was settling into a normal pleasant event that didn't make the least bit of difference to her.

Blythe didn't get home again to talk with her mother for several days, but when she did she found that her mother was most determined that they would all go to the wedding, and that she should have a new dress if possible. But Blythe declared that she had no time at all to go and select a dress. If her mother wanted to do it all right, but she simply couldn't get away, not if she was to ask for leave for the wedding. It was simply impossible.

Then the question of the wedding present came up and Blythe described the crystal ship elaborately, and saw that it entirely pleased her mother.

But she saw also that her mother did not look at all well, and she resolved that as soon as this wedding was over she simply must manage to get her mother away somewhere to rest. She would talk to her father the very next day.

So Blythe went to her night work in the hospital, and put the wedding and everything concerning it out of her mind. She didn't want to go to it, but she was going of course, and it was silly for her to care. She had a strange uneasy feeling that in some way Anne would try to be disagreeable, and she wasn't altogether sure but Dan might still be angry enough to mortify her in some way. However, whatever came would come and would pass, and what did it matter? She didn't love Dan, she couldn't have loved him ever, and she was glad he was going to be married and go away.

Then there came a warm happy feeling to her heart that there was someone she did love, someone she had a right to love, and who loved her. While she couldn't think of being married to him because he might never return to claim her, still she felt her life belonged to Charlie, and she was happy in the thought of him.

But quite early on that wedding morning everything changed. There came a telephone message for Blythe at the hospital from her father. Her mother was very sick and it would be necessary for her to come home at once. There followed days of anxiety when it was not sure whether the mother would pull through or not, and because nurses were so exceeding scarce, and because the hospitals were so overcrowded, it seemed best for Blythe to give up her course of training and come home to take care of her mother in this terrible emergency. Of course that would have been Blythe's wish anyway, and she was proud and pleased to be able to take over her mother's case, with the assistance of a part-time nurse after the first few trying days, when they able to get two skilled nurses, a few hours at a time.

Wedding? Why, they had no thought nor memory of the wedding, and at the hour when if she had followed the dictates of Dan Seavers she would have been marching up a church aisle to be married to him, Blythe was standing at the bedside of her darling mother, counting her pulse, watching the quiet breath that came so intermittently, trying to look brave when she saw the anguish in her dear father's eyes. No, Blythe did not go to the Seavers' wedding, and neither did any of her family, and the best thing about it was that her dear mother didn't have to know anything about it at all, not at least until it was far over, and no one could blame them for not being there. Everybody knew how very low poor Mrs. Bonniwell was, and no one would think of expecting any of them to leave their home.

So Anne Houghton had no opportunity to gloat over Blythe, or give one single triumphant toss of her head, or glint of her eye. Anne had chosen her path and would walk down it in pride, but not with any envious eyes turned in her direction.

So the organ rolled, and the flowers drooped, and the young men and maidens in uniforms or colorful chiffons, went carefully, measuredly up the aisle; but Blythe was not there to see.

"Why, where is Blythe Bonniwell?" asked someone of the bride as the guests went down the line. "Suely she is here somewhere, isn't she? I wanted to ask her a question about the work in the hospital. Has she gone down the line yet?"

Anne shrugged her shoulders.

"I really wouldn't remember," she said haughtily.

"With all this mob here how could I tell if one certain girl went by?"

"Why certainly she's here," spoke up the bridegroom. It wasn't believable that she hadn't come when all this show had been started just to impress her and make her understand what she had lost. "She accepted the invitation, didn't she Anne?"

"I believe she did," said Anne with utmost indifference.

"Well then, of course she's here," said Dan.

"*Why* of course?" said Anne amusedly. "Personally I'd be surprised if she came."

"I guess you don't realize she's one of my very oldest friends. Of course she's here," said the bridegroom fiercely.

"It may be so," said Anne with another shrug. "I don't recall having seen her. But then she isn't one of *my* very oldest friends of course," and Anne gave a little disagreeable laugh.

Dan motioned to a servant.

"Find Miss Bonniwell and bring her here," he demanded arrogantly.

"Aren't you making her rather conspicuous?" said the bride of an hour. "But then she probably likes that sort of thing. That's likely why she does it."

Mrs. Felton turned sharply from talking with Mrs. Seavers and answered Anne.

"Why, is it possible you hadn't heard?" she asked mildly as from superior knowledge. "Didn't you know that Mrs. Bonniwell was taken very ill this morning? Blythe was called home from the hospital to nurse her mother till another nurse could be found."

"Oh! Rilly?" said Anne affectedly with that haughty air of discounting the news. "But I suppose that's nothing but an alibi, isn't it? It might have been embarrassing for her to come, you know."

Mrs. Felton eyed the bride thoughtfully, like a cat contemplating homicide, and then she bared her nice little teeth and pounced.

"No," she said gravely, "it's not an alibi. I just met the doctor coming out as I was coming in here, and I stopped to ask how she was. He says she is very low. They are not sure she will live through the night."

Dan turned with a whirl on her.

"What's that? Who are you talking about? Who is not expected to live through the night, Mrs. Felton?"

Mrs. Felton looked the bridegroom over sharply.

"I was speaking of Mrs. Bonniwell," she said coldly. "You knew she was taken very ill this morning, didn't you? The doctor told me just now that she may not live through the night. 'She's a very sick woman, Mrs. Felton,' he said. 'You see she has been going too hard with her war work and all, and not stopping for proper rest.' "

"You mean that was *Bonny* they were talking about? Do you mean that was Bonny the doctor said might not live through the night? If that's so why didn't somebody tell me? Why she's one of my best friends. I ought to run right over there and see her."

"Oh, for heavens' sake!" said the bride, "can't you shut up? You've had too many drinks. Don't make a spectacle of yourself, whatever you do."

"But Bonny is sick, Anne, and she's one of my best friends!"

"Keep still, I tell you," said the bride in a low tone. "It's probably just an act. Can't you see? She would choose a time like this to get sick when she could take the attention away from us. This is some of that Blythe's doings, and I don't mean mebbe. I certainly will get even with her one of these days."

But Anne had her hands full that night to keep her tipsy husband within bounds, for constantly he kept returning to the subject, and it was plainly evident that it had greatly upset him to know that the Bonniwell family were permanently out of the picture, with a reason that everybody but himself seemed to have known all about.

"This is *awful!*" he said, more than once, as he mopped his forehead, and cast his eyes about to be sure that Blythe wasn't there somewhere.

But at last the festivities drew to a close, the bride retired to change to traveling garments, the guests assembled and made ready to catch the bride's bouquet, and pelt the newlyweds with rice and rose petals, and Dan's mother, still searching angrily to find a Bonniwell in the crowd, gave a hopeful glance at her husband and thought that it was almost time to go home and weep some more.

It was done. This great awful farce was over, and she could never again lift up her head proudly, for there would always be that terrible daughter-in-law!

Then the going away was over, and the guests who did not remain to dance, went out into the cool moonlight, to pass that quiet Bonniwell house among its trees, with its night lights burning and the doctor's car standing ominously outside the door. And then some of those guests looked at one another and said, "Why, it must have been true. I thought they were telling it about as a joke, didn't you? Anne didn't seem to make much of it."

And then they walked by with more reverent tread. In the morning with shocked voices they called up the doctor whose only response was, "She is still living, that is all."

Chapter 19

THEN BEGAN DAYS of tense anxiety for Blythe and her father, day after day the beloved one hanging between life and death, and death seemingly waiting impatiently at the door to take her.

Mr. Bonniwell spent much of the time in his home, even after the doctor gave a very slight hope of recovery, for the hope was so slight that death was still hovering near, and the tide might turn at any hour. The business could practically carry itself now if they only had their full number of trained workers. But of course, like all other businesses their workers were few, so many having gone into the war, or war work. But business or no business Blythe's father hovered very near the wife of his youth, while any danger threatened. So Blythe was not alone in her anxiety, and during that time of anxious waiting the father and daughter grew very close to one another, and often opened their shy hearts to speak of the things of eternity, which had hitherto been a closed topic so far as the family conversation was concerned. And often when one or the other had been absent from the sick room for a little while and would return, it was not unusual for the one who had stayed there to be found sitting with bowed head, and closed eyes. They came to understand that this meant an attitude of prayer, and that the prayer was an earnest petition for the life of the dear one. This prayer was gradually modified to include a clause, that at least the mother might live to know the Lord as they were beginning to know Him.

The two did not talk much about these things, but now and again a word would pass between them, which showed the trend of their thoughts, and a beautiful bond of sympathy grew sweet and strong between father and daughter.

There were several changes in the Red Cross class. Of course Anne Houghton was no longer there, and Blythe Bonniwell had been gone even longer from her place beside the window, where Mrs. Blake usually sat.

Mrs. Blake was still there, as quiet as ever, but very friendly with all the ladies. She was counted an old member now, and a certain halo shone above her from her friendship with the departed Blythe. Everybody respected the Bonniwells, especially now that there was no Anne Houghton to disparage her, and sneer at the woman with whom she had been friendly.

For Anne Houghton was no longer a poor relative in a stingy household, she was young Mrs. Dan Seavers, the wife of the handsome new officer at the camp, and she was engaged in arrogantly feeling her way into a new group, and making an impression that would serve her as long as she stayed in the place. But neither was she mourned in the Red Cross class she had left behind her, and the place seemed far more friendly since she left. People suddenly began to know that the quiet heretofore despised Mrs. Blake was a most useful and helpful member of the class, for she could not only do well almost everything that had to be done, but she was quite willing to show them the best and swiftest way to do it. Mrs. Felton was one of the first women to recognize this. Moreover it turned out that it was through Mrs. Blake that the latest and most accurate news of how Mrs. Bonniwell was progressing could be learned, for she was in daily contact with Blythe, and that added to their respect for Mrs. Blake. She seemed to be one who was a regular friend at the Bonniwell house, and so it was through Mrs. Blake that the Red Cross finally sent gorgeous flowers to Blythe when it was learned that her mother was decidedly on the mend, although it might be even months before she could hope to be around again, as in the past.

But in the meantime most amazing things were going forward on the "home-front" as Blythe gaily called their home life. The Bonniwell family were living as a family, in a simple homelike way, as they had not done since the

years when Blythe was a little girl, and they used to gather
at night around her little crib to hear her say her nightly
prayer. But that was years ago, Blythe would have told
you, and she scarcely remembered it herself. There hadn't
been any gatherings for prayer in that household since.

But one night, the night that Mrs. Bonniwell was first
allowed to sit up against her pillows for five minutes before
she went to her night's sleep, the most unexpected change
came about in that home.

The five minutes were up, and Blythe had rearranged
the pillows for the night. The father was sitting in the big
chair near the bed, as he usually sat while the mother was
dropping off to sleep. And now Blythe was putting away a
few things. Then suddenly the father's voice broke the
quiet:

"I'm going to read you a few words, Alice. Listen. I
think they will help you to sleep. Call them a pillow for
your head."

And then his voice dropped pleasantly into words they
all knew well, but hadn't been thinking about of late
years.

> He that dwelleth in the secret place of the most High
> shall abide under the shadow of the Almighty.
> I will say of the Lord He is my refuge and my fortress:
> my God; in him will I trust.
> Surely he shall deliver thee from the snare of the
> fowler, and from the noisome pestilence.
> He shall cover thee with his feathers, and under his
> wings shalt thou trust: his truth shall be thy shield and
> buckler.
> Thou shalt not be afraid for the terror by night; nor
> for the arrow that flieth by day;
> Nor for the pestilence that walketh in darkness; Nor
> for the destruction that wasteth at noonday . . .
>
> .   .   .   .
>
> There shall no evil befall thee, neither shall any plague
> come nigh thy dwelling.
> For he shall give his angels charge over thee, to keep
> thee in all thy ways.

Blythe had softly settled down in a chair near the door
as soon as she recognized what her father was reading,
and she watched the quiet face of her mother and won-

dered how she would take this. But then she knew of course she would accept in her sweet gracious manner just as she took her orange juice or glass of milk, something beautiful done for her because they loved her. Something in perfect harmony with a lovely life.

And then suddenly, even Blythe was surprised, for her father bowed his head, and in the same gentle tone that he would have spoken to her mother or herself he said:

"Oh Lord, we do feel to thank Thee tonight that we have passed a blessed milestone on the way toward the recovery of our dear mother, and we know that it has been in answer to our prayers that Thou art bringing health and strength back to our beloved one. We thank Thee for the verses we have read, precious promises that Thou hast made good to us. We ask Thee to help us henceforth to live a life that is pleasing to Thee, and that shall give glory to Thy name. Thank you, dear Lord. Amen."

There was an instant of silence, and then Blythe softly slipped from her chair, turned out all but the small night light as usual. But before she left the room she glanced at her mother to see if she was entirely comfortable, and she caught the vision of her mother's eyes opening, looking full at her husband, and then her wan face was wreathed in a lovely smile. Blythe's heart leaped up with joy. Mother not only had not minded, she had thought it beautiful! Could any joy be more desired just now than this?

And then she saw her father's hand reach out and take his wife's frail hand in a close warm clasp, and Blythe slipped away; wishing there were some way she might tell Charlie about it all, it was so wonderful. Her mother's and father's love story! Charlie would understand and love it too. Would it be too late in Heaven to find pleasure in talking over the beautiful things of the earth that had been left behind?

That night before she slept Blythe wrote another letter to Charlie, to add to the little pile in a lovely leather box which she kept locked and hidden away in a locked drawer of her desk. She liked to pretend to herself as she wrote, that these letters were going to Charlie on the next mail, although she knew that these were no letters for the eye of a censor. They were about intimate family affairs and must be held with a number of other precious confidences to talk over with Charlie in case he ever came back to claim them. But these letters in the box were pieces of her own heart that she was putting in permanent form to read over perhaps in the years to come, when the mystery of death had been solved, or when she no longer could even hope that Charlie would come back to her on this earth.

So tonight she wrote the tender letter, that was like painting a masterly portrait of her parents, with all the soft lights and shadows of the years in their faces, culminating in that few moments with the blessed words on the air, and the bowed heads, and that wonderful humble grateful prayer, like a golden atmosphere of praise sifting into the quiet evening silence. She painted it with pigments taken from her heart life, showing even the divine reflection that had come into her father's face, and glowed like a light in the darkened room, while he was reading and praying. Charlie hadn't known that father and mother through the years, and she wanted him to know them and understand them.

So she wrote her letter and locked it in the secret box, and then she knelt to thank God for that little holy time before her mother slept.

And in the room where Mr. Bonniwell sat long beside the bed with his wife's frail hand lying softly in his, it may be that God was there speaking to hearts that were tender and were thinking of Him.

Chapter 20

ALL DAY THE thunder of battle had been raging. There had been no let-up from sickly gray dawning, to the terrifying set of sun. A bright brass sun trying to set in the normal way through putrid black and green and purple snarls of clouds. The sky heavily frowning to a black night, and shaking a warning head at a cool slice of silver moon that occasionally gave a fearsome glance between the tattered clouds, just long enough to suggest what a night might be if peace were once restored. Was this sunset accomplished at the instigation of the enemy?

The enemy had brought fresh troops across that little winding river. Where did they get so many? Word had come from time to time through their intrepid informer that there was to be no rest that night. More troops were coming all the time. The darkness was making it possible for them to come by droves. There appeared to be endless numbers. The enemy had determined to hold this location, and the road to which it was the key, at all costs. And the costs would be plenty on both sides.

Hour after hour the intelligence continued to come, warnings of the next enemy move.

"That fellow's a wiz," Walter heard his captain say in a low tone to a fellow officer in a momentary lull of fighting. "I don't see how he stands it. He's been on alert since midnight last night. By all the rules of health he should have been dead long ago."

"Who is it? Some fellow you know?"

"I think they call him Charlie, though we're not sure. He never comes out for us to see."

"But how does he manage to get his intelligence across the enemy line to you?"

"He has three points of contact, two are up in tall trees, and when he can't get it over from one tree top or the other, he gives a flash from that far mountain over beyond, or he talks it over his telephone contraption down in a fox hole, some contrivance of his own. No one knows exactly but himself perhaps. Mostly I guess he stays in that fox hole all day, possibly altering its location from day to day, sometimes almost under the feet of the enemy."

"But what does he live on? Surely the enemy does not feed him?"

"No, I think he took a lot of those pill-foods, vitamins and the like, with him. Now and then they say he gets across to our own camp in the night when things are quiet probably, but always on the double quick to get back before he can be discovered. But he's been going a long stretch of hours this time, and scarcely a minute when there wasn't some news of some sort. After all, he's human, and a man can't stand everything. But I understand he volunteered for this, and expected to die when he came in. A pity a man like that has to be lost to the world because of these dirty dogs of enemies. But he's clever all right. Nearly all his means of service are his own device, and if he can't get us word by one method he'll find another. But he'll get to the end of course pretty soon. If all the hints he's given us today come true this night will almost see the finish of this engagement at least. He says the enemy is determined to hold this point at all risks, and *we'll* have to have reinforcements ourselves if the enemy continues to bring new troops. We *must win* this location! And Charlie can't continue to stand up in a tree getting news if a moon like that looks over a cloud for even only a second at a time, without getting caught by some sniper. Sometime soon the intelligence will cease, and we'll have to go on our own; and that will be good-by for Charlie! But there's no doubt about it we wouldn't have won all we have in this sector if it hadn't been for Charlie's magnificent work."

Walter moved quietly on in the darkness, his heart swelling with pride at what his captain had said of Charlie. For Walter had been convinced for some days that the work that was being done out there somewhere between the enemy and their own men, was Charlie's work, but this was the first time that he had heard the fact openly acknowledged. So, his captain had looked up the old friend from the home town, after all and was sure, but he hadn't told him. Probably wasn't sure but he, Walter, might lose his head and go out after Charlie and give him away perhaps. But there was a warm feeling around Walter's heart as he thought that his captain was acknowledging the worth of his hero too. And now, if anything happened to Charlie, and the intelligence should suddenly cease, he, Walter, would search among the dead most carefully for his beloved idol.

That night as the firing began again and the young soldier listened to the orders given, he knew that the worst was on its way, and if Charlie would ever need his help, it would likely be to-night.

The fighting was bitter indeed, and grew worse as the darkness drew on. Company after company of enemy troopers poured into the enemy ranks. There came planes, and other instruments of warfare, and now and again as Walter's duties led him back to the captain's tent Walter found that everything was happening as had been told them by Charlie that it would happen. Charlie was doing great work.

"God, be with him," he prayed in his heart continually. "If he is in peril protect him, if he is weary with the long battle give him strength, and if he needs a helper, send me, please, Father, God."

On into the night they went, till it seemed the morning would never come. Black night everywhere, for the moon had gone its way now, and the clouds were folded across till scarcely a star dared listen through the murky darkness of smoke and fire and death. It must be that the angels mourned as they looked down upon that night of carnage.

The firing had been incessant, the fight fierce on every hand. The dead were everywhere, and no man had time for rest. This was a battle to the death.

Walter had been everywhere, doing his duty without a thought of self or fear, and his heart was filled with prayer. "Oh God, keep Charlie."

Perhaps the captain understood how he felt and kept

him busy. Now and again came messages, signals from tree tops or the underground. Walter was waiting for a message from the captain to be passed on to his major when the word came, "Impossible to hold outlooks longer. Tanks are uprooting trees. Look out for 246. Coming down."

Walter's heart began to tremble.

"Oh, God, aren't you going to let him get through? Aren't you going to keep Your promise?"

He was praying so hard that unconsciously he had closed his eyes and bowed his head. His captain looked at him curiously, almost reverently, and a shade of pity went over his face. Then Walter looked up and caught his captain's glance.

"Captain, that's Charlie!" he said. And the captain bowed his head in assent.

"Yes, son, that's Charlie," he said, and there was infinite sadness in his glance. "Now, get this to the major as quick as possible. We must put in some men and stop that flank movement." Then he saw the alert look come back into Walter's eyes as he took the message with a quick "Yes sir" and sprang forward. The captain had rightly judged that the boy who loved Charlie so, would be quickest reached by duty, a message to be carried forward.

It was two hours later, and still blackest night when Walter heard a voice almost beneath his feet. Charlie's voice. He must have moved his underground radio. A hurried emergency station, trusting it would be heard. There! That was the voice again! "Keep it up till morning and we'll be more than conquerors. The enemy is on the run. Sorry I can't go on. They got me as I came down the tree. I'm getting out now. I'm done. Somebody take over. This is Charlie signing off."

Walter crept closer and called in that cautious tone they had all acquired when the enemy might be near:

"Charlie! Charlie! This is Walter! Wait! I'll come and get you."

But there was no sound but a kind of grating noise from underground like a heavy body pulling out, and Walter realized it was his business to report this to his superior officer at once. Reluctantly he turned away, marked the location by tree tops overhead as well as he could, and sped back to headquarters with his report.

The captain listened understandingly, gave swift orders for the next move in following the enemy. Then turned to Walter.

"Can you find that place where you heard Charlie's voice, son?" he asked.

"Yes sir, I'm sure I can. I looked up and got the location."

"Ah!" said the captain, "perhaps we don't look up enough."

"Sir?" asked Walter.

"It's all right, son, you did the right thing," he said. "Lead these men to the place. This man knows how to take over if Charlie left his machine still there."

"May I stay till I find Charlie?"

There was such pleading in the boy's eyes that the captain could not say him nay.

"Not too long, boy. We can't afford to lose you too. Charlie wouldn't want that."

"I'll be careful captain," said the boy, overjoyed to have the permission at last he had craved so long. And Walter went away into the blackness. Looking up he found his sky line, pointed out the place, and silently, in darkness they went to work, meantime keeping keen watch for stray snipers. And at last they found the machine which had brought so many of Charlie's messages to headquarters and saved so many lives, but they did not find a man inside the foxhole. Charlie had got out and crept away. Where? How far? Into more enemy fire?

The man who took over Charlie's work, crept inside the fox hole, sending his guards here and there to watch. But Walter stole away into the darkness, searching for Charlie.

The rest of the night he searched, coming to body after body lying dead on the ground, now and then finding one that he wasn't sure of, and turning his small pocket flash, to study the face, but none of them was the right one. How far had Charlie been able to go after he crept from that hole?

The morning was beginning to break, but the fighting had died away. Was it true that the enemy was on the run? But still he crept on. Mindful of his promise to his captain, he crept low, over the piles of slain, looking sharply at them one by one, telling himself that he must be sure. Charlie would have changed some perhaps, all these months of strenuous work! Oh, he must make no mistakes. Even the dead body of that beloved one would be better than nothing. He had a trust to keep for that girl that Charlie loved. She would ask him some day if he did everything that could have been done to find her lover.

On he crept, praying, "Oh God, guide me to him!"

Over the ridge he crept where the fighting had been the thickest all the day before, and last night. The slain were piled high, with no one to care, except those at home who would never know just how their dear ones went. Some of these dead were lads he knew, but most of them were enemies, fallen as they fought, together. Would God gather them and separate them according to His judgment? Walter was thankful it was not his task to judge any of them. Some of them were likely saved ones, and more of them had never known their God at all, or else rejected Him. But there they lay together, awaiting the judgment day and a just and righteous Judge.

Solemn thoughts were these to come to this young Christian as he crept among the slain, seeing only now and then one who stirred or moaned. And once or twice he lifted a dying head and gave parched lips a drink of water from his canteen. Till all the water at last was spent.

Then as the pale dawn crept into the east he saw below him the gleam of water. A narrow winding river. He would go down quickly and fill his canteen. It might be desperately needed before long.

So cautiously he crept on, careful to look above to the tree tops for his bearings, and keeping a watchout for any stirring enemy or sniper. But all was quiet. He must get out of here quickly. If there should be an enemy near by, now as the dawn was lightening, he would be an easy mark, here with the reflection of the bright water on his tired face.

Below him on a shelving piece of flat rock at the very brink of the river he saw a still form, prostrate, as if trying to drink from the river. But the back of the man's blouse was soaked with blood, a wide crimson gash, and there was crimson on the water where he had drank. Poor soul, he had likely been shot as he lay slaking his thirst after a terrible night of fighting. The thought hastened his own movements. He must go on with his search. It was important that he find Charlie before he lost too much blood. He must fill his canteen full and get on quickly.

He found a clear place in the water, filled his canteen, and started to go back up over the ridge, but something in the attitude of that quiet form lying at the water's edge startled him, something familiar. He could not get away from it, and in spite of his promised caution he seemed to have to turn back to look again at that man. Was he really dead?

Softly he knelt down and crept close; closer down to the river's brink where he could look into the man's face. He did not know why he felt he must do this, but there was something that compelled him; and so, bending low, he flashed the tiny light he carried for an instant into the soldier's face, and suddenly he saw that it was Charlie! Thin, emaciated, ungroomed, his hair heavy over the weary brow, but still it was Charlie. Charlie who had been out there meeting death day by day, all alone with God and death! Charlie whom he loved, and whom the girl back in the home town loved. Charlie!

Then suddenly the necessity was upon him to get Charlie out and away from this place, where if there was an enemy about he could so easily be seen. He must get Charlie, dead or alive.

Walter did not stop to question whether Charlie was still alive—just unconscious but alive—or whether he was dead. It made no difference now until he had him safely away from further danger.

So with strong young arms he went to work, lifting and drawing the thin body away from the bright water, turning him over, and trying to get the right grip to bear him away. No time now to make the usual tests to see if life was still there. He must get that precious body safely away first.

And so, slowly, working with all his strength, his heart calling upon his God for help, Walter at last succeeded in getting the man in his arms, and up across his shoulder, so that he could climb the ridge and get him back to friendly territory, back where there was a doctor and nurses, and a hospital not so far away. Panting and deliberate he climbed, knowing he could not complete the task if he used his own energy too quickly, climbing till he reached the top of the ridge, where he paused, and looked around him—still the same as when he came that way before, a field of dead men. He looked above and took his bearings again from the tree tops. Then turned and made his way laboriously until he came to the place where he had heard the voice coming from the ground, and there he found the guards, two of whom came at once to his assistance.

"Oh, that's bad!" said one. "Is he dead?"

"I don't know," said Walter. "Don't wait to find out. Let's get him quick to the doctor. I don't believe he's dead. God wouldn't let him die."

They gave him a strange look. Two of that guard did not know Walter, nor Charlie either. They were tired and hungry and had had a long hard night. They wanted it to end and get some rest. But they went silently, helping to carry that gallant tattered soldier, and they marched to headquarters like a funeral cortege bearing him as one would bear the body of a great hero, and laid him down tenderly on the cot that had been hastily prepared. Then the doctors and the nurses came quickly and worked, listened, made tests. Was the hero-conqueror still living?

But Walter Blake stood apart in the shadow of the dawning morning, and watched and prayed.

And over on the other side of the world a girl knelt by her bedside and prayed.

Chapter 21

"WE CERTAINLY MISS Blythe Bonniwell," said Mrs. Felton as she looked over the enormous pile of partly finished garments left from the last meeting. "Look at all these little nighties, all finished but the buttonholes! We certainly can't find anybody to take Blythe's place on buttonholes. Look at that one, will you? Somebody has just simply tried to *whip* over the buttonholes. Imagine it. Just about five stitches to a hole, too. They would never stay buttoned half a minute, and they would tear right out by the second day. Now, every one of those buttonholes has got to be ripped out and done over."

"But I thought that whole pile was finished," complained Mrs. Frazee, a worried frivolous little trifle of a woman who didn't do anything very well anyway, and simply *couldn't* make buttonholes.

Mrs. Felton looked up and immediately knew who had over-and-overed those buttonholes.

Then Mrs. Butler came in from the back room where she had been going over a box that was supposed to be packed and ready to go to headquarters in the city. Her arms were filled with a sizeable pile of unfinished garments. Obviously unfinished!

"Well, of all things!" said Mrs. Felton looking at the unfinished ones. "Where did you get those?"

"Out in the back room, all nicely packed in with the finished things. I caught a glimpse of a stain on the top one, and when I looked at it I found the whole lot was unfinished. Why look, only the side seams are basted up. Just *one shoulder* finished!"

"H'm!" said Mrs. Felton significantly, "Those are the

last ones that Anne Houghton worked on before she went out and got married. Don't you remember, she pricked her finger? That's the blood stain. She certainly was the laziest and the bluffingest gal I ever came across. I'm certainly glad she's married and out of the way for a while."

"For a *while?*" said Mrs. Frazee. "What do you mean, 'For a while'?"

"Oh, that kind seldom stays married very long. They always carry a divorce up their sleeves. That is unless they have a sub-normal husband with a wide patience, and if I know my onions I wouldn't judge Dan Seavers to be one of those," grinned Mrs. Felton.

"Well, I've seen some pretty dirty tricks from people, who ought to know better, and were brought up to have good manners," said Mrs. Butler, "but this beats them all. Sliding out of the work, and pretending it was all done, and then leaving all that stuff undone to go off and count against our group. But what gets me is, how are we going to get all this back work caught up in time to make our report!"

Mrs. Blake had come in while they were talking and now she spoke:

"Why," she said smiling, "I believe I know. We'll get Blythe to take these extra buttonholes home and do them. She has a lot of time on her hands when her mother is resting, and yet she has to be there lest she should waken. She was saying yesterday that she missed her war work, and wished there was something she could do at home in her extra time."

"Why, that's wonderful!" said Mrs. Felton. "Do you really think she would?"

"Surely I do," said Mrs. Blake happily, "I'll go to the telephone right away and ask her. I don't mind asking her in the least, because she said to me she wanted something."

So Mrs. Blake went to the telephone and explained how far behind they were, especially on buttonholes, and had no one who could make good ones, and Blythe accepted with alacrity. Mrs. Blake came back smiling.

"She says she'd love to do it," she said, picking up her work and dropping briskly into her chair. "I told her I'd bring the garments over with me when I go home this noon. Mrs. Felton, you get it all together. And put in *every*thing! 'The more the better' she said."

"Well, that's a great relief," said Mrs. Felton. "I think we can begin to take a new heart of hope about our report now."

The class became a busy happy place for the next two hours. They talked of war and how it would be when peace would come. They spoke of the boys coming home sometime. They spoke softly, guardedly, of some who would not come back.

"They say there's two or three from our town who are reported this morning as missing in action," lisped Mrs. Frazee. "I don't know who they are. At least I heard the names but I didn't know any of them. But of course it won't be a very merry Christmas for their families. That 'missing in action' is such a horrible thing you know. That might mean almost anything dreadful in this war. Prisoners of war, internment camps! They say they simply starve them there. And then so many seem to be taken out and shot or something. It really doesn't seem very Christmasy, does it? It doesn't seem a very good background for our Christmas party. Oh, dear me! And the favors are so very lovely and the invitations *handpainted*, and quite modern."

"It doesn't seem to me it's very patriotic to have such fool things as parties when this terrible war is going on," said Mrs. Butler, grimly. "I for one would much rather see them get up a prayer meeting, though goodness knows I'm not much for praying, and hardly ever go to prayer meeting myself. But somehow I can't see how people can be so frivolous when their relatives are being tortured and killed by the thousand, and we're all going without proper meat and butter, and working our heads off to win the war. And then somebody gets up a big party and they have a supper that would feed all the refugees in the nation. And they buy a lot of fool dresses that don't half cover them, and kite around flirting and smirking and eating and drinking just as if there was nothing the matter with the world, and some of their best friends weren't dying every day. Just as if they were doing it all to be patriotic. Personally I don't think it's *right!*"

"*Right!*" said little Mrs. Frazee in alarm. "You don't

think we ought to sit around and weep all the time till the boys come back, do you?"

"Mercy no, what good would that do?" said Mrs. Butler. "But I don't think we should get up big blowouts, and spend a lot of money, and eat up a lot of unnecessary food, when there are folks who are starving."

"But if we make plenty of money having parties, and buy a lot of war bonds with it, that would make it all right, wouldn't it?" Mrs. Frazee's big baby-blue eyes were lifted pitifully.

"You can't make a wrong thing right by doing good with it," said Mrs. Butler grimly.

"But, Mrs. Butler, you can't think it is *wrong* to have parties can you?"

"Well, there are times that are more suitable for parties than the present," said Mrs. Butler fiercely. "Personally if my son was out there fighting I wouldn't feel like going to a merry-making." Mrs. Butler's face had a self-righteous glow. "It certainly isn't good taste to be giddy when the nation is in sorrow."

"Do you mean the government is against parties?" asked Mrs. Frazee, "I thought they were saying we must keep cheerful."

"They do," said Mrs. Felton. "Don't be silly. You've got to go ahead with your party now it's started. Mrs. Butler just means we've got so much really necessary work to do in more practical lines that it seems a pity to waste time handpainting invitations, but maybe there are some people who couldn't do anything else, so why worry? Mrs. Butler, will you pass me those scissors? I seem to have left my own at home."

There was quiet in the room for a little while as the women thought over and sifted out the ideas that had been brought forth. Very few of those women in that room had stopped to think that this war wasn't just a game, just another function in which they could be delightfully active. Somehow life seemed to be taking on a more serious attitude, and they were not sure it was going to be quite so interesting.

Then at last with a little glad escape of a sigh Mrs. Frazee burst forth gaily with:

"Well, anyhow, it's too late to give up this party, isn't it?

The invitations are all sent and the tickets are paid for. It wouldn't be honest not to have the party now, would it?"

Then they all laughed. Mrs. Frazee was so delightfully childlike, so full of the little frilly things of life, and so empty where anything real was concerned. She couldn't even baste up a baby's nightie without getting the shoulders all hindside-before. No matter how many of them had to be ripped out and done over again, she promptly put the next day's shoulders all at loggerheads, and she finally cast them down in despair, saying:

"Well, I don't see what earthly difference it makes anyhow. Why won't they be all right when you get the sleeves sewed in?" And then she dropped down on the next chair and burst into childish tears. So, they finally decided that Mrs. Frazee would be invaluable pulling out bastings. And strangely she was pleased. Why, pulling out bastings was something she could really understand, and her heart thrilled as she worked away at it, feeling that with every basting that came out she was pulling down a whole battalion of enemy soldiers.

So Mrs. Frazee worked happily away at her bastings, jubilant over the fact that at least this party had to go on, this party on which she had spent so much time and thought, and for which she had developed so many original ideas. So she smiled to herself to think that what she used for a conscience was released from obligation to these women, at least, and she could go on and enjoy herself and her plans.

But the other women sat thinking, planning what the world should be when the war was over, and Utopia perhaps would arrive, which was a development of their part-pagan religion they had developed from within, communing with self and their own desires. It was so much easier for them to explain life and religion in terms of their own wishes than to try and understand a book called the Bible. They felt, as they put away their work, and got ready to go back to their world again, that they had been thinking some great thoughts, and that it was practically up to them as women to make the post-war world what it should be.

That afternoon Blythe, with her big bundle of babies' nighties by her side, and her gold thimble on her flying

fingers, sat in her mother's room, not far from the big
chair where the invalid rested, and made buttonholes, with
a lovely smile on her lips, and a happy light in her eyes.
She was so glad to have her mother getting well, and to be
able to do some real work again. The days of anxiety had
been long and trying, and it was good to have sunshine in
the home, and mother beginning to look as she used to
look when Blythe was a little girl. Mother with that rested
look on her face again, and no longer a strained anxious
expression.

Her mother watched her silently for a while, smiling to
think how lovely her girl was, and then going in her
thoughts over the last few weeks before she was taken
sick. At last she spoke:

"It's so dear to see you sitting there, Blythe, working on
those little garments."

Blythe gave a happy smile.

"Oh, but mother, it is I who should be saying that. It is
so nice to see *you* sitting there so rested and happy
looking, and really getting well after your long illness. It
was so dreadful when you lay so still and didn't know us
at all. But don't let's us think about that. I'm just glad,
glad, you are *really* better, and will be well pretty soon.
The doctor says it won't be long now. He told daddy so
this morning. I heard him."

"That's nice," said the mother, "but somehow I'm not
in a hurry. I'm quite content to rest here and not have to
hurry at present."

"I only blame myself that I didn't see how wornout you
were getting," said the daughter. "You know I thought
you liked all that planning and worry, and hustling from
one thing to another."

"Why, I guess I did," said Mrs. Bonniwell reminiscent-
ly, "but I'm glad I don't have to do it now. I just like to
lie and watch you sew those cute little nighties."

The mother was still for a few minutes and then she
said:

"Blythe, what about that wedding? Did Dan Seavers get
married? I don't seem to have heard anything about it.
Did it finally come off?"

Blythe laughed.

"Don't ask me," she said amusedly. "I wasn't there. I

was getting hot water bags, and hunting more blankets and trying to get you warm. You know, mother, if I hadn't been so frightened about you that I couldn't think straight, I believe I would have been grateful to you for creating a really good reason that nobody could question, why I didn't have to go to that wedding. But of course at the time I was too troubled to even think about the wedding."

"So it did come off! Well, to think of that! And you didn't feel badly about it dear, having your old friend go off with another girl?"

"Feel *badly,* mother! What do you mean? Did you ever think I wanted to marry Dan? Why mother, I thought I told you—"

"Oh, yes, I know you did. But I was afraid you might find out afterward that you had made a mistake."

"No," said Blythe definitely, "I did *not* find I had made a mistake. I did not *ever* want to marry Dan. He was a playmate in childhood, that was all. He never meant a thing to me. And I strongly suspect he has just the right kind of wife to suit his plans and ambitions. She'll climb as far up the social ladder as he wants her to, and she'll egg him on to get in everywhere and get ahead. And I, why mother, you don't know how glad I am that he and his wife are married and gone away from here. It seems somehow as if the atmosphere was clearer for right living."

The mother's face was thoughtful as she watched her daughter, and listened to her decided pronouncement. After a moment Blythe went on.

"But you know, mother, you ought to have understood all that after I told you about Charlie. You *couldn't* think that I could ever want to marry anyone else when I loved Charlie, and since he loved me. Didn't you understand that, mother?"

The mother hesitated before she answered.

"Well, dear, I wasn't sure about that. I thought it might be only a passing fancy, and that it would fade away."

"Oh, *no,* mother! It can never fade away. It is the real thing, mother. Love, the kind you and daddy have for each other. Could you have married anyone else, mother?"

"Why no, of course not, dear. But he was—well I'd

known him a long time, and I'd loved him a great deal."

"Yes, mother, that's the way I feel. Of course, we haven't had the fun together we might have had, because Charlie was too busy, and too humble, but perhaps we've loved all the better for that."

The mother was still again, and then she said slowly, half pitifully:

"But, my darling, this lover of yours was going out to war with the avowed expectation of dying, and I couldn't bear to think of my bright lovely daughter starting out her life in the shadow of death. Don't you see? Don't you understand how I felt, dear?"

"Yes," said Blythe, trying to speak gently, "I see how you looked at it, from an earthly point of view, but you didn't understand how great our love was, how great it *is*, I mean. Our love is a thing of our spirits, not entirely of our bodies and souls. Of course body and soul count some in any loving, but so many loves don't have anything to do with the spirit. Ours was deeply of the spirit. Mother, I love Charlie even more today than I did the day he went away, and I'm just as glad that he came to tell me of his love as I was then. Even a great deal gladder."

"But—even if he never comes back?"

"Yes, mother, even if he never comes back—to this earth."

"My dear! That's very beautiful! I dreaded sorrow for you, but I'm glad that you have found joy in these very hard times. I had hoped you might have forgotten him, but now—well perhaps I understand."

Blythe suddenly laid down her sewing and went and knelt beside her mother's chair, then stooping kissed her forehead and her lips.

"Thank you, mother dear. That's the sweetest thing you could have said to me. Now I can be really happy in loving Charlie."

For some time the girl knelt there by her mother with their hands tenderly clasped. At last the mother said:

"You dear, dear child!" and then after a moment, "And have you heard nothing more from—Charlie?" She hesitated over the unaccustomed name, yet spoke it as if giving her sanction to the relationship, and that brought great joy to Blythe's heart.

"Yes, mother, I've had a few more letters. Would you like to see them? Dad has read some of them."

"Yes," said the mother interestedly. "Yes, I would like to see them, that is if you don't mind, dear. If you think Charlie wouldn't mind."

"No, he wouldn't mind, I'm sure, and I'm glad to have you know him. I want you to know him as well as I do. I'll get them."

She hurried away to her room and brought the few letters that had come before the great silence enveloped him, and together the mother and daughter read them. And when the reading was over, and Blythe had told about the different ones, how and when they came, the mother handed them back.

"I'm glad you let me see them dear. I do not wonder now how you love him. He must be a remarkable young man. I surely feel that God has greatly blest you to give you a love like that, even if it was but for a little while. Some women never have such great love. I am glad my girl knows what love is."

After Blythe had put the letters away and come back to take up her sewing again they spoke about the different letters.

"But I don't understand about that little message that came wrapped in cellophane. Who did you say sent it?"

"Mrs. Blake's youngest son, mother. He used to admire and love Charlie when he was just a kid, and follow him around when he played football in the big college games, and when it happened that they met at a camp before Charlie went over, and were together for two or three days going to those meetings, Charlie knew that Walter was hoping to get home on furlough for a few days before he went overseas, and he asked Walter Blake to bring this to me, his last good-by. Wasn't that dear? But Walter didn't get his furlough after all, and was sent overseas unexpectedly soon, so after he got over there he sent the message to his mother and asked her to give it to me."

"His mother? Blake? Walter *Blake* did you say? Do you mean it is the son of that sweet little Mrs. Blake who comes in to rub my back for me sometimes when I am very tired? Why how dear of her! I shall like her all the better, now that I know this. I hope she comes soon again. I like the feeling of her strong warm hands. They are such little, gentle hands, yet they seem to have a power behind them. She was from your Red Cross class, wasn't she? Is that how you got acquainted?"

"Yes, mother. I felt she was the most interesting person in the whole class. I felt she was a real friend."

"She is," agreed Mrs. Bonniwell, "I like her very much. My dear, I wonder if this war isn't going to do a lot of things to the world, like getting people to know other people of like tastes and beliefs, and making them love one another, where formerly these same people were separated by social lines, and things like education and money? Things good in themselves, perhaps, if taken in the right proportion, but deadly when they are exalted beyond their place. When I get well, Blythe, I want to try and straighten out some of these differences between me and my neighbors, both rich and poor. And I would like to begin by getting very well acquainted with Mrs. Blake."

"Oh, mother! You're making me so happy!" said Blythe.

"What's all this?" asked Mr. Bonniwell, suddenly appearing in the doorway, "Let me in on it, won't you? 'Mrs. Blake' I heard you say. Is that the mother of the Walter-lad I know about, Blythe?"

"The same, daddy," said happy Blythe, pushing forward her father's chair and running to get his slippers. "Come sit down, daddy, and let me tell you what a wonderful mother I have, and what a sweet wife she's been all these years."

And so amid laughter, and sometimes a bright tear, they told the father all their talk, and the three of them were happy together.

"And now," said Mr. Bonniwell, "wouldn't it be nice, mother, if Charlie should walk in some day?"

"Indeed it would!" said the mother in a fervent sincere tone. "Some day *very soon.*"

"Oh, daddy! mother!" said Blythe, and suddenly sat down on a low stool between her father and her mother, and broke into happy tears. Then lifting a rainbow smile she said:

"That's the sweetest dearest thing you could have said."

Chapter 22

THE MEN WERE very tender lifting Charlie, though most of them believed he was already beyond help. But there was something about Walter's almost reverent handling of him, the way he looked at him, that caused them to walk cautiously. And when they learned who he was, that he was the guy who had given his life to make sure they would have the right information about the enemy, when they knew he had been living for weeks, hustling from one tree top to another, and back, down to his marvelous contrivance underground, that had brought the right intelligence, and made possible the several victories, one after another, through which they had been working; the guy that hadn't stopped for sleep, nor had much to eat, and had just gone on making it possible for them to win as they had done, there was no man there but would have done much for Charlie. They knew there were heroes among them, they had seen some of them, dying for the cause for which they were fighting, but this one in endurance and terrible persistence of self-sacrifice, had outdone them all. His name they knew would go down to history as a great one. He had all but accomplished the impossible.

They came solemnly and brought Charlie to their captain, and he gave one look.

"Is he still living?"

One nodded.

Then the doctor.

"This man might have a chance if we could get him to the hospital, but here, there isn't a chance."

"Would he live to get there?"

"I doubt it. He *might*."

The captain's glance rested on Walter, and his eyes kindled.

"Get him there!" said the captain quickly. "Where's Graham?"

"Took his truck down to the base with a load of wounded men."

"*I'll* get him there, Captain, if I have to carry him myself," said Walter, looking at the captain eagerly, determinedly.

A tender smile played over the captain's face.

"You *couldn't*, son."

"Yes sir, I could, if there wasn't any other way. He's *got* to be saved! There's a girl, Captain, and she *cares*."

"I understand," said the captain, "We all care. He must be saved, but it will be easier for him another way. Call Michelli. You couldn't stand carrying anyone that far."

"I—*could*—" said Walter with deep earnestness.

"Do you know, Captain," spoke up one of the guard who had been with them when Walter brought the wounded man to the top of the ridge, "At that I believe he *could*. If it hadn't been for Walt we wouldn't have been here now. He carried him all the way up the ridge on his shoulder."

"Yes," nodded the others. "He was *swell*. Just as careful!"

The captain's eyes glowed warmly.

"He *would*," he said in a soft voice. And then as Michelli came up and saluted, he turned and gave quick orders. Then turned back to Walter.

"You go with him," he said. "Stay by him as long as he needs you. And Michelli, see that the doctor looks Blake over too. He has blood on his sleeve. Has he been hurt?"

"Just a sniper's bullet grazed me. It's nothing," said Walter.

"Have it attended to at once. We can't take chances with our best men!" and the captain's voice was warm as he said it. "Now, *go!*"

The little interlude in the day's battle was over, the brief time when the captain had time to show his own human heart. The men walked out of his presence thoughtfully, saluting the man as well as the officer. A moment more and Charlie was on his way to any hope there might be for recovery, his head and shoulders resting in Walter's arms. Walter felt that the privilege of a lifetime was his now, and tenderly he performed any little service that was to be done. His heart was swelling with thankfulness that the captain had let him go.

"Oh, God," he kept praying in his heart, "it's up to You now. Please remember Your promises!" And then he looked down at the white face, and the closed eyes of Charlie, his beloved. It certainly looked hopeless, but there was God. God could do *anything*.

The days that followed were solemn days. The fighting was still going on in the distance. The enemy had returned with reinforcements, and renewed the battle, and wounded men were being brought in constantly. They gave an account of what had happened. They said the man who had taken Charlie's place was not as good, not as thorough, did not always get his information across in time to save the situation. They spoke in high terms of Charlie's exceptional work in the intelligence line, told what the captain had said about him. But Charlie was still lying unconscious in the curtained alcove which was as near to privacy as the primitive hospital afforded, and did not hear, nor care. Charlie was still hovering on the border, and there was sharp doubt as to whether he would not yet slip away from them. The wound had been a deep one, and complicated, and the hospital supplies were scant. There were so many things against his recovery. It was pitiful.

Walter listened to all the veiled talk about it, and sharply understood. It meant so much to him that Charlie should get well. It would mean so much to the girl—that is it ought to. Oh, was she good enough for him? Charlie was so wonderful!

But Walter's own less serious wound proved an unpleasant experience. He was not interested in himself. He desired to make little of his part in this affair. Yet the doctor persisted in dressing the wound carefully, and asking questions.

"You know, you may still be wanted for something important, boy," he said, "and you don't want this thing to get infected."

So Walter submitted, though he felt that he would rather the doctor would tell him more about the possibilities in Charlie's case than to waste time on him.

But there came a day at last when the frown on the doctor's brow smoothed out as he came to look at Charlie, and Charlie's "valet" as the soldiers now called Walter, felt hope springing very faintly in his heart.

"This wound is in better shape than I ever hoped it could be," said the doctor. "Now we can really begin to work on other things," and Walter smiled, a broad beam, just like sunshine.

But it was a slow process, that recovery. For Charlie was really very, very weary. He had gone without food so often because he hadn't time to replenish his pellets; or he felt, what did it matter whether he ate when there was immediate work to do which might make all the difference in the world with the way the battle went. You see Charlie was fighting his part of the war as if he were the *only* soldier, and he *had* to make it to victory. He simply had to, whether he personally played out or not, just so he lasted as long as he should be needed.

That idea had been so thoroughly ingrained into his mind that Charlie hadn't looked forward to anything, after he was once in action, except to die when the time came. And he knew he was ready to die, so there was nothing to worry about. But good soldier as that set-up made him, it did not conduce to build up a fine physique, though Charlie really used to have a very fine physique. The only trouble was he thought it could last forever, at least as long as it was needed.

Intensive feeding was the order of the day now, and little by little this was having its affect on the weary man who lay there with closed eyes, and no apparent interest in what went on about him. So there did come a morning when Charlie opened his eyes and looked up at the young soldier who was feeding him, and smiled. Vaguely at first. Then as he looked still harder and began to get the lines of the face and figure of the soldier standing beside him, he smiled again. More definitely. Then he spoke, in the old quizzical tone:

"That's you, Walt, old pal! How'd you get here?"

Walter grinned and winked one eye.

"Same way you did, Charlie. Eat your breakfast and don't talk. Them's orders, see?"

Charlie swallowed another mouthful, studied his young friend, and then spoke again:

"You in my outfit?"

"Something like that, buddy."

"I see. Well, how'd *I* get here? What happened?"

"Nothing to fret about. Captain just gave you a new location for a time."

Charlie looked thoughtful.

"Yes. I'm beginning to remember. They got me while I was taking a drink of water. Right?"

"Right."

"Had to climb the ridge. Couldn't make it without a drink. But how did I get up? Did I make it after getting hit?"

"Yep. You made it."

Charlie studied his face a minute.

"But I didn't make it alone, you old rascal. How did I get up?"

"Oh, I happened along, and we made it together. You see I'd been hit too. Same sniper got me. Now, finish this soup and don't talk any more or the doc will put me off duty."

That was the beginning of sanity again for Charlie, and the doctor was greatly pleased at the way the patient was responding to the treatment. But there was still a long way ahead, and Walter, to his delight, found himself detailed especially to look after Lieutenant Montgomery, and keep him quiet enough to really recover.

Of course the first question Charlie wanted to ask as soon as he began to get his bearings, was, "How was the battle going when you left?" And Walter had his instructions on that subject too.

"You are not to discuss the war. Tell Charlie, *when* he *asks*—no sooner—that *he* saved the day for us, and left the enemy in full retreat. Tell him Wheatley took over his work, what there was to do. Say it just that way, and you don't know any other details, see?"

That was all very well at first, but Charlie had too bright a mind, himself too vitally concerned, to be satisfied with no further details, and soon he was asking on every hand. It had however been made a rule of the hospital that the details of war were not to be discussed among the patients, so that helped. The patients were told that it would help in their recovery to take their minds entirely off the harrowing details of what they had been through. So Walter was able to keep a pleasant countenance and be as indefinite as the doctor wanted him to be. In due time Charlie began to relax, and to think of something else beside climbing trees, and discovering enemy's secrets, and crawling into holes in the ground to broadcast them to his officers who were waiting to know what they ought to do next.

And then one day Walter got a letter from his mother which greatly cheered the way. How it had found him he didn't know, for of course he hadn't been allowed to tell in his own letters where he was at the time, but it was wonderful to have a letter come wandering across the world and find him, even when he wasn't with his own unit. It was like as if God had sent it, God, the only One who really knew where he was, and how he needed it.

"They can call it the Army, if they like," he said as he sidled up to the chair near Charlie's bed, "or they can name it the government if they want, but *I* say it's God. Maybe God tells the army how to find us, or maybe He showed them how to make the plan for running this thing, but I still say it's God that saw to it that I got this letter. Would you like to hear a little of it?"

"Swell, buddy! Anything from the home town would be good to me."

"Okay. Mom's letters are always interesting I think. And I know she wouldn't mind you hearing them. She knows you, you know, so you can call it part your letter. Okay, here it is:

Dear Son:
    It seems a long time since your last letter but I suppose you are far away somewhere, and maybe not allowed to write at present. Your last letter spoke as if you were going into action soon. I suppose that word "action" means battle, but I try not to think about it. Just leave it with God to take care of you. You can't ever know what a comfort it is to me, now that I know you know God too, and are trusting yourself to Him.

I suppose you'd like to hear some news from the home town, but there doesn't seem to be so much any more. Nearly all the boys you used to know are either in camp or overseas, except Ray Donohue and Orville Casey. Ray has a bad eye, and Orville's limp is against him, so they are both working in defense plants. The girls you knew are working too, some taking hospital training, some Wacs and Waves, and some of those other letters they have. Nellie Casey is a secretary in the Warner Company, the three Brown sisters are working in the big grocery, have good positions. It's hard to get anybody to work anywhere now. Annie Holmes' kid brother Tom is delivering mail.

Dan Seavers was married a short time ago. I guess you knew him, his father is one of the rich men. Dan married a Miss Anne Houghton, a girl who used to be sewing in the Red Cross class. I guess you didn't know her. They had a big wedding in the church, and a fashionable reception, for all the world just as if there wasn't any war going on. Dan is an officer now and has an office somewhere out west I think. They went off in style.

You remember the Bonniwells? Blythe Bonniwell's mother has been very sick. They didn't think she would live for a while, but she is better now. Blythe had to give up her nurse's training course at the hospital and come home to care for her mother. Nurses are almost impossible to get any more.

You'll be surprised that I'm getting to be a frequent visitor at the Bonniwell house. First I went to take some buttonhole work to Blythe from the Red Cross, and then I found out I could help out a little giving Mrs. Bonniwell a massage now and then. But now, we seem to be real good friends. She likes me to come in and see her, and I like to go. She's almost as sweet as her daughter Blythe. And they are Christian people, *real* Christians I mean, the mother and father as well as the daughter.

My, I wish you could have seen Blythe's face the day I gave her that message from Charlie Montgomery! It shone like sunshine, and her eyes were so bright and happy. I just hope that boy Charlie is half as good as you say. He'd have to be wonderful to be good enough for her.

I suppose you don't know where he is any more. She told me the other day that it was a long time since she had heard from him. If you hear anything let me know, for I know she has her heart on him with all there is in it. And she's so gentle and sweet, waiting on her mother, sewing for the Red Cross, never seeming to care to go out any more the way the other young folks do. Just stays with her mother, and yet she seems content to have it that way. She has the happiest face I know and yet it is a kind of still happiness, as if the source of it was far away. Almost perhaps not till Heaven.

There is very little other news to tell you. Your sister is doing well in school. She has joined the Junior Red Cross and is interested in all their war activities, and very proud of her three wonderful brothers.

And your mother is praying for you Walter, yes and for your wonderful Charlie-friend, and hoping you will both, if it be God's will, come back to bring us joy, and to work for your Lord. Your loving mother.

There were tears in Charlie's eyes when the reading of that letter was completed, and he said in a husky voice:

"You have a wonderful mother, buddy. I wish mine could have known her. But they will some day know each other in Heaven. And mine will be glad that your mother is praying for me. But I cannot thank her enough that she has given me news of my lovely girl. Somehow that makes me almost sure she has not forgotten me. That she still loves me."

It was more as if Charlie were talking to himself, but Walter answered him, his voice half indignant.

"Of course she loves you, you poor simp! Could anybody forget you, Charlie?"

Charlie grinned.

"Not everybody is as foolish as you, kid," he said in the old teasing way.

"Well, I'll be willing to wager your girl is, anyway, if I'm foolish."

But Charlie's definite interest in getting well dated from the reading of that letter.

Before that Charlie had talked only of the time he would be able to go back into service, always with that solemn keen look of going into death once more. Not that he seemed to mind the death part. It was the job he had undertaken. But when he had spoken of it there was always that weary look around his eyes, as if he was too

tired yet to be eager for it, though more because of being
too tired to do the job right, rather than with the dread of
making death his daily companion once more. Charlie
wasn't really afraid of death any more. His intrepid spirit
had taken firm hold of the One who had conquered death.
But his wearied body wasn't yet up to the alertness he
needed to go back.

But one day he asked the doctor:

"Doc, when do I go back and help get this enemy
licked? Seems to me I'm getting pretty lazy lying around
here admiring myself."

The doctor gave him a keen, admiring, amused look:

"Not for a while yet, Lieutenant. You see you have to
give the other fellows a chance to get some of the stars
and hearts and medals of honor. You can't just think you
alone can do the whole job of conquering the world. No,
fella, you're due to stay here a while yet. And when I'm
through with you, and can give you a clean bill of health,
I think you're due for a furlough. You ought to go home
and rest up a while, get built up, before you talk about
going back and trying any more of your special kind of
tree-top antics."

That talk came just the day before Mrs. Blake's letter.
And that letter brought Blythe so clearly before him,
made him think that Blythe just *might* still be loving him,
made him sick with longing to see her again. And from
that time forth he began to ponder on what it would be
like to go home again.

Somehow it had been as if he had closed the door
definitely on the thought of any life for them together on
this earth, when he came away expecting to die. But now,
was there still such a possibility for them?

With the thought of going back home questions came
crowding that he had never permitted himself to think of
before. As long as his future was held by death, he had a
definite feeling that Blythe was his. But if he went back,
alive and fairly well, everything would be changed. Or
would it? There would be the question of what attitude
her parents would take. Even of what attitude she herself
would take when she saw him again. There would of
course be the question of marriage, the natural normal
outcome of loving, the usual, honorable matter of asking a

girl to marry when you had told her of your love. It was one thing to admit love for a poor fellow who was going out to die, but it might be quite another thing to marry him if he came back. Was her love great enough for that? What had he to offer her? A broken weakened body, and a life that was all disorganized. Could he take care of her as such a girl ought to be cared for? He just hadn't contemplated his own possible return to normal life again, although she had said she was praying for it, but his mind had been so thoroughly filled with the idea that he must die that he had kept the thought of such joy for himself out of his mind. He knew if he dwelt on such possibility it would unnerve him for the work he had to do, and he had vowed to be a conqueror. He must not let anything stand in the way of putting his very best into his job of helping to make the world free from tyranny.

For a couple of days after Walter read him his mother's letter Charlie was very quiet and thoughtful, and at last one day Walter, who had an uncanny way of reading his idol's mind, asked a question right out of the blue. He asked it quite casually, as if it were not very important, but he waited breathlessly for the answer.

"You two going to get married when you go back home?"

Charlie gave him a startled look, and then in a minute answered quietly:

"We hadn't talked about marriage," he said, "I was going out to die, not to come back. All that has passed between us was on that basis."

"Sure," said Walter as if he thoroughly understood. "But that doesn't count now. God's letting you go back. And my mom always told me that the right kind of a guy asked a girl to marry him when he told her he thought a lot of her. It sort of implies that, doesn't it, when you tell a girl you love her?"

Charlie was still for a long time. Then he said:

"But I've got to be sure she still cares. The situation is changed you know."

"Oh, sure," said Walter like a connoisseur in marriage, "but you know she does. You've got to take all that for granted. You've got to trust she's got the same kind of love you have for her. Why wouldn't she care, I'd like to know? You're the same guy that went away, only you're ten times grander. You've got citations and things, and you're a lot wiser I suppose. 'Course she cares just the same, only more perhaps."

Walter was embarrassed but he felt it was something that ought to be said. But the silence this time was longer still as Charlie considered his future.

At last Walter burst forth with another question.

"Aren't you going to write to her? You can, now, you know. They send mail out from here every day. I think you ought to think of her and how she must long to hear from you. Mom seems to think she cares an awful lot. You could at least let her know you're still alive."

At last Charlie said thoughtfully:

"I suppose I could. I hadn't realized. I've looked on myself as dead so long. Well, bring on your implements. Got a pencil and paper? I don't know what kind of a stab I'll make at writing, with this arm still bandaged, but I can try."

So Walter brought the writing materials, and noted a lighting of Charlie's eyes as he set about writing.

It wasn't a long letter, for the right hand was pretty well hampered yet by bandages to help support the wounded shoulder, but he finished it, and lay back with his eyes shut while Walter hastened to mail it. Charlie lay there thinking over what he had written, wondering if it was the right thing. He still had a feeling that perhaps he was presuming to come back from the dead this way. They had planned on meeting in Heaven, yes, but what of this earth? Would that change the situation for her? He still was greatly conscious of her wealthy parents for whom he had much reverence, of her social position, and delicate rearing. Somehow those things had seemed to fade away when he held her in his arms, when he wrote her those letters, but now after his long enforced silence they had returned. And so he had written briefly, out of his own heart-hunger, yet still protecting her from even his love.

My darling:
    It seems that I am getting well of my wounds and am being invalided home in the near future. Do you still want me back, or would it be a relief if I didn't come?

Forgive the question, but I had to know. When you gave me your love it was with the knowledge that I would not likely return. My love is still the same. The greatest joy that earth could give me would be if you would marry me and we might spend the rest of our lives together. I could not ask you this before, because I did not expect to return. With this in mind, do you still want me to come?

I shall be letting you know later of my orders, and I am sending you all my love.

May the peace of God abide with you, my love.

Yours, Charlie.

After the letter was gone Charlie got to worrying about it. Just the act of writing it had given him the touch with Blythe that he needed to bring him back to normal again. Perhaps his letter had been unworthy of a real trust in the love she had given him. And yet he had to give her the chance to speak plainly. Perhaps he ought to have waited until he could ask her face to face. It had been a weakness in himself to write that letter. He should have waited till he got back, but somehow he shrank from bearing the uncertainty all that time on the way home. Well, he had evidently grown soft. It hadn't been fair to the great love she had promised him that he should have written so. He would write her again at once, taking it for granted that she loved him as he loved her.

And so he wrote another letter and filled it with his great love, and told her of the joy that the thought of her was bringing him and that he might hope to see her at some time not too far off.

When Walter came back from mailing the other letter he had the second one ready, and Walter rushed out to see if it could still be gotten into that day's mail. When he returned he found Charlie with his face wreathed in smiles.

"God is good, isn't He Walt?" he asked in his old cheery way. "I hadn't thought there was anything yet ahead on this earth for me, but now I see God is handing it out to me, and I've been too self-centered to hold up my hands and take it. Thank you for your part in showing me what I was doing. Bless you!"

And so the joy light came back into Charlie's eyes, and his recovery became more marked day by day.

"Boy! you really are going some!" said the doctor when he came in to see him one afternoon. "I think I can soon give you a clean bill of health. I'm writing your captain today, and I'll tell him. Maybe your orders will be coming along soon. Do you still want to get back to your job?"

A sudden blank look came over Charlie's face for a minute, but then the brightness surged back.

"Why, yes, if I can go back of course I want to go. I want to be a conqueror. Of course, you had got me all steamed up to get home for a while first, but if I'm needed back in action I'm ready to go."

"Good boy!" said the doctor happily, "I knew you were a conqueror. You certainly have the victory over yourself more than anybody I know. Ready to go back, even when you were all set to get home. Well, don't worry, we're not sending you back at present. You're to go home. I got the orders this morning, and you can begin to get ready. Your plane reservations are all secured. You start day after tomorrow, and your buddy goes with you. So there you are. And I understand your citation for a purple heart is on the way. Now, are you satisfied?"

"Me? A purple heart?" grinned Charlie. "What have I done? I came out here to conquer the enemy, and I haven't done that yet."

"Well, you did a good deal toward it I understand, and your time has come to rest a bit now, so get ready to go. We'll all miss you here. You've kept the place cheery, both of you, and by the way, Walter gets a silver star," and the doctor's smile included Walter.

So then, as soon as Walter knew definitely, he went out and sent a cable to his mother. And his mother, dear soul, hurried over to tell Blythe.

The cable reached the home town even before the two letters, and the entire Bonniwell household was filled with a great joy. Blythe beamed like a ray of sunshine, her mother seemed happy and content and her father made quaint jokes and looked up ships and times of plane landings. They would telephone when they reached New York, Walter had said.

So Father Bonniwell arranged to take the family and

Mrs. Blake over to New York to meet the conquering heroes and take them home. There hadn't been so much joy in the Bonniwell home for years, for all of them were looking forward to knowing and loving the new son whom they had never seen.

And Mrs. Blake was overjoyed at the pleasure of going with them to meet Walter. It was greater happiness than she had ever counted on having on this earth.

As the great ship of the air started on its final lap toward home, Charlie grew very silent. All his "inferiority complex" as Walter called it, returned upon him, and he began to think what a terrible thing it would be if Blythe had lost her love for him during the long absence. How was he going to bear it? His solemnity grew with each hour they flew across the great wide sky.

At last Walter came over to him as he sat staring out at the flying sky, and said "Hi, Lieutenant! Seems to me you've lost your faith!"

"Lost my faith? What do you mean, Walt? I still have my faith, thank the Lord."

"Oh, no," said the younger soldier. "You haven't! You don't think God is able to carry this thing through to the winning. You think God would take all this trouble to get you well, and bring you back, and then let you lose in the final inning? That isn't like you, Lieutenant."

Charlie looked at him astonished. Then he smiled.

"I guess you're right, kid. I didn't trust, did I? I'm not much of a conqueror after all. I set out to win, but I lost faith. Well, from now on there's to be no more of that. I'm trusting to the end. I'm putting myself into God's hands to do with as He wills. I guess He who began it is able to carry it through, and I'm ready to leave it with Him."

A smile of satisfaction rested on the younger soldier's lips as he repeated smiling, "More than conqueror, through Him that loved us."

A little while later they got out at the airport, and there were the dear ones waiting for them, and Charlie hadn't any more doubt about whether he was wanted.

There stood Blythe, watching for him to come, and she went straight to his arms like a homing bird, and was folded close, regardless of interested watchers. In fact the whole family had a beautiful glimpse of the lovelight on those two faces, and all their hearts were rejoicing that it was so.

Walter was folded in his happy mother's arms, too, and presently Charlie and Blythe came out of their spell long enough to introduce the new son to his new father and mother, and the Bonniwells felt that their cup was full. This young soldier was as good, if not better looking than the pictures of him they had seen, and his whole attitude was just what they had been led from his letters hopefully to expect.

There were outsiders at the airport, waiting for the plane to Miami Beach, Florida and among them Mr. and Mrs. Dan Seavers.

"My word, Dan! Look at that perfectly stunning soldier kissing that girl. My but he's good-looking! Find out who he is, Dan. I want to meet him. See! He's wearing a purple heart and the other one has a silver star. They must be some heroes!"

Dan looked and frowned. Where had he seen that good-looking face before? And who was the girl he was kissing?

"My word, Dan. The girl is Blythe Bonniwell! Can you imagine it? Somehow she always did have good luck getting all the good lookers."

Dan looked again in blank amazement, and a wave of envy went over his narrow little soul. Blythe was looking very beautiful, and she was definitely not for him and never had been.

"Come, Dan, let's go up and speak to Blythe and she'll have to introduce us," said Anne, taking Dan's arm firmly in her white glove. "I'm dying to find out who that good-looking lieutenant is."

"Well, I'm not," said Dan in a gruff ugly tone, "and I guess if that's the case you'll have to die, for I don't want to meet that lieutenant, nor the girl, and what's more I won't. If you want to meet them you'll have to go alone," and Dan jerked his arm from her grasp and walked away.

But then the Bonniwells got into their car and drove away, and the Miami plane arrived and took the others away, but Dan was ugly all the way, as he thought it out, and finally realized that the handsome lieutenant was none other than the boy who used to star in his marks in high school, and became a great football player later in college. Charlie Montgomery, the boy who worked for his living and starred through college! Dan had never liked him, because he was entirely too conscientious to get along with, and wouldn't be bossed!

But on the road to the home town the Bonniwells were having a wonderful time, and no longer did Charlie doubt his girl's love. He was filled with a great wonder and delight, and the things that had troubled him seemed all to have melted away. Was it always so when one trusted it all to God?

Novels of Enduring Romance and Inspiration by

GRACE LIVINGSTON HILL

☐	12928	TOMORROW ABOUT THIS TIME	$1.75
☐	12846	BEAUTY FOR ASHES	$1.75
☐	12847	THE ENCHANTED BARN	$1.75
☐	13890	THE FINDING OF JASPER HOLT	$1.75
☐	12225	IN TUNE WITH WEDDING BELLS	$1.75
☐	12226	MARIGOLD	$1.75
☐	12227	MATCHED PEARLS	$1.75
☐	12228	COMING THROUGH THE RYE	$1.75
☐	12929	THE GOLD SHOE	$1.75
☐	12167	THE OBSESSION OF VICTORIA GRACEN	$1.75
☐	12559	LADYBIRD	$1.75
☐	13062	STRANGER WITHIN THE GATES	$1.75
☐	11836	JOB'S NIECE	$1.75
☐	11329	DAWN OF THE MORNING	$1.50